Q.E.D.

Lynn Brock

First published: 1930 London

This edition published 2023 by

OREON

an imprint of

The Oleander Press
16 Orchard Street
Cambridge
CB1 1JT

www.oleanderpress.com

A CIP catalogue record for the book
is available from the British Library.

ISBN: 9781915475268

Cover design, typesetting & ebook: neorelix

Q.E.D.

Chapter One

Simon Wyckham Melhuish, having eaten everything eatable of a large orange, two bananas, and a good-sized bunch of grapes, sighed deeply, raised his seraphic eyes from his plate, and considered with thoughtful impartiality the grave, good-looking man who sat at the other end of the dining-table.

"I say, Daddy," he inquired with delicacy, "what's an ordinary G.P.?"

Dr. Sidney Melhuish was, as nearly always at mealtimes, a little abstracted. The long day's work which had begun before nine that morning, had ended but five minutes before he had entered his dining room at a quarter to eight. He was tired, preoccupied with reminiscences of an unusually large number of unusually serious cases, a little worried by incipient earache – with him a chronic trouble in winter-time. As a matter of fact, he had plugged the complaining ear with cotton-wool just before he had left his consulting room. For all of which reasons his son's question remained unanswered.

The child's arched eyebrows straightened in a frown, his clear, pitiless gaze studied again with absolute detachment the clean-cut, handsome, tired face bent at the moment over the peeling of an apple. On the whole, he decided, *not* a satisfactory father to come down to "after-dinner" to. Not a very satisfactory Daddy anyhow. Always out on his rounds or shut up in his consulting room; always busy... too busy to go for walks or do shopping or play games about the house or laugh or make proper jokes or do anything but be busy. Too busy even to answer questions – even to look up from peeling his apple. He had always been like that, Simon Wyckham had always realised. But tonight the truth was acute to the pitch of injury. In the matter of Daddies he had been very, very unlucky.

Of course, Daddy had been very busy that day. He had got home late to lunch from his morning round. Since two o'clock the front door bell had never been still – Clegg, the butler, never out of the hall. Of course Daddy was tired. Of course Daddy *mustn't* be bothered or disturbed by small boys. Small boys, having eaten their "after-dinner," must just kiss the greying temple bent abstractedly to their "good-night" and retire upstairs to bed, no longer appreciated or of importance. Of course... all that. Mums... lovely, jolly, understanding Mums, who could be coaxed into allowing almost anything else – who was never tired, never busy, never dull – even she was strict and solemn and uncoaxable where Daddy was concerned. As long as Simon Wyckham could recall, Daddy's busy-ness and Daddy's tired-ness had been the things that made all the other things not matter to any one in the house. All that... of course... had to be.

But... *why?*

Why couldn't this Daddy be things and do things and allow things, as other Daddies did? Why couldn't he, say, sometimes... well, make faces... or sit on the floor and do things... or even go for walks with the dogs and Mums? Why – to come down to the grievance of the moment – couldn't he answer a perfectly sensible and interesting question?

Abruptly, as if the lights in the room had suddenly grown many times brighter, the child saw a new and for evermore unchangeable truth. He did not like men with black hair and dark eyes and pale, hard, serious faces.

Absorbed in the novelty and certainty of this perception, he leaned back in his chair, breathing a little noisily and rubbing his knees with his hands under the table. A further prolonged scrutiny of his father's face confirmed him absolutely in his disapproval of it. Upon considered thought he decided that, of all the faces he could think of, belonging to persons conceivably eligible as Daddies, the best and most completely satisfying was Uncle Wyck's. Uncle Wyck – the more intimate relationship had been bestowed upon him in reward for highly honourable discharge of the duties of godfather – had a brown, light-hearted face with grey eyes that sparkled and danced when they smiled, and crinkly yellow hair. Well, not yellow exactly; but not anything like red. And *what* faces he could make with his face...

Simon Wyckham's voice took on a note of sharpness as he repeated his question. Definitely, he had decided that he was dissatisfied with Daddy... so dissatisfied that he wanted to show it a little. He stretched, rather truculently, for another banana.

"What's an ordinary G.P., Daddy?" he asked again, with a loudness which alarmed himself somewhat.

Dr. Melhuish had finished his apple. But he was still chasing its pips round his plate slowly with the extreme point of a fruit knife.

"An ordinary G.P.?" He smiled his grave, abstracted smile. "An ordinary greedy person." He raised his eyes at last, as Clegg re-entered the room, and caught sight of the third banana, already half-skinned. His smile faded to severity; excess of any kind always offended him. "An Extraordinary Greedy Person named Simon. You've had quite enough fruit. Run off to bed now."

Slowly and rigidly the small boy disentangled himself from his chair. His question had been a perfectly sensible and interesting one, inspired by an overheard remark of his nursemaid's which he desired to have explained. But not only had the question not been answered properly; it had been turned into one of Daddy's jokes – the kind that only Daddy himself thought funny. With stony deliberation he turned away from the table and, without a glance towards his father, went stiffly to the door.

The deliberation of the exit and its omission of the usual final ritual of farewell, aroused Melhuish from his abstraction. His eyes followed the child with growing curiosity and tenderness, until the door had been slowly opened and the small figure was all but through the aperture.

"Simon. Come here."

That curt summons could not be disobeyed. His son turned and went slowly back to him. Offended because the third banana had been forbidden? Much more probably dejected because his mother – who was up in London for a few days – had not been there to make the usual gentle fuss of his "after-dinner." For Simon Wyckham, his father was perfectly aware, his mother held the keys of all happinesses – he himself the faintest of interests. Long ago he had resigned himself to exclusion from their alliance; he had no time to take a share in it, no art to win one, no pliancy to bind about a small boy's heart. That was so – beyond his helping. Simon was his mother's, beyond enticement, even if one thought of attempting it . . which one never did... now.

But discipline was discipline. The wide eyes that looked up into his were those of a rebel.

"Forgotten something, haven't you, Simon?"

A silent struggle – little wriggling hands – little flushed cheeks – a long, difficult swallow. Clegg, who worshipped the child, coughed deprecatingly, observing his distress.

At length:

"Goodnight, Daddy."

Melhuish waited. But tonight, it was clear, Simon Wyckham did not intend to kiss him.

"Goodnight," he said gravely, with the faint smile habitual to him, and nodded dismissal. Clegg, moved by unwonted agility, reached the door in time to open it to its widest for the child's departure. Slowly, unforgiving, Simon Wyckham went out of his Daddy's way – for good and all.

Clegg came back from the door, when he had shut it with meticulous care to make it seem as little like an exclusion as possible. His stolid face had reassumed the special urgency reserved for telephone calls which disturbed his master's meals.

"Lady Larmour is on the phone, Sir. She said it was very urgent or she wouldn't have disturbed you, Sir."

With the quick, neat, unhurried movements habitual to his carefully trousered legs, Melhuish obeyed the summons. Clegg, following him to the consulting room, overheard the brief monologue which followed.

"Dr. Melhuish speaking. Lady Larmour? Yes. I'm sorry to hear that. Vomiting blood? Quite impossible to say, of course, until I've seen him. Yes. Quite right... admirable. I'll go out to him at once. Not at all..."

"Shall you want the car, Sir?" Clegg asked, as the swift preparations for possible contingencies began.

"Yes. At once."

The reply was so curt that the butler felt apology necessary for his question.

"The reason I asked, Sir... you can't hardly see your hand before your face outside, Sir, with the fog. Halliday was saying only a few minutes ago he supposed the car wouldn't be going out again tonight."

"Fog? Nonsense. I wish Halliday was as anxious to do his work as he is to suppose that he's not going to be asked to do it. Tell him to bring round the car at once. I may be late. Wait up for me. I shall have some letters for post."

When, a few minutes later, the butler opened the hall door, the grey wall of the fog replaced it with a barrier, all but as opaque, that sagged forward swiftly and flowed like dense smoke into the hall. Clegg eyed it dubiously, then, perceiving that his employer had taken a cigarette from his case, struck a match for him, the last service he was to render him. A moment later the hall door of Dr. Melhuish's comfortable, well-appointed house had closed behind him – for it, a last service to its master also.

Coughing a little – for his throat still remembered that it had been gassed in 1915 and disliked fog extremely – Clegg went back to the deserted dining room and, upon consideration, drank a glass of port. For him, too, as for all the servants, the house was not the same when its mistress was away. While he respected its master, his master, he admitted to himself while he sipped his port, got on his nerves at moments. Silly, for instance, getting on to Master Simon that way, when he might have seen that the poor little chap was a bit downhearted at not being taken notice of.

And speaking of Halliday that way... to him. Sneering at him – even if Halliday was a bit slow and lazy. And "I may be late. Wait up for me. I shall have some letters for post." With a letter-box not ten yards from the hall door steps... if the letters had to go that night, which they probably hadn't. Vomiting blood.... It might be two or three o'clock in the morning before he got back. It often was... and later.

Though it wasn't so much the things he said. But things could be said without making you feel that you didn't matter no more than a . . well, than an empty decanter.

There was just one more glass in the particular decanter which had suggested the comparison. Clegg finished it and, a little cheered, remembered that his mistress would return from London in the afternoon of the morrow.

He went back to the consulting room to extinguish the lights. A sheet of note paper lying on the writing table caught his eye – the beginning of a letter evidently interrupted by the dinner gong.

"DEAR GORE, My wife, who hopes to see you while she is in town, will give you all our news. This hurried scribble is merely to tell you that I met an old friend of yours today. While on my..."

Chapter Two

THE PERSON TO WHOM that letter had been begun sat just then at a table at the Ritz, smiling across the debris of dessert at – as no doubt she was perfectly aware – the prettiest and smartest young woman in a roomful of decorative femininity. Through the smoke of his cigarette he noted the fact with entire satisfaction, if without the least admixture of self-complacency.

Pickles was thirty-five – more than halfway towards thirty-six. She looked... what? Not a day older than twenty, despite seven years of matrimony... and Simon Wyckham. Not a line, not a wrinkle in that delicious skin. No sign of tarnish in the gold of that imperious little head. No tiniest possible suspicion of that double chin which... as he had known since her pigtail days – had always been the most dreaded of all possible evil chances that life might hold for her. And, best of all, no dulling of the keen tempered spirit that was Pickles. Still the little witch of – Lord, how many years ago since he had first fallen in love with her – in the very first vacation of his Harrow days. Still one eyebrow a little higher than the other when she smiled.

Ah – if... If he had been a clever, steady successful medico instead of a penniless, rackety young subaltern... If the poor old Governor had left stocks and shares alone. If everything had been different... except Pickles... what would she have said if he had risked it that night before he went off to India? Well – he hadn't. Thank heaven, at any rate, she had never known that he had funked it...

Happy – secure – lovelier, he thought, now than she had been ten years ago – a child – the best of husbands. Splendid...

"The Doctor up to his eyes, I presume, as usual?" Mrs. Melhuish sketched a gesture with her long fingers.

"My dear Wyck, except at dinner... sometimes... I haven't seen Sidney for weeks and weeks. However, I've given up the struggle. After all, *I* don't really matter in a world of sickness. Rude health bores Sidney. I suppose that if I developed pernicious anæmia Sidney would be most attentive. By the way, he sent you his regards – his most flattering symptom of esteem. Sidney, as you know, is not good at saying unmedical things. However, he always means the ones he says."

Gore laughed. He was very fond of Sidney Melhuish, apart from the customary respect of the male for another who knows his job. But he was aware that Pickles' husband was not a gushing person.

"If you ever catch him trying to say one he doesn't, Pickles – get on the phone and order your widow's weeds straight away. How is he? Fit?"

"Quite, I believe. And, I trust, quite happy. Poor dear, it's a shame to make fun of him. Goodness knows what horrors he's looking at now... now... while I'm..."

Her long eyes – green flecked with gold – true witch's eyes – swept the room and the table in reproach. "It makes one feel rather a shabby sort of sneak, sometimes, when one thinks of people like Sidney, Wyck, doesn't it?"

Her smile came back.

"However – I don't come up to London Town on the Spree *very* often, do I? And it's very sweet of you to have given up a whole evening to me. Please believe that I am not ungrateful... if slightly boring. May I say... without embarrassing your sensitive soul... that you look extraordinarily attractive tonight. So clean... and nicely brought-up. I'm so glad I invited myself to dine with you this evening. I feel just right this evening for saying something I've been wanting to say to you... oh, for ages. Give me another cigarette and I'll say it... before I chill down.

The cigarette, however, had been lighted a long time before Mrs. Melhuish, it seemed, could quite decide upon her gambit. Her companion's grey eyes – very shrewd eyes, despite their twinkle – awaited it with respectful tranquillity. But they opened a little when it came.

"You're getting on, you know, Wyck. Why don't you do something with yourself... while there's still time?"

He surveyed her face again carefully. It was quite grave now. *This*, then, was why she had offered herself for a whole evening of her little spree's six. That little outburst of self-reproach, apropos of her husband's devotion to his patients had been preparation... for *this*. Now, what under heaven in the affairs of Wyckham Gore could concern that little golden head to such portentous seriousness?

"I do," he urged provisionally.

But her cigarette swept the protest aside with an impatience that was very nearly angry.

"Oh, *that* – Good God, Wyck, I'd rather that you swept crossings."

"Dirty things crossings. Dangerous too, nowadays. Besides, *do* they sweep 'em now? Haven't seen a crossing sweeper for..."

This time the cigarette – and the green eyes – were angry beyond all pretence.

"Oh dammit, Wyck, do cut out the cheerful idiot business for five minutes." The cigarette, half-smoked, was ground to ruthless ruin. "You know it yourself. It's a shame. It's a sin. You... with your brains... with your record... with your . . with everything..."

"No, no," protested her host. "Much. But not, surely, all."

But Mrs. Melhuish was well under way now and deaf to humorous interruption.

"It's a shame... a sin... a scandal. You, who might have done anything... *you* . . a private detective. After all, no better than any of those wretched, hateful creatures who go sneaking and spying round area gates and hotel offices..."

"No better whatever whatsoever," agreed the culprit, unabashed. "Indeed I regret to say that only this morning I... er... did a lot of sneaking round hotel offices."

"Trying to get some wretched creature into trouble. I suppose."

"Trying earnestly. And for nothing at all so respectable as matrimonial misconduct... which, by the way Gore & Tolley don't handle."

"Some thief."

"No. Merely a little typist whose mother – probably quite mistakenly – persists in thinking her undeserving of being strangled in a ditch. You may have seen the case in the papers a couple of months ago – down in Sussex?"

"Mud and murder. Ditches and dirt. Wyck – doesn't it hurt *you* at all? Are you really just smugly self-satisfied and complacent – perfectly happy nosing in the muck? Are you? Answer me."

"Happy? I'm not bored. I get paid... usually. Quite well, sometimes. And if I do occasionally get people into trouble, I get them out of it sometimes."

A stupid slip. Pickle's colour had warmed a little.

"I'm not likely to forget that, my dear boy," she said gently, and slid her fingers across the table to him. But instantly her eyes were accusing again. "Though that's only because it was I who was in trouble. I should have hated you to do for any other woman the very things you did for me. Yes. I hate your doing what you do. I hate it. I often lie awake for ages and ages at night, hating it."

"Now, now."

"I assure you that when some idiot of a woman in Linwood, who knows you and all about you, rushes up to me in a shop and screams out: "My *dear*, Barbara, *can* you give me Colonel Gore's London address? Such a dreadful thing has happened. Our

chauffeur has gone off with all my husband's warm undervests...
or something of that sort."

"Now, now, Witch. This interlude began as tragedy... not
farce. Now, consider. In this world, Pickles, the supply of pegs is
very large. The number of holes, round and square, is comparatively limited. Middle-aged pegs with military and naval pasts
and nothing else, are not preferred. Yet, for them, daily bread
is necessary – daily butter desirable. Of course, there is the gas
oven or the good old Webley. And, naturally, better dead than
hated. But even then the lady of the shop would happen – and I
should be both dead and hated. I perceive that I am exasperating
you. But don't forget that I can sometimes even wangle a little
jam out of the mud."

Barbara Melhuish tilted a scornful chin from its resting place
upon her fingertips.

"The fact is, my dear Wyck, you like this horrible peeping and
spying business of yours. You've acquired a taste for garbage...
the habit of the rubbish bucket. As if the best of life wasn't
horrible enough and ugly enough and cruel enough to satisfy
anyone. Well – I've said it."

"How long has it taken you?" he asked, a little curiously.

"I've always wanted to say it – ever since you started. But I
made up my mind that I would last February."

"February?"

"Yes. After watching that poor angelic-faced creature sitting
in the dock for three whole days, while you did your best to hang
her."

His face hardened.

"Miss Gretta Higgins? I didn't know that you were such an
adherent of the lady's. Though I believe I do remember now
having noticed a rather marked silence with regard to her on, I
think, the only occasion we have met since the trial – bar this
one. My dear witch – *my* interest in Miss Higgins—"

"You did your best to hang her. That was your interest in
her. It was *you*... from beginning to end. If you hadn't poked

and burrowed and done all the dirty work for them beforehand, what could the police have done? What would there have been for counsel to say? What could a hundred witnesses have said against her, if *you* hadn't put the words into their mouths?"

"Tut-tut. Pish-pish."

"Who but you could have trumped up that absurd story? For you know in your heart—"

"None. And I don't."

"You do. You *know* that it was absurd – far-fetched – impossible. Just a frantic determination to be clever and to prove yourself right. Who *would* ever have thought of it, if you hadn't invented it? No one."

"Q.E.D."

"Thank heaven, you *didn't* pull it off that time."

"*I* did. Your gratitude, I presume, is intended for the jury and the unfortunate judge."

"Fortunately there are some decent-minded, fair-minded, human beings in the world. But it's the solemn truth, Wyck, that when I hear your name mentioned now, I go hot and cold all over. I'm beginning to lose my temper, I think. What time does our show start?"

Now Messrs. Gore & Tolley, like most people, had had their share of little failures. But the failure upon which Mrs. Melhuish had just laid an accusing finger – the affair which, just a year before, had been known all over the man-in-the-street's world as the Mendip Mystery – had been a big one. Also it had earned for the senior partner of the firm – then in its sixth year – an, at times, extremely unflattering publicity in the press and a great deal of rather trying banter from his friends and acquaintances. Gore had not been able to conceal from himself the fact that the business of the firm had fallen off noticeably in the ten months following the trial which had resulted in the acquittal of its central figure. Various little official courtesies and facilities, hitherto graciously afforded, had been summarily curtailed. Gore had found it more comfortable to resign membership of the most valued of his clubs. And now – this...

Until their taxi deposited them outside their theatre, Mrs. Melhuish's escort preserved a silence as profound as her own. Then he said, somewhat hurriedly: "Er... eight-thirty, I believe."

She stole a glance at his profile. Never had she seen it look so nearly fierce.

Well – that was *something* to the good.

"Conscience stirring faintly, Wyck?"

He nodded curtly as they went up the stairs. "Yes. I made a mess of that business. Never mind... I may tidy it up... yet. In which case, no doubt, the affected parts will chill down or warm up, as the case may be – permanently."

"They have," said Mrs. Melhuish concisely. "We will now talk, perhaps, of quite other things. Do unclench your teeth. Every one will think I am your wife."

The twinkle came back to his grey eyes as he looked down at her.

"Bad Witch. Got my goat, that time. Well I may be a private detective. But God forbid that I should be taken for a wizard. They are unclenched."

And so, for that time, the little discussion dropped. Little did either of them guess, as they made their way to their seats, how soon they were to be reminded of it.

***

Before he fell asleep that night, however, Gore's thoughts occupied themselves for a little space with that angelic-faced creature of whom Mrs. Melhuish had spoken so feelingly. Had he been asked just then to summarise Gretta Higgins' career for insertion in a national biography of living celebrities – she had been one at least for three days – his summary would probably have read as follows. The probable criticisms of his friend, Inspector Lord, are inserted in italics.

GRETTA HIGGINS. Born 1900, Port Elizabeth. Daughter of Michael Higgins, M.B., F.R.C.S.I., and Pauline Higgins. Descended on mother's side from family of Westmouth furniture dealers and farther back from John Hare, the accomplice of William Burke, in the Edinburgh murders of 1828. (*Insufficient evidence.*) Educated Loreto Convent, P. Elizabeth. Came to England, 1920. Enrolled as probationer at St. Waldo's Hospital, London. Joined staff, 1923. Excellent nurse; for some time operation-sister. Character highly satisfactory, steady and reliable. Personal appearance and manner most prepossessing.

At end of 1925 sent down to Wraxton, Somerset, to attend a Miss Greston, only surviving daughter of Mrs. Greston of Wraxton Court, in an attack of cerebral meningitis. Known to have corresponded there with a half-brother in S. Africa, Paul Brazil. Brazil a rolling stone and adventurer with a long history of more or less dubious enterprise; arrested for I.D.B. 1925, Jo'burg; 12 mos. Imprisonment. Miss Greston ordered long sea voyage early in 1926, upon which her nurse was to accompany her. Miss Higgins, who had great influence over her patient, arranged that the voyage should be to S. Africa. At Durban a mine owner named Louis Tanquered introduced himself to Miss Greston at her hotel, made himself useful and agreeable, returned to England by same boat with Miss Greston; married her at Southampton without knowledge of her relatives. She had then about £10,000 a year in her own right; two lives only stood between her and her mother's estate, Wraxton Court. Valuable coal mines on this property made its estimated value about £50,000 a year. The two lives were her mother's and that of Philip Greston, a boy of four, the only son of a deceased only son.

Tanquered – alias Paul Brazil – took a place on the Mendips in Somerset, with his wife's money – and settled down to the life of a country gentleman. A keen sportsman, he quickly made himself popular with his neighbours. Miss Higgins, whose influence over Mrs. Tanquered was now absolute, went to live with the newly-married couple permanently. In November, 1926, the boy Philip Greston was asked on a visit to Tanquered's house. He died there, supposedly killed by a load of gravel fallen from a cart which he had contrived to tilt back while at play. Probably he was strangled by Gretta Higgins before she tilted the load of gravel over him. (*No evidence whatever.*)

Mrs. Greston received frequent invitations to the house. She was a confirmed invalid and very nervous at night, when her maid always slept in her room. (*Suggestion without a scrap of evidence.*)

Not very long after the tragic death of her nephew, Mrs. Tanquered – a very neurotic and difficult girl, who had quickly discovered that her husband and she entertained no real affection for one another – formed an intimacy with a Mr. Boyne who lived in the neighbourhood. Without doubt from that time her purse strings closed themselves to her husband. Equally without doubt, Gretta Higgins perceived that her half-brother's fascinations had lost their spell, and that, as a means of retaining a secure hold upon a now certain prospect of £60,000 a year, he was now of no value whatever. (*No proof*) He realised this himself and was annoyed about it. Finding his half-sister unwilling to act as friend at court in the extraction of money, he was foolish enough to threaten her with his suspicions as to the truth of young Greston's death. (*No proof whatever.*) It is probable that he had had no hand in this, and that Gretta Higgins managed it unaided; she is a most capable and enterprising young woman, physically very strong, her hands being unusually large and powerful for a woman. She decided then that her brother was both a nuisance and a danger, and that he stood seriously in her way. An opportunity to put him out of it presented itself on the night of November 27th, 1928. She took it. (*No proof*)

On the afternoon of that day a private inquiry agent named
Gore was to have had an interview with Mr. Boyne at the Bower
of Bliss Inn, a lonely little house of call in the wilds of the
Mendips. Mrs. Greston's suspicions had been aroused with regard to her son-in-law; she had spoken to Mr. Boyne concerning
some information received by her concerning Tanquered of a
very serious nature; as it involved her daughter, she had asked
Boyne to consult a reliable firm of inquiry agents and to have
Tanquered's history looked into – the investigation, obviously,
being one to be made without recourse to the police. As it
fell out, however, Boyne was unable to keep the appointment
made by post with Gore; he was hunting that day and received
a serious fall not far from the inn, to which he was carried
unconscious.

Hearing of his accident, Mrs. Tanquered hurried to the inn
accompanied by the inevitable and capable Miss Higgins. In
angry pursuit of her, arrived Tanquered shortly after. She refused to leave Mr. Boyne; and after a stormy scene Tanquered
announced his intention of staying there until she made up her
mind to go home with him. It was a poor, dingy, uncomfortable
little place; but at any rate he found enough brandy in its tap to
enable him to settle down to one of his periodical bouts. About
ten o'clock at night – a night so stormy that most of the roads in
that exposed hill-country were blocked by fallen trees and that
Gore, unable to return to Westmouth in his car, decided to sleep
at the inn, – Tanquered was left, dead drunk and asleep, in the
tap. In the small hours of the morning he was found dead on
the floor, strangled and with two serious wounds in his head,
inflicted obviously by a bottle.

The discovery was made by Gore, who had been awakened by
some noise and had gone downstairs. He had found, kneeling
on the floor of the tap beside the murdered man, and holding a
broken bottle in his hand, the landlord of the inn. This man, it
was well known, held bitter ill-will against Tanquered, and bore
no very good reputation. A brother of his had been suspected

for a time of having had some hand in young Greston's death and had been shut up in a lunatic asylum, mainly through Tanquered's influence with the local authorities. A belt which Tanquered had been in the habit of wearing under his clothes, was found in one of the landlord's old coats; various other circumstances pointed definitely to him as the murderer. Gore, who found himself the chief witness against the man, did not believe that he was guilty, however, and set himself the task of discovering who was.

The inn had lodged several other guests that night. The suspicion of the police – and of Gore – hovered over most of them before it crystallised for the latter into a conviction that the hands which had strangled Louis Tanquered had been those of the lovely and capable Miss Gretta Higgins. Assisted by the professional advice of his friend, Dr. Melhuish, he succeeded in building up a theory sufficiently convincing (*plausible*) to induce the police to arrest her (*unfortunately*). She was tried at Taunton in the following February and triumphantly acquitted. Fortunately the landlord's innocence had by that time been established beyond doubt. Against none of the other guests of the inn of that night who still survived – for two of them had since died – was there any sufficient evidence to warrant action. And so the affair terminated.

No trace was discoverable of a large number of valuable uncut diamonds which it was believed had been contained in the belt worn by Tanquered. It is certain that Gretta Higgins knew that he carried them about with him in his belt; it is probable that he did so as a precaution against her enterprise; it is certain that she removed them from it. (*No proof whatever. The man from whom he had stolen them in S. Africa was at the inn that night.*)

Also without doubt, before her arrest, she murdered subsequently two other people – those other two guests of the Bower of Bliss whose evidence was not, unfortunately, available at the trial. (*No proof.*) The evidence of these two people would have hanged her; so she got rid of them. (*No proof.*) Miss Higgins is as direct in her theory as capable in her practice.

Ears of remarkable beauty and delicacy of detail. Eyes grey (*there are no grey eyes*); iris-black; marked outer black rim to pupil. Lashes black, long-smudged effect. Nose neither straight nor tilted. Mouth perfect cupid's bow, very scarlet, no salve. Hair jet black, very silky. Eyebrows noticeably highly arched, very finely drawn. Chin resolute. Skin and complexion like a child's. Figure, legs and feet perfect. Hands appalling – huge for a woman, bony spatulate fingers, stubby nails, brutal. Voice lilting. Face perfect oval; expression unusually candid and spiritual. Very Irish type. Teeth small, very even, very pearly. No make-up of any sort. Indifferent to sex-appeal; practically sexless. Height, 5' 6 1/2". Weight 8-4. Temperament gay and abnormally optimistic. Keeps her hands out of sight.

But the Colonel, as has been said, would have made a somewhat prejudiced biographer.

Chapter Three

As MELHUISH OPENED THE door of his car, two figures emerged from the fog and all but collided with him. One was a somewhat elderly woman in nurse's uniform; the other he recognised as one of several fellow practitioners who lived in Victoria Square, and paused to greet him. "Homeward bound, Biddulph, I hope?"

"Hullo, Melhuish. Pretty thick, isn't it? No, I'm on the warpath still. You also, I presume?"

"Yes. I've got to go across the Bridge."

"Across the Bridge?" The other wheeled towards the nurse." Here's your chance, Nurse. Doctor Melhuish is going your way. He'll give you a lift, I'm sure, if you coax him." He explained to Melhuish. "This lady wants to get to Cumberland Place. She has rather lost her bearings for the moment, I'm afraid... Perhaps you'd...?"

"Certainly," agreed Melhuish, and held the door of his car open. "Get in, Nurse."

But the offer was declined with thanks; it was only a little way; the nurse felt sure that there was no necessity to trouble Dr. Melhuish. She disappeared into the fog again, walking smartly, one hand clutching her attaché case, the other groping along the area railings for guidance.

"Something urgent?" Biddulph asked, lighting his cigarette.

"Sir William Larmour has been taken ill suddenly."

"Sir William Larmour?"

There was faint surprise in the other doctor's voice, tinged with a slight acidity. In ten years Sidney Melhuish, an outsider from the north, had succeeded in building up the largest physician's practice in Westmouth's most important residential suburb, and – since it had gradually absorbed most of the wealthiest patients in a wealthy neighbourhood, the most lucrative. Of course... an extremely clever, hard-working fellow, Melhuish, like all these northerners. Admitted. But just a little luckier than seemed to his colleagues in Linwood – most of them ousted from some field of regular and valuable income – quite deserved. Sir William Larmour, for instance, Chairman of United Westmouth Breweries, had been Posnett's patient up to twelve months ago. Of course, Posnett *was* a bit antiquated. Still...

"Must be very suddenly, then. My wife saw Lady Larmour and Sir William at some show at the Alexandra Hall this afternoon – chamber music, or something of that sort. What's the trouble?"

"Haemorrhage, I understand from Lady Larmour over the phone. I know nothing more definite."

"Ah, well, even three millions won't buy a smooth passage to the incinerator, I suppose. You're chancing a head-on with a motor-bus, I perceive. I'm relying on Shank's mare. Wish I could wangle a lift from you. But I'm bound the other way – anæsthetic at St. George's Home – due ten minutes ago. Night, night, Melhuish."

"Goodnight, Biddulph."

Despite the earliness of the hour – it had been half-past eight precisely when Melhuish had left his consulting room – the short, usually busy streets by which his car made its way towards the Suspension Bridge (Linwood's link with the select outlying district called Woodleigh, a suburb of the suburb) were practically deserted. Two dim yellow eyes marked a meeting car, of which nothing more was visible; a dim yellow blur marked a still open shop, forlorn and hardly more stationary than the crawling vehicles. Familiar as Halliday, the chauffeur, was with every turning and shopfront, it was only at the expense of a caution exasperating to his employer that he succeeded in reaching, without a collision or the necessity to reverse, Cumberland Place, the straightforward thoroughfare at whose farther end lay the river.

From that point he progressed at improved speed, his Klaxon blaring continuously. It was, however, ten minutes to nine when he halted in front of the two small lodges at the east end of the Suspension Bridge, challenged by one of the keepers on duty.

"Return or single?" the man called out. Then, recognising Halliday, who crossed the Bridge with his car two or three times a day, as the chauffeur of a yearly ticket holder; "Sorry, Harry. I didn't recognise your bus at first. Nasty night."

The tide had turned a little after eight, but two hundred and fifty feet below them, the river was still busy with traffic eager to escape from it before it dwindled swiftly to a muddy ditch. Muffled by the fog, an incessant clamour rose from the two long processions of craft, large and small, bound for sea or dock, which were creeping past one another warily down there in the narrow, dangerous channel. Anxious boomings and blarings, startled hootings, menacing screams... a whole orchestra of discordance swelled in the depths and mounted toward the frail, invisible fabric that spanned the gorge. The bridgekeeper, a cheery R.N.R., grinned as he jerked his peaked cap towards the medley of raucous sound.

"Glad I haven't to take a big 'un down the Horseshoe Bend tonight, mate."

Halliday, yielding to his ill-temper at being taken out on such a night, had stalled his engine and found some difficulty in restarting it. He nodded now and moved on cautiously. One more light, high in the air, was visible ahead of him – the arc-lamp, as he was aware, in the lower arch of one of the massive towers carrying the bridge's twin set of ponderous triple chains. Beyond that light, until he reached the corresponding lamp at the farther chain tower, two hundred and thirty yards away, no light save those of his car would show him his way – an economy on the part of the Bridge Committee which was destined to assume a sinister importance within the hour. The bridgekeeper, looking after him, watched his tail-light fade into the fog, his Klaxon blending itself with the confused din from the river as it receded. Another light on the car attracted the man's desultory attention for some moments, one fixed apparently on the rear off wing, presumably as an additional precaution due to the badness of the night. He knew Halliday, as he knew most of the Linwood chauffeurs, and was aware that he was a somewhat nervous sort of fellow. The light on the wing disappeared from his view and his mind simultaneously.

"Oi-oi-oia. Oi-oi-oi-oi-oiiiiiiiiyah."

The official turned an ear towards the scream of a wildly-whooping siren.

"That'll be that big Russian that went up last week, Bill," he remarked for the benefit of his colleague, silhouetted against the cosy light of the nearer lodge's open door. "She'll be lucky if she gets down channel on the ebb."

Although one of the city's more important westward exits, the volume of wheeled traffic passing over the Bridge was, save during the days of summer, comparatively small – on winter nights, a mere trickle. Since dusk, when the fog, thick all day, had assumed the density of black cotton wool, barely fifty vehicles had crossed from the east end, still fewer from the west, leaving an average interval of, roughly, three minutes between each. Until eight p.m. eastward bound tolls were collected and tickets issued (or, if return-tickets, checked) at the west end, where there were two more lodges. After that hour, however, the lodges at that end were closed until the morning, and all vehicles and foot passengers challenged at the east side. As cars had been known to rush the exit at that end at night and evade the payment of sixpenny toll, until the gates were closed at midnight, for prudence sake, one or other of the men on duty usually remained outside his lodge at the edge of the narrow passage between it and its fellow. Tonight, however, it was unlikely that anything on wheels would rush in any direction. The two keepers returned presently to their fire and resumed an interrupted discussion as to the merits of Westmouth City's newly-acquired outside left, disturbed after a few minutes by two pedestrians passing eastward – a youth and a maiden, too absorbed in one another even to look at the smiling official to whom they exhibited their return tickets. They had just passed on their way, arm-in-arm, when trotting footsteps turned the keeper's head again towards the Bridge. To his surprise, the arc-lamp suspended from the wall of the lodge revealed the burly figure which emerged from the fog a moment later as that of the driver of the last vehicle which had gone across.

"Hullo, mate. Trouble with your bus?"

"No. Bloke thrown a fit or something on the Bridge. Guvnor told me to cut back here and ring up for the ambulance."

With the promptness of the senior service, the Bridgekeeper made for his telephone, while his colleague found him the number he wanted. The ambulance summoned, they turned to hear fuller particulars.

"'Bout halfway across, I was, or a bit more, going slow, when I see a bloke right under my bonnet, holding up his arm. He sings out as a bloke's had a fit or something, and the Guvnor got out. I couldn't see the bloke – he was on the footway, as far as I could make of it – and the other bloke – this chap as stopped me – he said as he'd nearly walked on the bloke's face. Of course me blurry old engine stopped, and the Guvnor got on to me for trying to start it. "Stop that confounded row, will you," he says, "get out and go back to the Bridgekeepers' lodge and phone for an ambulance. Wonner he didn't tell me to put the bloke in the bus and reverse her back here with him. I thought he might, and I needn't tell you I wasn't having any of that on the Bridge tonight. So out I nips quick, and bungs off back here 'fore he could think of it. Gotta match, boss?"

The chauffeur lighted a cigarette and warmed his hands at the fire for a moment before he went out into the damp-sodden darkness again. A furniture-dealer's lorry, westward bound, drew up outside as he did so, and he lingered while the driver paid his toll to warn him that a car was stopped halfway across the bridge. When the heavy vehicle lumbered forward on its way, he followed at leisurely pace in its rear, having called out a "See you later" to the bridge officials. They went back to the fire and the merits of outside lefts, but after a while abandoned that topic for a discussion as to the advisability of one or other of them proceeding to the scene of the mishap to render possibly needed assistance. On the one hand their assigned duty was to challenge traffic at the bridge-end; on the other, they might be considered responsible for anything that occurred at any point of the bridge. But, again – there were three persons already on the spot to do anything that could be done for the casualty until the arrival of the ambulance – probably in the course of the next five minutes at latest.

Ultimately, however, Glennie, the younger of the two, left the lodge and proceeded westward along the bridge. Two footways for pedestrians bordered the central carriage-road; he took the south footway.

A car travelling eastward passed him at the nearer chain tower, and a little way farther on he thought he heard hurried footsteps on the farther footway, moving in the same direction as this car. Its noise, however – for it was evidently in bottom gear – made him uncertain upon this point. He continued on his way, without encountering anyone, as far as the west chain tower, somewhat surprised to see Dr. Melhuish's car, somewhat more than halfway across the bridge, standing deserted at the near side of the central roadway, with no light whatever showing. Concluding that its owner and driver were on the other footway, he climbed on to the roadway over the separating framework of the bridge, climbed from there on to the north footway, and went back eastward again, towards his starting point. He met no one, however, until he reached the east lodge where he found his colleague and Halliday, the latter in a state of puzzled perturbation.

According to the chauffeur's account, he had gone along the central carriageway behind the lorry until he had reached his car and had found to his surprise that its lamps had been switched off. He had tried to switch them on, but had failed, and, without light of any sort, had been unable to make any investigation as to the cause of this failure. Believing that he would find his employer attending to the stricken man on the north footway, he had made his way on to it, but had walked nearly to the farther end of the bridge and back again to his car without finding any trace of him or of the man who had stopped the car, or, indeed, of any person whatsoever. Much mystified, he had made his way back to the east lodge and consulted the keeper, Hudson, whom he found there. He had seen the car which had passed eastward; it was clear that his footsteps had been those which Glennie had heard.

Accompanied by the latter, who had provided himself with a pocket torch, he went back along the north footway again. Three youthful soldiers, faring towards the city, met them near the farther end, but stated that they had met no pedestrian as they had approached the bridge and, as a matter of fact, had seen no one for more than five minutes of pretty rapid walking. They had, however, seen the lorry going west and the car going east; in addition to these, another car going westward had passed them about a half-mile the farther side of the bridge, travelling very fast for such a night. They could not, of course, say where this car had come from, or whether it had come across the bridge – which both keepers doubted – or turned out of one of the side roads. Nor could they give any information as to its appearance or passengers. They were of opinion that it had turned down Hornham Hill towards the city, but could not be sure about this, having paid no particular attention to the sound of its retreat when it had passed. In any case, Halliday maintained, nothing was less likely than that his employer should have gone off without warning him, especially as he was on his way to an urgent case. There appearing to be nothing else that he could do, he borrowed Glennie's torch and proceeded to investigate his switchboard disconsolately, his final belief being that Dr. Melhuish had gone on foot to Sir William Larmour's house – barely a quarter of a mile distant – and his own intention being to follow him.

"Like as not some small car that could turn on the Bridge came along, and they stopped it and put the bloke into it and took him off to orspital. I suppose the Guvnor got fed up when he saw my lights gone. Or maybe he couldn't find the blinkin' ole bus. I had hard work to find it meself."

To the first part of this theory the level-headed Glennie made two obvious objections. No tracks of a turning car were findable. And why should the supposed small car – however small – have gone to the trouble of turning in the narrow roadway of the Bridge instead of carrying on the way it must have been going originally? Going by Linwood, it would reach any of the hospitals just as quickly, if not more quickly, than by going back along Woodleigh Road and down Hornham Hill. To these arguments Halliday vouchsafed no answer. His attention was concentrated entirely upon the production of the choicest flowers of blasphemy in the extensive garden of his vocabulary. For he had discovered that the fuse had disappeared from its clips behind the switchboard and that both leads running from it were detached.

He was describing in lurid detail precisely what he desired to do to the individual responsible for this outrage – for it was impossible to suppose that mere accident could have caused such comprehensive damage – when, without warning, a large saloon came out of the fog and, despite Glennie's shout, crashed into Halliday's vehicle, burst its petrol tank and pushed it up against the iron framework at the edge of the roadway, the radiator of the assaulting car, despite its fender, being badly damaged. The occupants of the latter emerged one by one – four farmers bound for home after a successful and convivial day in Westmouth's markets. While they expressed, in vivid chorus, their opinion of people who left cars standing without lights and listened to the mournful duet of the leaking radiator and the ruptured tank, Glennie, concerned by the danger of several gallons of petrol let loose upon the bridge, flashed the light of his torch over the roadway in an endeavour to discover the extent of the dangerous area and the likelihood of the spirit draining into the bordering gutters. The ray of the torch fell upon an object lying in the roadway, at the side farther from the two stationary cars. He crossed and picked up a grey Homburg, new but soiled by contact with the greasy surface of the road and so badly dented that a portion of the crown had been flattened to the brim. He returned with this find to the illumination of the rearmost car's headlights.

"Some chap's lost his tile, by the look of it."

Halliday paused from acrimonious dispute with his four assailants to glance at the hat.

"I believe that's the Guvnor's tile." He grabbed it and examined it at close quarters, his conviction growing quickly. "It *is*," he decided finally. "Or if it isn't, it's another the spit of the one he had on him."

At that point one of the farmers snatched it from his hands.

"Blast you and your hat. Here – what are you going to do about it, that's what we want to know. Get a move on and shunt that b – old tin can of yours out of the way, quick, or I'll send you where this's going."

He crumpled up the Homburg and, amidst the laughter of his friends, pushed off Halliday's angry hands and kicked the hat into the fog, across the footway. It disappeared beyond the breast-high ironwork fencing which protected the outer side of the footway; nothing more was heard of it for over two months, when the captain of a Norwegian timber-ship handed it over to the Westmouth police with the explanation that it had fallen on to the deck of his ship when on its way down the river on its previous homeward voyage.

Halliday's car was completely out of action; the front wheels of the other, forced askew on a bent front axle, were so badly damaged that any hope of steering it without disaster for fifteen miles on such a night – even if its owner was willing to risk an empty radiator – had already disappeared. Leaving the disputants to a wrangle which seemed unlikely to lead to any profitable result, Glennie returned to his lodge and got busy on the telephone. Within half an hour the breakdown lorry from a garage in Linwood had arrived and towed the two crippled cars off the bridge to a position of comparative safety, from which it then removed them, one by one, to cover for the night in the garage workshops.

In the stress of his accident and of the subsequent salvage operations, the mystery of their original cause and of his employer's disappearance, had faded from Halliday's disturbed mind. His car under shelter, however, he rang up Sir William Larmour's house on the garage's phone and learned to his surprise that not only had Dr. Melhuish not arrived there, but that he had not been expected to arrive there, no member of the household being in the slightest degree indisposed. Still more perplexed, Halliday returned to Victoria Square and consulted with Clegg, who, however, was positive that the call which had taken his employer out had been one from Lady Larmour. The two men sat up until half-past one by the fire in Clegg's pantry, discussing the matter desultorily until drowsiness overtook them. Halliday then went off to bed; Clegg, having waited vainly another half-hour for his master's return, followed his fellow servant's example shortly after two o'clock.

He was awakened a little more than two hours later by the insistent ringing of the front door bell. Huddling into a dressing gown – for he had decided to sleep in the greater part of his day attire – he made his shivering yawning way to the hall door and opened it, expecting to find his employer's familiar figure at its other side. Instead, a stalwart figure, caped and helmeted, appeared in the aperture, the bas-relief of a policeman of whom the posterior half merged in the background of the fog.

"Morning. You are Dr. Melhuish's butler?"

"Yes."

"You probably haven't heard yet," said the constable with calm matter-of-factness, "Dr. Melhuish was taken out of the river shortly after three o'clock this morning, dead. There's a chauffeur lives here over the garage named Harry Halliday, I understand. I want to see him."

For a few moments Clegg was too staggered for speech. His hands vaguely gathered his dressing gown a little more closely to his plumpish curves. He stared at the policeman's stolid, glistening face helplessly.

"Come in, officer," he said at length. "I'll get Halliday, if you'll wait here. Out of the *river*? How the deuce did the Doctor get into the *river*?"

Doctors didn't get into rivers. Butlers didn't get into rivers. No respectable person thought of being found in a river at three o'clock in the morning...

But the policeman had no explanation to offer. He appeared merely bored and wet. The butler drifted away slowly in search of Halliday, repeating as he went the query:

"But how the deuce...?"

The thought uppermost in his still drowsy mind was that the whole thing was most unreasonable and likely to deprive him of a good job. For Mrs. Melhuish would almost certainly not require a butler whose principal duty had been to attend to the patients and the never-resting telephone of a doctor's house.

He wondered if *he* would be expected to pass on these unpleasant tidings to his mistress over the phone. A trunk call – probably a matter of half-an-hour's wait. How would one say it? "I regret to have to tell you, 'm, that the Doctor's been taken out of the river, dead." Jolly sort of thing to have to say.

In any case, no more sleep tonight.

Chapter Four

THE TRAGEDY WHOSE DETAILS startled the readers of the Westmouth papers that morning was given some prominence also by the London press in briefer form. The summarised account which Gore read with horror at breakfast in the *Telegraph* sent him in haste to his telephone. Mrs. Melhuish, he was told, had learned of her husband's death at half-past four in the morning and had returned to Westmouth by the first fast train. The friends with whom she had been staying had insisted upon providing her with an escort, fearing a possible breakdown on Mrs. Melhuish's part in the course of the long journey. A wire from Westmouth, however, had informed them that she had arrived there without mishap, although she had not opened her lips once during the two-and-a-half hours' run.

Gore could see those lips. Nothing, he knew – no grief, no pain, no fear, no loss – could ever extort a whimper from them. That had always been her creed... drilled into her partly, perhaps, by three ruthless brothers and countless boy chums... but bred in her blood. He had seen once a not very skilful vet try to set a broken ankle for her on the roadside – the result of a cropper over one of the stone walls of the Berkeley country. She had smoked a cigarette tranquilly while the bungling, flustered little beggar had striven vainly with his raw-meat paws to get the loose ends of the two bones together....

He had seen her in worse trouble than that – seen her face the probable loss of everything a woman holds valuable – her husband, her home, her friends, her reputation. Not a whimper... the gamest, pluckiest little witch in the world.

But *this* was terrible, devastating. The abrupt, merciless obliteration of the man who, he knew, had been half of all the world held for her of value. More than half. Wrapped up as she was in her boy, her love for him, Gore had always seen, had been an afterthought of her love for Sidney Melhuish. And Sidney Melhuish was now a dead, meaningless thing, lying in a mortuary... gone from the clasp of those long fingers of hers for ever.

Terrible. Ghastly. Incredible.

Words... futile and exasperating. Oh damn everything. He got into a taxi, breakfastless, and rushed off to the London offices of Westmouth's most important morning paper, the *Hour's Mirror*. On its centre page he found the story told in full.

The body had been found – by merest accident, since the discovery had been made in darkness and fog – lying on one of the steeply-pitched mud banks forming the bed of the river, a little below the Suspension Bridge. The manner of its finding was in itself curious. A belated tramp-steamer bound for Cardiff had been caught by the fall of the tide and had gone aground. There being no likelihood of getting her afloat until the next tide the captain had decided, since there was some danger of her kneeling right over on the shelving bank which had entrapped her, to send a couple of steadying cables ashore at the east side of the river. The two men told off for this task – one of very considerable difficulty, since it involved crawling without guidance across a wide stretch of liquid mud in which they might at any moment sink breast-high – had made the first part of their journey in a boat rowed by a third member of the crew. When this smaller craft had also stuck fast in the mud they had left it, armed each with a plank, and had succeeded with the aid of this primitive equipment in reaching the bank and eventually making the hawsers fast. Their return journey to the waiting boat had been all but accomplished when one of the planks, as it was slid forward along the mud, had struck an obstacle which had proved, to their dismay, the body of a man. With the assistance of reinforcements from the crew, this flotsam of the tide had been brought ashore, under the eyes, as it had happened, of a policeman on patrol along the riverside. An examination of the dead man's pockets had revealed them empty. His head had received severe injury; his spinal column had been fractured; he had been dead before he reached the water. The marking on his linen had revealed his identity. The newspaper report was disposed to regard the murder as having been committed for the sake of robbery.

Two people had vouched for the fact that a telephone call had summoned Dr. Melhuish to Sir William Larmour's house in Woodleigh – Clegg, the deceased's butler, and Dr. Biddulph, a professional colleague. On the other hand, it was quite certain that that call had not come either from Lady Larmour or from any other person in Sir William's household. It had not been possible, so far, to ascertain from what instrument the call had emanated. But that its intention had been to ensure that Dr. Melhuish would pass along a certain definite route at a definite time, appeared certain. His only alternative route to the Larmours' house would have involved an inconceivable detour of several miles. No casualty amongst those brought into any of the hospitals that night had been collected from the Suspension Bridge.

The eastward-bound car – that which had passed Glennie just before he had found Dr. Melhuish's car standing deserted and without lights – had not yet been traced. Nor had the pair of pedestrians who must have actually passed Dr. Melhuish's car as it was moving along the bridge. The driver of the furniture lorry and his mate, however, had already been found and had given one important piece of information.

They had made out Dr. Melhuish's car – which they had expected to come upon on their near side, having been warned by Halliday – in time to avoid running into it. Its lights, they stated, had then been out; but both of them were of opinion that someone had been standing close beside it, leaning into it through the open offside door. This could not have been Halliday, who was then following the lorry some distance behind it. As they moved on slowly towards the west end of the Bridge, someone, running hard, had passed them on the footway at their near side. Neither of them had seen the runner, but both had heard his scurrying feet. The lorry driver had changed up after passing under the west tower and, as he had done so, he and his mate had heard a car getting under way some little distance ahead of them – perhaps thirty or forty yards – and had seen its lights appear suddenly, as if they had just been turned on, and then disappear into the fog.

Examination of the bridge itself had afforded no enlightenment as to the supposed outrage, the motive for which, apart from the unconvincing theory of robbery, remained unintelligible. The *Hour's Mirror* concluded its account by reminding its readers that the deceased physician, held in the highest esteem in both his personal and professional capacities, had a few years before been associated indirectly with another dastardly crime which had shocked not just the city of his adoption but the entire country.

With very mingled feelings, as he hurried through the revised edition of breakfast which his man Stephens provided, Gore reviewed the discussion of the preceding evening, so oddly apropos. Poor little dear... Even while she had proclaimed her hatred and abhorrence of a mere friend's association with life's darker side, her own man had been on his way to a death of diabolical cruelty.

A phrase of his own recurred to him, like a slap in the face – that damned, idiotic remark of his about widow's weeds. His brown face screwed itself up in a spasm of bitter self-reproach. *She* would remember that phrase – never forget it.

Well, there was nothing she would need *him* for. Relatives and friends by the dozen would gather about her and make anything easier that could be eased. Lord, he supposed, would be in charge of the business – a keen, excellent fellow – the shining light of the Westmouth Detective Division, whom Gore had come across in connection with the Mendip case, in the preceding year. But – viewed dispassionately, even – an incredible business.

Melhuish, of all people in the world, to die that way. Not, perhaps, very popular with his brother-practitioners in Linwood but beloved by his patients, esteemed by everyone. A man devoted to the highest of human endeavours – a man whose life had been as an open book. Who, conceivably, could have planned a dreadful death for such a man? Why, conceivably, could they have planned it?

For of course no one person, unless a veritable Hercules, could have accomplished it. Melhuish, if slight of build, had been wiry and active; a determined, courageous man, still in his early forties. The iron fencing which guarded foot passengers from the two-hundred-and-fifty-foot fall to the river, was, as Gore remembered it, rather more than breast-high. To lift a struggling eleven stone man over that barrier would be a task possible, perhaps, for a professional wrestler, but for any other assailant of even greatly more than average physique, a sheer impossibility. Two assailants at least, there must have been. Under the canopy of heaven... who?

***

He had a talk with Inspector Lord over the phone that afternoon in German – which Gore spoke intelligibly, Lord fluently, in addition to French, Italian, Spanish and Russian. Lord's side of the talk was not voluble, however; it was made perfectly clear that the Westmouth Detective Division's star performer felt entirely capable of clearing up the Suspension Bridge affair without the aid of outside suggestions. He had, at the moment, no particular line in sight. He hoped, not very convincingly, that Colonel Gore would look him up any time he happened to be in the neighbourhood of Westmouth. At the conclusion of the conversation Gore had acquired no fresh information and the conviction that half-a-crown and his best Deutsch had been wasted.

He sent Mrs. Melhuish a wire and a brief note, but received no reply. He had expected none. She had rarely answered his rare letters.

Chapter Five

MESSRS. GORE & TOLLEY were looking just then for three fiddles (amongst them the celebrated Silver Strad) which had disappeared mysteriously from the collection of a well-known amateur. Gore travelled up to Birmingham that evening, and was away from London for three days. It was not until he got back to town on Monday, November 25th, that he saw the intervening issues of the *Hour's Mirror*, which, however, contained no fresh information concerning the Suspension Bridge tragedy. A small paragraph tucked away at the foot of an unimportant page did not catch his eye. Nor, if it had, would it have interested him in the least. Chance, however, was to bring under his notice the minor tragedy which it reported.

His trip to the Midlands had been so far successful that negotiations for the restoration of the three stolen violins had already been opened at long range. Nothing of interest awaited his return to his headquarters. He spent an hour or two in rather irritable debate with what appeared to him a foolish and entirely futile temptation and finally made a dash for the best train of the day to Westmouth.

After all, Pickles need know nothing of his nearness to her. A little caution would enable him to keep out of her way – especially as it was unlikely that at present she was much out of doors. Even if she did learn that he was in Linwood, she could hardly resent the quite natural desire of one of her oldest friends to hear at first hand the latest news of progress – if any was being made – towards the clearing up of her husband's death. Lord had been stiff over the phone. But Gore thought he understood very well just why. He had persuaded Lord once into biting of more than he could chew. Lord was determined that that would not happen again. It was unlikely, however, that – with a little enticement – he would refuse to give a sufficiently straight hint as to what was being done. *If* anything *was* being done. There were several ways, unfortunately, of being given oversize mouthfuls to chew.

A quiet elderly man alone divided his smoker with him for the greatest part of his journey down, and, after an inspection of the bag of clubs above his head, struck up a conversation with him. Learning that Gore's destination was Linwood, where he himself resided. He returned to the golf bag – to him, evidently, the symbol of life's most absorbing interest.

"Every morning – not Sundays, of course – but every week-day morning, wet or fine, for thirty years, with perhaps the exception of twenty days in the year, I've played eighteen holes. I'm seventy-seven – and for thirty years I haven't had as much as a cold in my head. There – what do you say to that, Sir, as an advertisement for the royal and ancient game?"

Gore was suitably impressed. He gave his considered opinion that his companion did not look a day more than a remarkably fit and youthful fifty.

"Where do you play?"

"On the Downs. You know, perhaps, that we have a Linwood Downs Golf Club.. Not, perhaps, quite up to championship standard. Though I'll venture to bet that if a man could do a seventy-six over the lies on Linwood Downs, he'd beat Bobby Jones anywhere else. Talking about lies, I had a funny experience a few mornings ago. Or rather, rather a nasty experience, really…"

There was no help for it. Gore started another pipe and listened to the story amiably – the last thing in his mind being that it had any concern with the purpose which was hurrying him towards Linwood. Shorn of digression and comment, it was this.

The morning in question – that of the preceding Friday, Gore's first day in Birmingham – had been, alike there and in Linwood, wet and blustery. Undeterred, however, Gore's acquaintance – a retired tea-planter named Gardiner – had sallied forth on to the Downs with three other members of the club, contemporaries in age and enthusiasts of equal energy and regularity who had made up a morning foursome for more than a quarter of a century. If the game which they played was not of a kind to cause Mr. Bobby Jones serious uneasiness as to his laurels, it was played with a zest, genial but rigorous, which faced all difficulties with philosophical fortitude. In a driving, icy rain into the teeth of a gusty icy wind, the four gentlemen pursued their customary way, playing, as usual, for a penny a hole.

Now Linwood Downs, as all the world knows – Sam Weller walked across it once – forms an extensive grass plateau, high above the river, agreeably dotted with clumps of timber and bushes and thickets scattered at haphazard over its surface. Amongst these the golf course follows a clear and unmolested path... but not always, alas, the golfers. On this particular morning Mr. Gardiner's partner and Mr. Gardiner had both been suffering from severe pulls, much aggravated by a crosswind. Going to the third, therefore, they found themselves considerably to the left of the green and cut off from it by a tall and wide clump of thicket which reared itself some forty yards in front of them. It was Mr. Gardiner's partner's shot for the green and the ball lay in an uncharted tract of long grass. Taking his trusty mashie niblick and thoughtful stock of the thicket, he fixed his eye firmly on the ball and hit at it, with the intention of lofting it over the thicket and dropping it, on the other side, if not into the hole, at all events with puttable distance of it. The club, unfortunately, cut under the ball, which rose almost vertically in the air, from which it descended – after some time – into the thicket.

Following it, they saw, as they came up to the bush, that it formed, partly by nature, partly by human adaptation, one of those densely sheltered bowers much in request, at suitable hours and seasons, by amorous couples and compulsory sleepers-out. Penetrating into the darkness of this little grotto, they saw, lying on the ground, an aged and very ragged and dirty man, whom at first they judged asleep. Beside him lay a beer bottle and a small basket containing some bread and butter, an apple, and some pieces of cheese rind. But the salient fact of the moment was that the golf ball of which they had come in search lay in the battered and sodden hat which rested on the ground at his inner side.

Mr. Gardiner himself had at once detected a curious smell, not any of the customary smells of dirty old men. His companion, however, who happened to be an ardent photographer, had not only noticed the smell, but had at once recognised it as that of cyanide of potassium. When he had looked at the sleeper's face more attentively a growing suspicion had induced him to pick up the empty beer bottle and sniff it. His next proceeding had been to endeavour to ascertain whether the man was still alive. His next to state, with emphasis, that he was dead.

A mounted policeman, one of those picturesquely cloaked cavaliers who patrol the Downs with vigilant dignity, had passed across the vista of an open space a few moments before. His attention had been attracted, and the tenant of the thicket delivered into his charge. Both the policeman and the four gentlemen had at once recognised him as one of those dingy prowlers, for ever employed upon mysterious quests in retired nooks and corners, who were a familiar feature of the Downs.

But at this point a difficulty had arisen. What was to be done about the ball that reposed in the dead man's hat? Had that ball reposed upon the ground, the opponents had contended, it might have been picked up and dropped at the farther side of the thicket from the green, with a penalty of a stroke. To this Mr. Gardiner and his partner had agreed. But when their opponents had urged that, being in a hat, it must be considered not merely out of bounds but out of play absolutely, and that its owners, consequently, must lose the hole, Mr. Gardiner and his partner had disagreed vehemently. Their opponents had played one more and were still off the green. Nothing was less deserved than that they should win the hole – or, if a fair and reasonable interpretation of local rules was adhered to, less likely.

"It was a nice point, I think," commented the narrator. "And, of course, the policeman settled the matter by taking the hat and the ball while we were arguing about it. So we decided to halve the hole in the end. But it *was* a funny lie, wasn't it?"

Gore nodded, diverted by the gentle humour of the story's telling. "Rather an elaborate funeral feast for a Downs suicide," he smiled. "And rather an extravagant method. Usually, I think, they dive off the rocks free gratis and for nothing. But beer... *and* cheese... *and* cyanide of potassium... a whole bob's worth, at least. Poor old beggar... Well... I hope he's got good value for it."

"I've known him for years by sight," said his companion. "I understand that his friends on the Downs called him Woodbine, because he spent most of his time hunting about under the seats and so forth for the remains of cigarettes. The policeman found a couple of handfuls of cigarette ends in his pockets. Nothing else, except a badge or a locket of some sort, which I suppose he'd picked up somewhere. Not even a solitary match for all those lovely smokes! Perhaps that's why he decided to go somewhere where he could always be sure of getting a light."

The conversation turned to Linwood's sensation of four days' back (Mr. Gardiner, who had known Melhuish well by sight, had seen him in his car on the day of his death, in the neighbourhood of the Downs) and then to indifferent matters. The luckless Woodbine faded from Gore's mind long before the train slammed its way into the gloomy vault of Westmouth's terminus. One more unfortunate; Linwood Downs had known plenty of them in its countless time.

Installed, at all events temporarily, in a comfortable little hotel on the borderline between the city and its western suburb, he made a prolonged attempt to find Inspector Lord on the phone, without success. The evening being a fine one, he decided then, for lack of anything more interesting to do, to visit the scene of the tragedy and, possibly, have a chat with the Bridgekeepers. As most of them were probably officials of long service, there was just the chance that one of the men on duty might remember him and prove willing to provide some scraps of information not given by the local press.

This hope was in some measure fulfilled. Glennie, the man he was most anxious to interview, happened to be on duty that evening, and found no difficulty in recognising the appearance, if not the name, of the tall, spruce gentleman who entered into affable conversation with him. Learning that he was speaking to a personal friend of the late Dr. Melhuish's, he narrated with succinct vividness the story of the tragedy as seen from his own viewpoint.

From him Gore learned for the first time of the finding of the bashed-in Homburg hat and its subsequent disappearance. Glennie's estimate of times was that Halliday had returned to the east lodge from eight to ten minutes after he had passed it in his car; that he had remained about five minutes at the lodge; that then perhaps seven or eight minutes had elapsed before he, Glennie, had gone along the Bridge, and a further seven or eight before he had got back to the east end of the Bridge and found Halliday there once more.

"So that, whoever did it, Sir, they must have had a good ten minutes to do it in, at least. Poor old Halliday was talking to me this morning about that. He's in a proper state the way the police have been on to him about it."

"Really?"

"Yes. He's got it into his head they think he may have done it, because they keep on worrying him about the times. They say – how was it, if he was sent back in a hurry to telephone that it took him so long to get to it? Of course *he* says, on account of the fog and because he was trying to start his engine for a good bit before he was sent back to telephone. But they won't be satisfied with that, seemingly. If you ask me, Sir, the trouble is that Halliday didn't take any notice of the man that stopped the car, really. But afterwards he kept trying to think what sort of a chap he had looked like, and persuaded himself he'd seen what he didn't. Anyhow, he's told the police two or three different stories, and that's started them guessing about Halliday himself. Seems he was a bit queer a few years ago and was shut up for a while. Of *course*, they've raked that up..."

"As a matter of fact, did he give any description of the man who stopped the car when he came back to telephone?"

"No. Not then, Sir. Just told us a bloke had stopped it. Afterwards – I mean, after it was all over and he was waiting for his car to be towed away – he told us then that the man he'd seen in front of his lights was a big chap in a blue rainproof coat, with a cap pulled right down over his face, and a pair of big white wash-leather gloves. He noticed the gloves especially, he said, because he thought the chap was a policeman at first. But he's changed most of that since. He says, now, that the chap was wearing a bowler, he thinks, and wasn't anything out of the ordinary for size and had a thick blue cloth overcoat on – what you'd call a Melton. Only thing he *hasn't* changed is the gloves."

"Not very helpful," Gore commented. "Anyhow, someone stopped him, and said someone else had been taken ill on the footway. The footway on his off side?"

"Yes, Sir. Of course, I needn't tell you, if there had been fifty people ill on it, he couldn't have seen one of them from where he was in that fog. Dr. Melhuish got out of the car, then—"

"Almost at once, I take it?"

"So it seems, Sir. And he and this man went across the roadway together. Halliday was starting up his engine again, and Dr. Melhuish came back to him and told him to go and telephone for the ambulance.

"He spoke pretty sharp, and Halliday nipped out pretty smart, I expect, and started back here. He says the last he saw of the Doctor, he and the man with the gloves were climbing over on to the footway. But he didn't pay any more attention to them. In fact, he says, he could hardly see them from the side of the car, when he got out."

"He heard nothing suspicious?"

"Not a sound, sir."

"Anything noticeable about any of the cars that went across just before Dr. Melhuish's – anything that stuck in your mind?"

But Glennie and his mate had discussed that point exhaustively and were unable to recall anything that had attracted their attention or that – looking back – appeared now suspicious. Their joint recollection was that, about three minutes before Dr. Melhuish's car had come along, a new Morris Cowley saloon, dark blue or green, had crossed westward, driven by a chauffeur in livery and containing two ladies and an elderly gentleman; a couple of minutes before that the two-seater of the Vicar of Woodleigh, driven by one of his daughters, had gone over the same way; and a few minutes before that the van of a dairyman at Portsham had preceded it. Beyond that, their recollection did not go with any certainty. Of another thing, however, they were both quite sure. No tall or fairly tall man, in a blue overcoat of any kind, with a large pair of white gloves of any material, had bought a ticket from either of them that evening.

From the Bridge Gore walked back through the once familiar streets of Linwood, yielding to an impulse which induced him to take Victoria Square on his way. As he came abreast of the steps of the Melhuishs' house its hall door opened. For a moment the possibility of an abrupt encounter with its mistress disconcerted him. But the figure which came down the steps was that of no slim, fleet-footed witch. The hefty young man who descended them slowly and with unmistakable dissatisfaction in his every movement, was Inspector Lord.

"Hullo. Run me to earth, Colonel, have you? I heard you had been looking for me. Which way are you going?"

"Yours," replied Gore. "You're dining with me this evening."

The other laughed. "Cheaper to buy an evening paper, you know. You'll get exactly as much out of it – which is just damn-all."

"So bad as that?"

Lord nodded, hesitated, then decided on bluntness definitely, as they moved on side by side.

"You knew Melhuish intimately?"

"I knew him. He wasn't a man, I think, who allowed anyone to know him intimately."

"Mrs. Melhuish?"

"Oh, yes. I have known Mrs. Melhuish, I believe, since her perambulator days. Perhaps I ought to say that my interest in this affair is due to that fact. Not to any passionate desire to butt in... as it may possibly seem to you."

The winning modesty – not to say diffidence – of this disclaimer, moved Inspector Lord's nicely cut lips to a sardonic grin.

"As if anyone could dream of such a thing, my dear Colonel." He abandoned irony. "Rats. Now look here. I'm open to a trade. I'll give you what I have for something I haven't... quite."

"Everything I have," Gore assured him, "is yours. I needn't say that offer includes my profound sympathy. Poor Melhuish has been dead nearly five days now. Unfortunate that nothing has turned up, isn't it. I expect your Chief's beginning to get a little peevish."

The offer of a cigarette and the lighting of two gave this poisoned dart a little time to do some rankling. He twisted it gently, then:

"Nothing doing with Halliday, of course?"

Lord took swift stock of the agreeable profile revealed by a streetlamp.

"Oh. So you've been busy already. Though I don't expect you'll tell me anything I don't know about Halliday."

"I will," smiled Gore. "He shuts his eyes every time he changes down. He drove me up on to the Mendips one day, just about this time last year. I noticed that little weakness of his, I remember. Now, you know, a chap who closes his eyes because he thinks he's going to hear a grinding noise is incapable of…"

"Blow Halliday and his eyes," snapped Lord. "If he'd kept them open that night… I'm not interested in Halliday. I never was, personally. The person I am interested in is – Mrs. Melhuish. She was mixed up, wasn't she, with a chap called Barrington, who got done in down here a few years ago?"

Gore stiffened, despite his determination to be agreeable.

"Mixed up?"

"It was the year before I came down to Westmouth. But I've had a talk with Long, who had charge of the case. Of course you'll remember all about it. As a matter of fact, I believe it was your first experiment in… er…"

"—butting in," Gore supplied. "Yes."

"Mrs. Melhuish had been pretty intimate with this fellow Barrington, hadn't she?"

"Everyone in Linwood knew him well, I believe."

"Yes. But Long tells me that there was something more to it than that with Mrs. Melhuish, he always thought. It was known that he had been bleeding quite a lot of people around here. What I want to find out is… was Mrs. Melhuish one of them?"

Now, how the devil, had that mess of five years ago – cleaned up, as Gore had believed, and wiped out of Pickles' life for ever, without even the breath of a suspicion touching her – been dragged to light again? Barrington – Frensham, his confederate – Thomson, his tool – all three were dead and done with; it had seemed certain for those five years that none of those three tongues had told Sergeant Long (he was an inspector, now, Gore learned) of Pickles' secret. As certain as that from Sidney Melhuish's lips no one had ever heard a whisper concerning it. The Melhuishs' servants...? Twelve months ago, at any rate, their butler and one at least of their maids had been survivals from the date of the Barrington affair. Impossible to feel sure about servants, of course .

Possibly the intelligent Lord was just guessing, on a ground-work of suspicion supplied by his friend, Inspector Long. In any case he had to be handed the lie, in sugar. Or perhaps more neatly in vinegar.

"My dear Lord, you know as well as I do the attitude of the upper lower male mind towards the upper middle female who happens to be unusually pretty, unusually smart and quite indifferent to his existence. He is just sufficiently complexed to find consolation in believing that the grapes are... shall we say... over ripe. I remember Long well . . he was a sergeant then. Excellent fellow for pinching drunks and blocking the traffic and all that, but... well, I suppose you've seen Mrs. Melhuish...?

"Yes. Just now... I certainly agree that she's a very charming person. Also that she was speaking the truth... almost... when she assured me that she could think of no one who could have any motive for serious enmity against her husband or herself...."

For a moment Gore's imagination ran riot foolishly. He saw himself kicking Inspector Lord, very hard down a very long passage in which turning was not possible. He only said, however, mildly:

"Almost? Don't tell me that Long has succeeded in infecting your mind. . . Anyhow... what's the big idea? Obviously Barrington didn't pull this job. Nor did Frensharn. Nor did Thomson. And that about exhausts the possibilities of *that* little lot, doesn't it?"

"Frensham had a couple of pals working with him, Long says. You yourself gave him that bit of information, which, I presume, was correct?"

"Quite accurate," Gore agreed. "But they, I think, were just a pair of amateur thugs picked up by Frensham for a special job...

as a matter of fact, the job of knocking me out for a minute or two."

"They faded away, when Frensham went off the cliffs, I gather?"

Gore shrugged. "Not to spend five years planning revenge because one of their pals chucked another over the cliffs, dear boy. By the way... that reminds me... Coming down in the train I heard a sad little story about a gentleman called Woodbine. You've heard it too, I expect. Care to drop into the Club? I'm a member still, I believe. They used to give one quite a decent little meal..."

Lord declined, however, the renewed invitation to stay on for dinner at the Club. But he consented to a comfortable armchair before the blazing fire in a still empty lounge and some brown sherry which soothed effectually his slightly ruffled soul.

"As you mentioned our friend Woodbine," he said, after some moments, "I wonder if you've ever seen anything like this before. Rum little gadget. We found it in his pocket."

He took out a little packet of tissue paper, unrolled it, and handed its contents to Gore – a circular badge of silver. Inside the circle was a triangle, intersecting a square. In the square was a monogram consisting of the letters D, E, and Q, interlaced with such intricacy that it was not possible to determine in what order they were intended to be read. At the back were pin and catch of unusual solidity. The diameter of the outside circle was a little over an inch and a half.

"Looks like a problem in what we used to call Euclid in my days," Gore smiled. "The letters make 'Q.E.D.' one way. That was always the most satisfactory part of propositions in Euclid, so far as I was concerned. The happy ending for me, always... and, one presumes, for the original owner of this little affair. Not, probably, Woodbine the Weary?"

"No. A pal of his says Woodbine found it on the Downs a few days ago. You can't think of any club or association or mathematical body of any sort that those initials would fit?

Didn't strike me about the Q.E.D. idea. What's it... *Quad erat*
something or other?"

"*Quad erat demonstrandum*. Meaning, 'And that's that.'"

"Euclid, you say? Never heard of it."

"He died a little before your time," Gore explained. "What
are you carrying this treasure trove round for?"

Lord explaining that he had interviewed Woodbine's friend
that afternoon with reference to it, Gore handed it back to him.

"Only thing I can make out of it is that it was made in the
States. Those serifs and counters are American. Worn for a considerable time evidently. Also belonged at some time to someone who attached value to it and wore it because he did. He had
a new pin and catch fitted to it... both very strong... evidently
determined not to lose it. Of no value in itself... clumsily made
– design of monograms poor and confused. So the value must
have lain in wearing it... or in some association with other values.
Possibly a college club. Sorry I can't be more helpful."

He steered the talk back to the Suspension Bridge and gradually elicited from his companion the unwilling admission that
beyond questioning Melhuish's servants and the bridgekeepers,
running down the furniture lorry which had crossed immediately after Dr. Melhuish's car, and looking into Halliday's
record, nothing had been done... for the very simple reason that
nothing else to do had suggested itself. The spoof telephone
call could not be traced. No one could give any information
as to Melhuish's private life, it seemed, except possibly Mrs.
Melhuish, since he had evidently been an extremely reserved and
reticent man. Mrs. Melhuish had treated the suggestion of an
enemy malevolent to the point of murder with contempt (Inspector Lord had evidently had an uncomfortable quarter hour
with Pickles that afternoon, and had not yet quite recovered
from it) and had also scouted the theory of murder for robbery's
sake. Her husband had never carried more than a couple of
pounds at most about with him; nothing had been taken from
his case, left in the car; if his watch and stethoscope and clinical

thermometer had been taken from his pockets they had been taken to convey the idea of robbery as motive for the crime.

"So…" Lord concluded, frowning at another glass of sherry held against the firelight ruefully, "what the devil *can* we do?" He meditated, and returned visibly to his solitary hope. "I don't know. I'd like to be quite certain that there is nothing in Long's idea. You see the danger is always that one refuses to accept the obvious. Now – if there's anything obvious about this business, it is that Melhuish had already been closely connected with another murder in Linwood within the past five years. Even the newspapers got on to that point at once. Barrington was murdered just outside Melhuish's house – with a Masai knife taken from a trophy in Melhuish's hall. He had been dining at Melhuish's house that night. I quite admit that Melhuish had – actually – no more to do with his murder than I had. Still, you can't get away from it, there was something odd in the way the whole affair seemed to centre round him and his house. Barrington's body was left outside his house in a car, next day… or the day after, wasn't it?"

"Yes."

"Thomson was employed by Melhuish as a temporary chauffeur. You can't get away from it. I want to know what became of those two birds – those pals of Frensham's, whom no one ever heard anything about afterwards. And I'm going to find out that first, if I can. The obvious thing to do …"

He rose, declined another invitation to stay and eat at the Club, and held out his hand.

"By the way," he said, "I don't know if you've heard or not. You were one of the last people poor old Melhuish had in his mind, apparently. He began a letter to you evidently just before he went out, that night. I saw it lying on the table in his consulting room. Well… we shall meet again, I expect. Staying down here long this trip?"

"No idea at the moment. I'll look you up from time to time, if I may. Good hunting. So sorry you won't grub with me."

When his guest had departed, Gore spun a penny solemnly. It fell tails. He put it back into his pocket and took out another. That one fell heads. Six minutes later he was standing on the steps of the Melhuishs' house in Victoria Square.

Chapter Six

Clegg's face lost something of its gloom at sight of the caller.

"Mrs. Melhuish is not at home, of course, Sir. But I'm sure she will see *you*, Sir. At all events, I'll chance it. Though I know she's terribly upset the way the police have been bothering her, poor lady. Bothering all of us, the silly ijits. I'll just run up and let..."

Gore stopped him. "Not just for a moment, Clegg. I'm going to take a great liberty first. Dr. Melhuish wrote a letter to me that night, I understand, just before he went out..."

"He began it, Sir... just before dinner. He never finished it, though. Only a few lines, Sir. It's lying on his table now."

He led the way to the consulting room, and indicated the unfinished letter silently. Gore picked it up and read it – re-read it – and then made a copy of it, replacing the original on the writing table to the butler's surprise. A little morocco-covered engagement book lay beside it, still open at the last page filled in – that containing Melhuish's appointments for the day of his death, Wednesday, November 20th. Gore noted that the name Larmour closed the list.

In reply to his inquiry as to whether Dr. Melhuish had not kept a more formal register of visits to and from his patients, Clegg produced the usual practitioner's ledger – kept, in this instance, with the orderly neatness which had been one of the dead man's many virtues. This book, too, had been entered up for November 20th, Sir William Larmour's name forming the last entry which Clegg had seen his master make before going out that night. Having compared the two lists carefully, Gore made a copy, adding to each name, with Clegg's impressed assistance, an address extracted from the Westmouth Directory. The list was a long one; this business took some little time. He was writing the last address, when Clegg, in the act of replacing the Directory on a shelf, turned his head towards the closed door.

"The mistress, Sir," he warned the visitor.

No doubt, having seen through the partially-open door that the lights were on in the consulting room, Pickles had suspected further activity on the part of Inspector Lord or his subordinates. Her expression, as she opened the door, was one of frozen anger. But at the sight of the tall, tweed-clad figure that had risen to greet her imperious entry her face changed, and her shadowed eyes flooded with the light of an incredulous relief.

"Wyck..." she said in a whisper, choked already. Before his hands could catch those she held out to him, she had burst into a storm of such sobbing as he had never before seen anguish a sane human being. For five days of impotent despair that storm had been gathering... Clegg, alarmed, drifted from the room, and stood afar off in the hall, fingering his chin, and eyeing the shut door of the consulting room doubtfully.

It was a long time after Colonel Gore's usual dining hour when that door opened again. To Clegg's intense relief, his mistress, who had existed entirely on tea and cigarettes for the past five days, ordered, with a ghostly something of her old self in voice and smile, the immediate preparation of a meal of some sort... the legitimate one of the hour having fallen into abeyance. Still more reassuringly, she made at all events a pretence of eating with the guest. True, there was another little outburst of tears when Master Simon appeared, by special request of his godfather, for "after-dinner." But the worst was past, Clegg felt. Something had been bound to go, he had felt. Well... better red eyes than the blazing green fires that had scared everyone in the house stiff for five days... *and* nights. The nights had been the worst. Clegg had spent most of them listening to his mistress roaming from room to room ceaselessly – upstairs to the master's room – downstairs to the study – across into the small sitting room – on into the big sitting room – out to the consulting room – back to the hall, where *his* things still hung – upstairs again, only to begin the same old thing all over once more. Got on your nerves, that sort of thing, after six or seven hours of it every night... You never knew what you might hear next, when she went into his bedroom... or into the consulting room... with all those bottles about... Clegg's smile was benign as, from the shadows at his sideboard, it rested discreetly upon the three faces warmed by the table's rosy lights.

He had a good night that night. No opening or shutting doors, no softly-moving feet, took him out of his snug bed. His face beamed as, at half-past ten next morning, he admitted Colonel Gore again.

Even at that moment Gore had not decided in what guise he was to present himself to the eyes which, he knew, the sound of his voice had turned towards the other side of the study door. Last night the only references to Melhuish had been the pitiful incoherences of a woman for whom life had, temporarily at least, lost all meaning, all sanity, and all purpose. His business had been to listen – to offer the clumsy soothing of the male – to avoid like death itself any slightest suggestion that the affair could hold any possible interest for him in a futile and purpose-less future, any emotion for him save sympathy with that past the memory of which was now to be all that life held for her. She had spoken furiously of the callous invasion of her grief by the police; he had gone away last night without even telling her of his meeting with Inspector Lord.

And this morning? Could he expect to find her looking at things through eyes any more matter of fact... any more re-signed? After all, what could it matter to her whether or not some scoundrel or scoundrels continued to live, or died at the end of a rope? Would a hundred hangings give her back her man... let her hear his key in the door even once more – hear even once more his quiet voice call her "Babs" – see even once more his slow smile dawn as he looked at her? Even to suggest prying into his private affairs would almost inevitably bring on another nerve storm.

Better by far, Gore decided, as he delivered his hat into Clegg's keeping, to keep right out of the deeps and to devote his visit to persuading her to a change of scene and association. Time would heal the hurt... everything passed. Perhaps then she would regret, if no vengeance had been taken for her. But, this morning, what more idiotic to think of offering her than a desire to help her to vengeance. He went into the study, sworn to go out of it in ten minutes without having mentioned Melhuish's name. The second thing he saw in the room was Melhuish's unfinished letter in Pickles' hands.

She held it out to him.

"I have seen it," he said gently, and tried to persuade her fingers to release it. But she continued to stare at the few lines of neat small handwriting as if she expected to hear a voice complete their unfinished message.

"Sidney never wrote to you, did he, Wyck?"

"No."

"This was the first letter he ever wrote to you, then?"

"Yes."

"The first... and the last. That's strange, Wyck... And he had been very busy all that day, Clegg says... He hated writing letters. He'd never have thought of writing one that evening unless there had been some special reason... some very special reason..."

She stared again for a little space, frowning. Then her eyes looked up quickly. "*That's* what you were doing last night at his table.... Going through his appointment-book...?"

He nodded. That quick, brave little brain of hers had steadied itself... there would be no hysterics this morning.

"Everyone whose name is on his list for that day will have to be seen, of course," he said, tentatively. "Inspector Lord didn't say that had been done... I'll see that it is. He saw your husband's letter on his table; he told me so himself. But naturally he was not to attach any significance to it. I'll try to start him on that job straight away, if I may use your phone."

"But Inspector Lord couldn't possibly know who is an old friend of yours and who isn't.... I mean – Sidney met someone or came across someone that day whom he thought you had some special interest in... Of course I know that any day he was likely to come across half a dozen people who were old friends of yours. There are plenty of them in Linwood still. But... why should he have written to you about *this* particular one... It's odd. It seems to *me* odd, Wyck... I can't get it out of my mind that... that... Oh, my God... why did I leave him? Why did I go up to London? If I had been here... he would have told me... I could have stopped his going out that night. It is I – I who have killed him..."

The absolute conviction with which she said the words was worse than any tears or hysterics could have been. He did his best – but she refused to be comforted. It was useless, he knew from long experience, to attempt specious argument with Pickles; she knew perfectly well now... somehow or other... that just the suspicion which she had put into words had flashed into his own mind the moment he had read those few precisely-written words. That "old friend" must be found. And... of course she was right... the only person who could do the finding was himself. He left her, still staring stonily at the unfinished letter, and, after some delay, succeeded in getting Lord on the telephone, and arranging that the latter would call at Victoria Square in an hour or so. Collecting the little appointment-book from the consulting room, he returned to the study.

One comfort awaited him there – the swift turn of a golden head. She wanted something done – she looked to him to have it done. Tacitly *that* point had been settled.

Name by name, the appointment book's list for November 20th was gone over and debated. Well as Gore had known Linwood in the years before the War – his family had been settled in Westshire for several generations – he recognised few of the names. The lean years since 1914 had wrought many changes; the houses where he had dined and danced were now broken up into flats and filled from basement to chimney pot with strange wreckage. Of the twenty-seven patients visited by Melhuish on the morning of November 20th, and the twenty-three who had called to see him in the course of the afternoon, but two were personally known to Gore. Even to Mrs. Melhuish most of the names were unfamiliar. Linwood's population was now largely a floating one; her husband had rarely spoken of his patients, even to her.

Melhuish's meeting with the "old friend," however, had been an unexpected one, obviously – and therefore quite possibly, had taken place in just one of those houses in which it had seemed unlikely to occur. At any rate, all these people must be seen. There was, of course, the possibility that the meeting had taken place, not in any house, but in the street, along Melhuish's way that morning. But Halliday, summoned to the study, was quite positive that, at all events while in the car, his employer had spoken to no one save himself. That morning – following a night of hard frost – had been very nearly as foggy from nine o'clock on to about eleven as the night of that day had been. He gave it as his opinion that, even though necessarily the car had been driven slowly, it would have been difficult for Dr. Melhuish to have recognised anyone on the footpath in passing. On the other hand, as usual when several calls were to be made close to one another but in different streets, Dr. Melhuish had at different points along the way left the car to wait at a convenient place while he performed these shorter journeys on foot. The meeting might have taken place in that way unwitnessed by Halliday – or anyone.

With some difficulty the chauffeur was induced to evolve from his memory the points at which he had waited that morning. Already, however, that morning had begun to blur, confused by reminiscences of countless other mornings on which he had done the same things at the same places at the same times. Gore tested him with Melhuish's list; it was quite certain that from Halliday's unaided recollection no one could ever have discovered with any accuracy even sixty percent of the addresses to which he had driven his employer on that particular morning.

While they waited for Inspector Lord's coming, they made out a chart of Melhuish's movements on his last round, with such approximate times as could be elicited from Halliday. They had just completed this when Lord arrived, arrayed with a smartness which attracted Gore's attention. It was to be quite clear that Inspector Lord, at all events, suffered from no social complexes.

His keen, good-looking face displayed a careful lack of enthusiasm as Gore tactfully indicated the line of action suggested by the unfinished letter. The ironical smile which he affected received the mild hint that Colonel Gore should accompany him upon the proposed round of inquiry.

"Well, frankly – I should prefer you didn't, Colonel," he said. "Though, of course, I can't prevent your running round asking questions on your own. But in the first place, I honestly don't think any importance whatever is to be attached to the mere coincidence that Dr. Melhuish intended to write to you – even if it was for the first time – on that particular night. If I may say so, Mrs. Melhuish, I think that that letter was to have been written to Colonel Gore, simply because Dr. Melhuish happened to have been thinking of you – as he very naturally would whenever he had a free moment. He remembered that you were to see Colonel Gore in London – he remembered that he had met some friends of Colonel Gore's that day... very probably also an old friend of yours... you have many friends in common, I feel sure... and so it just came into his head to fill in a few moments while he waited for his dinner gong by dashing off a few lines to Colonel Gore which would probably come to your eyes also. I'm not trying to be ingenious. I'm simply holding on to the obvious... for the present. I put it to you frankly, Colonel... amongst all your friends, old, new and middling... can you think of one likely to commit murder for any reason whatever?"

"Several of 'em," replied Gore promptly. "That argument is neither ingenious *nor* obvious, Lord." He turned to Pickles. "Had Dr. Melhuish written to you that day?"

"Yes. His letter got to London after I had left, next morning. I can get it for you.... It was written just after lunch... There is nothing whatever in it about his having met any old friend either of Colonel Gore's or of mine – though he mentioned Colonel Gore in his letter—"

"I should like to see it, if I may."

"Certainly."

Lord turned as the door closed behind Mrs. Melhuish. "Sorry, Colonel – but there's nothing in this, you know. Of course we'll make the round – and you can come along with pleasure if you really want to waste a morning rather tediously. But what I had *hoped* you had to tell me was that you had got some information from Mrs. Melhuish for me... along the lines we discussed yesterday."

Gore considered. After all, *no* faintest indication of a track must be left untried.

"I'll ask Mrs. Melhuish the question I gather you asked her – if you wish," he said, politely— "What was it, by the way, precisely?"

"Whether she or her husband had heard or seen anything recently of any person whom either of them knew to have been in any way connected with Barrington."

"I see." He turned to Pickles, who had re-entered the room and repeated the question verbatim. She shook her head impatiently but decisively.

"No. Here is my husband's letter."

Lord read it and then passed it to Gore, without comment. Written after lunch – for it referred to the arrival of a patient during that meal – it supposed that Mrs. Melhuish had already seen Colonel Gore, but said nothing of any intention to write to him.

"One concludes then that, as Dr. Melhuish's morning round was over when he wrote, this old friend of yours must have turned up between lunch and dinner time."

"If so, one concludes wrongly," said Gore rather sharply. "The last words Dr. Melhuish wrote were 'while on my.' The next word he would have written would certainly have been 'rounds.' The old friend was met that morning..."

"Why not 'while on my way,' for instance? Dr. Melhuish may have gone out in the afternoon."

Inspector Lord had a first little triumph. Clegg was summoned and stated that Dr. Melhuish had gone out for something over half an hour that afternoon – a most unusual interruption of his afternoon's usual routine, which had filled the waiting room chock-a-block – to visit a patient who had been operated upon that morning, a Mrs. Hayling, who lived close at hand. Lord threw out a spread hand.

"There we are. He met the 'old friend' on his way to Mrs. Hayling in the afternoon."

He turned to Pickles.

"I should like to go through any correspondence Dr. Melhuish may have received on that day or the days just before... in fact, any papers you can let me see..."

"My husband kept all his letters and papers in the consulting room. Nothing has been disturbed, I believe. . . The butler will bring you the keys of the safe. I found them in my husband's dressing room."

"I hardly like to trouble you, Mrs. Melhuish – but, of course, it might be of assistance if you would help me to go through any letters and so forth there are..."

The invitation deliberately excluded Gore, but, in obedience
to a glance from Pickles, he followed them to the consulting
room and assisted as spectator at the depressing little investigation which followed. It had evidently been Melhuish's habit
to keep all letters, docketed and filed alphabetically, for several
months at least after their receipt. For a couple of hours Lord
occupied himself with the contents of the files and the safe,
occasionally asking a question which was answered as tersely. A
collection of chequebook stubs underwent careful examination
but, save in one instance, no recent payment by cheque of any
considerable sum was to be found. The exception was one of
£125 to someone named Dorch, on November 18th.

The investigator looked enquiringly towards Mrs. Melhuish.

"I have heard my husband speak of a Dr. Dorch," she said. "A
patient of his. I know nothing more about him... except that I
believe he lives up somewhere near the Downs, and has a good
deal of money. Oh yes. His daughter married a Dr. Simpson, I
believe, who is on the Infirmary Staff."

"The name Dorch was on the list of appointments for that
morning," Gore recalled. He consulted his list. "Aloysius I.
Dorch, D.Sc. Yes. Quite right. He lives at ' Wavertree,' Downshill Road. Let's see what he does."

The Directory, however, afforded no clue to Dr. Dorch's
occupation, and the payment of £125 to him remained unexplained until, going through some loose papers in a small drawer
of the writing table, he came upon a brief note signed with the
unusual name, and dated November 19th.

*"MY DEAR DOCTOR, – Thank you for your cheque for
£125. I enclose the Corpus delicti. Yours truly,*
ALOYSIUS I. DORCH."

"Q.E.D. as we used to say."

Inspector Lord's Latin had rusted somewhat. The word
delicti he did not recognise, the word *corpus*, however, he did.

Concluding, rather hastily, as he told Gore afterwards, that this communication must relate to a payment for anatomical or pathological specimens or something of the kind, he refrained from reading its contents aloud in Mrs. Melhuish's presence. He handed it, however to Gore to inspect. The latter's comment was interested, but unexpected.

"Rather curious that we should have been discussing those very initials yesterday, isn't it?"

"What initials?" Lord asked, puzzled for the moment. Then he saw, and the ironic smile produced itself once more.

"Still more remarkable that Mr. Dorch's own initials should be A. I. D.," he said dryly. "I don't think we are likely to get much of it from your friend Euclid, though, Colonel. However, we can ask Mr. Dorch about this cheque when we see him this afternoon. It's half-past one now. Suppose we make a start at half-past two?"

At the appointed hour the tour of inquiry was begun, accordingly, its course, following Gore's chart, beginning a few doors from the Melhuish's house, working up and down the neighbourhood surrounding Victoria Square and striking then northwards towards the Downs and another ganglion of Roads, Avenues, Places, Terraces, and Gardens. The succession of failure to failure soon became monotonous in its total lack of result.

But the investigators continued on their way patiently, undeterred by the marked coldness which in several cases greeted the intrusion of a police official. The majority of Dr. Melhuish's visits that morning had apparently been brief. The middle-aged lady who had had a stiff neck and the elderly gentleman who had had one of his usual bouts of indigestion, were alike surprised and a little indignant that they should be supposed capable of throwing the least light upon a murder. More trying still were the patients who wanted to hear all about their pet physician's death, or who had "pretty good" ideas of their own on the subject to expound at length for Inspector Lord's guidance.

The November afternoon wore in to a frosty dusk swiftly. Darkness had fallen before their task was more than half-completed. It was getting on towards six o'clock when, having skirted the southern edge of Linwood Downs, they arrived at a short row of large detached houses, each surrounded by grounds of just sufficient extent to cut it off effectually from sight and sound of the road and of its next door neighbours. A wallplate informed them that at this point the semi- rural avenue which they had been following became Downshill Road for a space. The first house of the road was Wavertree, and at sight of it Gore recalled that, as a very small boy, he had once been a guest at a Christmas party given by tenants no doubt long ago scattered over this world and the next.

A smallish, dapper man came out of the gates as they arrived at them, passed them, and then, seeing that they had turned into the short drive, came back.

"Excuse me – but did you wish to see Mr. Dorch? He is away at present for a day or so, in Liverpool."

"Well, yes," Lord replied. "I should like to have seen him for a moment. However – if he's in Liverpool, obviously—"

"I am his secretary – my name is Ross. Perhaps I could be of some assistance to you...?"

"Mr. – or should I call him Dr. – Dorch?"

The secretary shrugged. "Dr. Dorch holds the degree of Doctor of Science. Some people call him Doctor – some Mister..."

"I understand he was a patient or a personal friend of the late Dr. Melhuish's?"

"Both. Dr. Melhuish has attended him for many years – nine or ten."

"Dr. Melhuish called here to see Dr. Dorch on the morning of Wednesday last – the day of his death."

"Yes. He saw Dr. Dorch that morning for a few moments. Dr. Dorch has been having some trouble from neuritis lately. Nothing very serious. My recollection is that Dr. Melhuish stayed only a very few minutes with him on Wednesday morning. Dr.

Dorch will be very greatly shocked to hear of his death... I don't suppose the Liverpool papers will have reported it."

"What is Dr. Dorch's occupation or business? Scientific work, I presume?"

"Yes... His interests are chiefly scientific. Though I suppose one would hardly describe them as an occupation or business." The secretary interjected a suave question. "May I ask your name?"

"I am Inspector Lord, of the Westmouth Detective Division. What I wished to ask Dr. Dorch was whether, while Dr. Melhuish was here on Wednesday morning last, he met or saw any other person than Dr. Dorch himself."

The secretary's face was invisible in the darkness of the drive, but his surprise was audible.

"Myself – the servant who let him in and out – I cannot think of anyone else besides Dr. Dorch. May I ask the reason of the question?"

Lord laughed. "Never expect a policeman to give a reason, Mr. Ross. That is quite sure, however... Dr. Melhuish met no one at this house that morning, except the persons you have mentioned?"

"That is so."

Lord turned to Gore. "Care to have a look at Dr. Dorch's parlourmaid, Colonel? I gather that his secretary and you have *not* met before."

"I think not. But perhaps we had better inspect the parlourmaid."

"The parlourmaid happens to be a butler," said Ross stiffly. "I'm afraid I don't quite understand. Who is this gentleman? Also belonging to the Detective Division?"

"No – unfortunately. This is Colonel Gore – a friend of the late Dr. Melhuish's. We should like to see the servant whom Dr. Melhuish saw on Wednesday morning."

"With pleasure," the secretary replied. "But unluckily, he is out at the moment. If you could call a little later – say between seven and eight, I expect he will have got in by that time. He gets Monday afternoons off."

"We can see him tomorrow morning," Lord decided. "Just one more question, Mr. Ross – sorry to detain you. Do you know anything of any business dealings between Dr. Dorch and the late Dr. Melhuish?"

"Business dealings? No."

"Dr. Dorch would perhaps not view them in the light of business dealings exactly. Scientific people keep as far away from the word business as they can, don't they? But it's possible, perhaps, that Dr. Dorch may have supplied Dr. Melhuish with some pathological specimens – or some apparatus – or something of a scientific sort...? The reason I ask is that Dr. Melhuish made a payment by cheque to Dr. Dorch on November 18th of a hundred and twenty-five pounds. Perhaps you can tell us what that was for?"

The secretary reflected. "I remember now a cheque of Dr. Melhuish's passing through my hands within the past week. But I'm afraid I can't remember that Dr. Dorch made any remark to me about it, except that it was to be lodged in the ordinary course. Probably, I should say, settlement of some commission with which Dr. Melhuish had entrusted Dr. Dorch. Dr. Dorch is, as you are possibly aware, a well-known authority on pictures and china and silver and so forth. He attends important sales from time to time, and buys either for himself or for friends who prefer to rely on his judgment. It may have been something of that sort. However, when Dr. Dorch returns, I will ask him about it. I expect him back the day after tomorrow at latest. I could ring you up – Inspector...?"

"Lord. Thank you, Mr. Ross. Good evening. We'll come along tomorrow morning, then, and inspect your parlour-man."

At their next place of call, however, the allusion in Melhuish's letter was explained.

At the door of a shabby little flat at the top of a tall converted house in Tenby Road, they were received by a worn-looking, blowsy lady with a furiously-howling infant in her arms – her latest and seventh grandchild, she explained. Upon learning the motive of their visit she ushered them into a tiny, shabby sitting room, from which she removed five more grandchildren by main force. She indicated then a thin, bleary-eyed middle-aged man, in dressing-gown and slippers, who had been reading an evening newspaper by a sad little fire with the aid of a bottle of stout and a villainously odoured pipe. At sight of Gore, this individual sprang to his feet and held out his hand warmly "Gore – well, I'm damned. My dear old chap, how the devil are you?"

Recognising with some difficulty the blotched, flabby face whose wavering smile strove to conceal its embarrassment, Gore shook the proffered hand. He had last seen the face being violently sea-sick on a leave boat on a stormy day in 1916; on the whole it had looked more attractive then than it did at the moment. But, if never the face of a friend, it had once been the face of one of his subalterns. He stayed for a little while to listen to its owner's misfortunes since his demobilisation – Lord, with the ironic smile well in evidence, had made his escape as soon as possible, in high good humour over his third little triumph – and, having learnt that the seven "blinkin' kids" were the offspring of a widowed sister, who apparently supported the menage, lent him a fiver and departed into the darkness, pursued by gratitude perfumed with Guinness.

There could be no doubt, he told himself, as he walked towards his hotel and dinner, that the little mystery was solved. His old friend had at all events asked Melhuish on that Wednesday morning whether he ever saw anything of "old Gore" now, knowing that they were friends. That seemed to settle the matter.

On the other hand – Melhuish had been attending one or other of the "blinking seven" apparently for several years back.

The old friend – his name was Jolliffe – had had no job, it seemed, since the war, and was probably at home most mornings when the doctor had called. Melhuish must have known, in all probability for a considerable time past, that his patients' uncle claimed ancient friendship with Colonel Gore. But he had never judged the knowledge worth passing on... until the night of his death. Why *then*?

Discreetly Jolliffe had been induced to remember what he had done on last Wednesday evening. He had not gone out – on account of the fog – and had read a French edition of a novel banned by the censor in England, lent to him by a "little girl." He had found it disappointing and had gone to bed early. As this account had been given in the presence of his sister's mother-in-law, it was to be presumed that Mr. Jolliffe, at any rate, had been nowhere near the Suspension Bridge round about nine o'clock on Wednesday evening.

Gore got Inspector Lord on the telephone before bedtime that night.

"Well, that seems to be that."

"In fact," agreed Lord, "Q.E.D. No need to trouble the he-parlourmaid at Dr. Dorch's – nor any other kind anywhere – I think?"

"No. There's just one thing I forgot to ask you this afternoon. Have they inquested our friend Woodbine yet?"

"With all the honours – yesterday. Why?"

"Suicide?"

"As Latin appears fashionable in this part of the world just now – why not *felo de se*? Anyhow suicide was what it worked out at. What's bitten you now, Colonel? Think Melhuish may have hired Dr. Dorch to do Woodbine in – and that Woodbine was the '*corpus delicti*'?"

Inspector Lord waited for a chuckle. He got only another question. "Found out where the old chap got the cyanide of potassium? It was potassium cyanide?"

"Oh yes. No... I'm afraid nobody seems to have worried about that. It's not hard to get, you know. Why?"

"I think it might be just as well to find out – if you can."

"Hardly worthwhile now. Probably impossible. I keep on asking why. Please tell me."

"Chiefly because I learned from the American consul half an hour ago that Dr. Dorch is an American subject. So is Mr. Ross, his secretary – though, as a matter of fact, he is an Englishman."

There was a silence at Inspector Lord's end.

"Well – what about it?" he asked at length. But this must stop, he decided. "Now look here, Colonel. This is a killing, in Linwood – which is, though it doesn't know it, a place in real life. Every killing in real life is a damn silly thing, done by a damn silly fool – just that – not a – not a detective novel. Don't worry. This particular damn silly business is being looked after all right, thanks all the same. Goodnight."

Unruffled, but in rather rapid tempo, Colonel Gore's voice got in a last question.

"Was the basket Woodbine's basket? Where did his friend say he..."

But at the other end silence, dead and disgusted, remained the only answer.

Chapter Seven

A TALK WITH PICKLES next morning made it quite certain that, to her knowledge at least, no faintest echo of her sinister adventure of five years before had ever disturbed the smooth happiness of her life with Sidney Melhuish. That danger, at least, seemed to exist only in Lord's imagination. Gore remembered sufficient of the two men to whom Lord had referred to remain convinced that they had been not at all gentlemen to run any serious risk – two shifty-eyed shabbily-flash fellows of the type always to be found hanging round obscure bars and billiard rooms. Frensham, to do him justice, had been an intelligent and very wary individual, very unlikely to have admitted a pair of such palpable public house bums into his confidence. He had enlisted them for a special purpose – a little bit of blackjacking, unattended with any real risk. His death had, no doubt, induced them to remove themselves promptly from the neighbourhood of the Westmouth police's interest in Frensham's known associates. And there, so far as they were concerned, it was pretty certain that their connection with the affair had terminated for good and all.

The payment of £125 to Dr. Dorch remained unexplained. Pickles knew of no intention of her husband's to make any purchase of so considerable a value. In neither pictures nor silver nor glass nor china had he taken the remotest interest. And yet, it seemed, the article for which this payment had been made had accompanied Dr. Dorch's letter of November 19th. Clegg was quite sure that no parcel of any size had been delivered by post at the house on any day of the preceding week.

Gore took Dr. Dorch's letter from the drawer to which Lord had returned it.

"As far as one can judge from the fold, it was contained in an envelope. But of course the envelope may have been contained in a parcel.... In any case, I rather think I'll go round and see Dorch on Thursday. He's expected to get back tomorrow. What about a run up to the Mendips this morning? Do you and Master Simon good, wouldn't it?"

But she shook her head. "It would be good of you to take Simon. You know he adores going anywhere with you."

And so Simon Wyckham and his godfather spent a long, splendid morning – not on the Mendips – but at the Zoo, which, as Simon Wyckham decided, was more 'citing. Having expended immense sums on buns and nuts and biscuits for its inhabitants, they left the gardens and proceeded towards the head of Tenby Road, proposing to travel by bus to Uncle Wyck's hotel where, by special permission, his godson was to lunch. Their way to Tenby Road lay by Downshill Road. As they approached the gates of Wavertree Gore noticed, drawn up before them, a large furniture van, the loading of which was being supervised by Mr. Ross and a manservant.

He stopped to ask if a definite date for Dr. Dorch's return had yet been fixed. Ross – by daylight a sallow-skinned, dapper little man with high cheekbones and oblique dark eyes of different colours – replied that he had not heard from his employer in the interval, but assumed that he would return next day. He indicated, then, the tall manservant who stood beside him.

"This is the man Inspector Lord wished to see – Peterson. He is quite certain that, except Dr. Dorch and myself, he is the only person Dr. Melhuish saw when he called here last Wednesday." He explained to the servant. "This is Colonel Gore – the gentleman I told you about—"

If Gore was very certain that he had never seen the man Peterson before, he was equally sure that he had no desire whatever to see him again. Some blend of black and white and yellow had produced him – it would have been difficult to give the product a definite colour. His eyes – the most absolutely devoid of all expression, save insolence, that Gore had ever seen in a human being's head – were mere slits. He shifted the chewing gum with which his heavy jaws were busy and nodded familiarly.

"Sure, Colonel," he said easily. "That's right. The Doctor he jus' ran in an' out, looked at de boss's arms while he was shakin' hands with him, said 'much better' and beat me to the street door. Some sprinter the poor guy was, I will say."

No need to ask where Dr. Dorch's butler hailed from. Mainly Chinese after all, Gore decided. He nodded to Ross as he thanked him, and went on his way with Simon Wyckham.

His godson was rather silent until they were seated in their bus.

"Uncle Wyck," he said then, "wasn't that man in the dress suit rather cheeky to you?"

"Was he? Nasty fellow."

"He was like a big monkey with the long arms," reflected the child. "Why did he call Daddy a poor guy?"

This was dangerous ground. For Simon Wyckham supposed that his daddy was away on his holidays. His godfather changed the subject swiftly, and for a couple of hours dismissed Dr. Dorch and his household from his thoughts.

When he had delivered up his charge safely in Victoria Square – Mrs. Melhuish was engaged with some visitors, the maid informed him – he found himself at a dead end. Partly to satisfy a need to do something, partly because he had learned by experience the danger of concluding that two and two always make the right four, he decided to complete the interrupted tour of inquiry of the previous afternoon. At his third place of call, a residential hotel close to Tenby Road, the first person he saw, as he followed a maid across the entrance lounge, was an old schoolfellow whom he had last met at the Eton-Harrow match in 1913.

It was true that this gentleman had never even heard Dr. Melhuish's name until then, this being his first visit to Linwood for something like twenty years. But that another old friend should turn up at a second address on his list suggested to Gore at least the possibility that the "old friend" of Melhuish's letter might still be found before the list was exhausted. Until nearly seven o'clock he pursued his quest, therefore, doggedly. But Chance had exhausted her stock of coincidences for that day. He had seen no one else whom, to his knowledge, he had ever seen before when the last hall door closed behind him and, in a drizzling rain, he set out for his hotel.

He found Lord there, awaiting his coming in his sitting room. On Lord's knees rested a small fibre basket of an inexpensive kind.

"Hullo, Colonel. Hope I'm not *de trop*. But I thought, as I was up this way, I'd drop in and see you. You were interested in Woodbine's basket, I think, last time I spoke to you. A rather curious thing has turned up in connection with it. You remember I mentioned to you that we got some information from a pal of Woodbine's about that little gadget we found in his pocket? Well – I've just got some more from him. I thought you might like to hear his story at first hand. So I brought him along. He's waiting round the corner. Perhaps we had better interview him in the open air."

Standing beneath a lamppost, gazing gloomily into the darkness, they found a seedy, elderly man whom Lord introduced as "Bullock."

Mr. Bullock explained that he had known the late Woodbine for something like thirty years. During that time they had met regularly every morning on the Downs in the course of the only regular business which either of them seemed to have had in life, the search for treasure trove. Not, evidently, a lucrative business; still, most mornings – especially in summer – something turned up; and occasionally there was the reward of a real find – a cigarette case... a gold pin... a vanity bag – once, even, in Mr. Bullock's career, a purse with three five pound notes and nearly a pound in silver. His smile was demure while he explained that, as he had heard of no one claiming this treasure, he had not troubled the police about it.

But that had been many years ago. His only find of real value during the past five years had been a gold upper-plate, for which a dealer had given him a quid.

"Must have been busy, a bloke as didn't miss *that*," he commented. "But it's mostly buttons and hairpins and used matches and butts of fags. Woodbine was dead nuts on fag ends. Told me one time he picked up twelve hunnerd of 'em in one day, summer three years back, after the flying exhibition—"

He was induced to narrow his reminiscences to the morning of Friday, November 22nd. As a rule, it appeared, he and Woodbine had worked in partnership, for company and old friendship's sake, and, meeting at a spot consecrated by long habit, shortly after seven o'clock in winter, shortly after six in summer, had started out upon a quest which had occupied them until about one o'clock, when they had separated for the day. During the two weeks preceding his death Woodbine had had a temporary night job as watchman at the scene of some road repairs in a remote part of Westmouth. On this account he had been usually about half an hour later than his accustomed time in arriving at the meeting place; after a couple of mornings Bullock had given up waiting for him and had started off on his morning round alone.

Pretty close on seven o'clock on the morning of that Friday, he had arrived on the Downs, just as the first light was showing in the sky. As soon as it had been clear enough for his purpose, he had begun his search, although heavy rain had begun to fall just then. Following the course of thirty years of habit, he had gone from bush to bush, exploring every bit of cover which might have contained human occupant since his last visit to it.

This was, of course, a long game and a slow one, even when one knew every inch of the broken ground at the south and east borders of the Downs, where the game was always begun. He had been engaged upon it for about half an hour when, reaching the top of the slope along which he had been working, he had come out upon the level ground. The bush or thicket in which poor Woodbine was to be found some hours later, was then about fifty yards from him and, as it was a favourite nesting place, he had gone towards it, both for the purpose of exploring it and to find shelter from the now heavy rain while he lighted his pipe.

While he was still some little distance from it, however, a man whom he described as a "stiff-built chap with no hair on his face, and his mouth in front of his face, medium height same as meself," had emerged from the bushes which there covered the slopes on his left hand thickly. At that hour of the morning few people were ever to be seen on the Downs – the majority of them workers moving along regular paths towards early jobs. Many of those who crossed his beat Bullock had known by sight for months – in some cases for years. This man, however, he could not recall having ever seen before, though he had judged him from his dress and general appearance a kind of worker fairly often encountered between half-past seven and eight – a chauffeur living out. He had been walking at a smart pace, as if late; but reaching the thicket towards which Bullock was moving, he had halted there, and remained standing in front of the opening in it, lighting a cigarette. This sudden slackening of speed had attracted Bullock's attention; funny games, he was aware, were likely to go on any time of the day or night on the Downs. He had slackened speed and sheered off a little; the man, he had thought, had looked at him in a suspicious "nasty sort of way." He had ventured, however, a morning greeting, as one early riser to another, and had said that it looked like they'd have rain all day with the wind south-east. To that the other early-riser had made an answer which had struck Bullock as highly humorous. He had said:

"Rain? Rain's what there's going to be nothing today but, Sonny."

To that conclusion Bullock had already come himself. The Downs had looked extremely unpromising that morning. Having strayed onwards for a short while, he had turned about and gone back towards his starting point, on the chance of meeting his pal Woodbine and discussing the wisdom of further operations. And, as a matter of fact he had met Woodbine coming in pursuit of him. He was absolutely certain that at that time Woodbine had had no basket.

Knowing that Bullock was ahead of him, Woodbine had naturally not lingered on his way to make search in places which had already been thoroughly investigated. Before they had parted – for Woodbine had been determined to defy the weather – Bullock had handed over to him some cigarette ends which he had collected; he had also, he was pretty sure, repeated, for his benefit the humorous remark made by the chauffeur and told him of his meeting with its author. Woodbine's night job had stopped off that morning; he had arranged to meet Bullock at seven o'clock next morning at the usual place. In Bullock's opinion, he had then no more intention of doing himself in than he had of trying to set the Downs afire. But, that, none the less, had been the end of their long partnership.

"You'd know this man who spoke to you, if you saw him again?" Lord asked.

But Bullock was a little dubious about that. "Well – if I heard him speaking, I might," he said at length. "He spoke like a Yank, what I made of it."

He was persuaded to repeat the humorous remark about the rain, which his first version had given in good broad Westshire. The second reproduced what it was clear the talkies had taught him to regard as the customary intonation of "Yanks" – a blend of Cockney and adenoids in slow motion.

"He was standing near this bush, smoking a cigarette, when you last saw him?"

"No. I saw no sign of him when I turned back. He must have gone away. Or perhaps he was inside – in under the bush. Anyway, I saw nothing of him, and I passed fairly close to the bush going back to meet Woodbine."

"Was he carrying anything when you saw him?"

"No. He had his hands in his pockets."

"He couldn't have had that basket, for instance, under his coat – or under his arm?"

"Not as I saw, he didn't have it nowhere."

"Anything remarkable about Woodbine's appearance?" Gore asked.

"Remarkable, sir? Well – I needn't hardly say he wasn't no oil painting to look at, any more nor meself. Only thing you'd notice about him was he always carried two sticks. One to help his left leg what got broke a few years ago, and t'other with a nail in it for picking up bits of things with. That's the only way you could say there was anything out of the ornery about poor old Woodbine."

"What about that little silver affair he showed you, and said he had found. When did he find it, do you know?"

"Last Thursday morning – day before he died. He—"

"Did he say where he had found it?"

"Yes. He found it on the Downs – near the path we always came up by from the top of Tenby Road. Not on the path exactly – in the grass a bit beside it. He showed me the place that morning – Thursday morning – when we were going back. Matter o' that, I wasn't so far off from him meself, when he found it, only I didn't know it 'count of the fog being so heavy that morning."

"On the Friday morning – the morning you saw this chap you think was a Yank," Lord asked, "did you see anyone else near that bush while he stood in front of it – near it – or in sight of it?"

But Mr. Bullock, it appeared, had now given all the useful information at his disposal. He departed shortly into the darkness the richer by two half crowns, leaving their donor his address. Gore and Lord, warned by a booming gong, returned to the hotel to make hurried preparations for dinner. The dining room was crowded; it was not until they were back in Gore's sitting room that the curious significance of Bullock's story was discussed. Inspector Lord's smile had tempered its irony this evening with unaffected good humour. True, he had elicited Bullock's story by the merest accident; still, he had elicited it. If the Suspension Bridge affair still remained a baffling puzzle, the case of Woodbine promised to develop – in spite of a Coroner and his jury – into a sensation quite sufficiently startling to distract the attention of his superiors and of the Westmouth press, which had grown rather peevish during the past few days.

"Well, now, Colonel," he said, when his Partaga was going satisfactorily, "let's see what this works out at. Firstly... Woodbine found this basket – and presumably its contents – in the bush where he died. That's almost certain. He was not a hundred yards from it when he left Bullock. He knew Bullock had been over the ground between, twice – he wouldn't begin his own hunting until he got to where Bullock had turned it down. If the basket had been anywhere along that hundred yards, Bullock would have seen it, either time he covered that ground. So Woodbine found it in that bush – probably made up his mind to chance it and drink the beer almost straight away – and was dead in less than half an hour after he left Bullock. That fits in with the doctor's report. He'd been dead for a couple of hours or so when he was found.

"Now – someone left the basket there. Why? Forgotten? Very unlikely. Left there to get rid of it? Unlikely. Only good reason why anyone would have wanted to get rid of it was because he knew there was something in the beer. But if he knew that, he wouldn't leave it where someone was bound to find it, and probably drink the beer – he'd pour the beer out on to the grass

– or if he wasn't careful enough to do that, he'd have chucked it somewhere where it wasn't likely to be found, unless he wanted it to be found – and drunk."

"Quite. Now why should anyone have wanted that to happen? Of course, I know that there have been several cases of poison being laid for dogs on the Downs fairly recently. But you want a very special kind of madman or scoundrel to lay a trap of this sort for two-legged game. I'm not denying there are plenty of both about. But let's suppose this wasn't a case of mere wanton malice. Let's suppose it was a deliberate, thought-out plan to do someone in. The question is – whose plan was it – and who was intended to be done in? Hardly Woodbine. Woodbine was worth just about as much dead – to anyone – as he was alive."

"I wonder," Gore mused. "Bullock was scared away from that bush. It's quite clear anyhow that he felt he was being scared off. As soon as he went near the bush this beggar in the leggings came out of the bushes at his left in a hurry, and made for the place where the basket was and stood in front of it. If he knew that the basket was in there and if he knew that Bullock wasn't the person he wanted to find it, that's just what he would have done. But poor old Woodbine *wasn't* scared away. You've got to remember that the number of people likely to go to that spot at that hour – in the ordinary course – would be extremely limited. A couple of mornings' watching would have told anyone interested, in fact, that the only two people likely to go there at that hour were Bullock and Woodbine – either together or separately. Bullock wasn't allowed to go there – Woodbine was. And don't forget that Woodbine was easily recognisable. He carried two sticks."

"We don't know that this chap in leggings wasn't miles away by the time that Woodbine got to that bush. Bullock said, in fact, that he didn't see him near that bush as he came back to meet Woodbine."

"Well, but – the fellow came out walking quickly in a certain direction – the direction in which Bullock went after he was scared away. The natural thing to expect is that when this man left the bush, he would have gone on in the direction in which he had been hurrying at first. Hurrying, not to get out of the rain – because he hurried out of plenty of shelter. But Bullock would have seen him if he had gone in that direction. He didn't. Why? Because our friend the chauffeur went back to his hiding place to wait until someone else came along, – someone with two sticks, probably, with luck. You've seen this bush?"

"Yes. Quite a good hiding-place. I suppose you could get a dozen people into it – standing up. I took Bullock up there on my way here."

"See into it from outside?"

"No. You've got to go a little way into the opening. Besides, of course, it's pretty dark in underneath. A chap standing outside, where Bullock said this chap stood, might stand there all day and see nothing of twenty baskets inside. However – the first thing to do is to find the gentleman in the leggings. Medium height, burly, clean-shaven, prominent mouth, fawn raincoat, black leggings, grey cloth cap, American accent... perhaps. I'll get busy on that at once."

Lord rose with regret from his armchair. "But why the devil anyone would want to dope a poor old devil like that for – over seventy years of age – practically down and out since he was born, I suppose. A most inoffensive old chap, too, I believe. I've been to the place where he lodged. Appalling. Eleven other people sleeping in the room with him – men, women, and children. Better off now, poor old blighter."

Gore offered no comment upon this reflection. He had taken from the basket the apple and the remains of bread and cheese, which it still contained (Inspector Lord had informed him that the beer bottle was now in other hands) and had then removed the folded sheet of butter paper with which the basket was lined. Underneath this he had found a farther packing for the bottom of the basket, a folded sheet of newspaper which he had spread flat, and was regarding with attention. He handed it to Lord after a moment.

"Rather curious, isn't it?"

Lord looked at the sheet. "What is?"

"As you see, it's a sheet from a copy of the *Chicago Tribune*. So that perhaps, after all, that shover *was* a Yank. Got that badge with you, by any chance? You have. Good. Let's have another look at that lettering."

They considered the monogram which formed the centre of the little silver ornament carefully. Though poorly executed for professional work, and devoid of any attempt at ornateness, the lettering was of good design, with that pleasant fatness and boldness which lends a special charm to the American poster and the American postage stamp. To this fact Lord agreed, if somewhat unwillingly.

"You're not suggesting, are you, that this little gadget brought Woodbine his other bit of luck? The thing's not worth more than a couple of shillings. And anyhow it was left in his pocket. It wouldn't have been, if it had any value for anyone."

"Did the press get hold of the fact that it was found in his pocket, by the way?"

"Nothing in the local papers about it at any rate. But of course a crowd collected at once round that bush. No doubt dozens of people saw the mounted man turning out his pockets, as far as that goes. Why?"

Again he waited for a reply. Very carefully Gore had removed from the bottom of the basket a short black hair, and seven or eight much shorter white ones. These he had laid carefully on a sheet torn from a grey writing block and was now examining them through a pocket lens.

"A lady with extremely fine, black hair and a wire-haired terrier – *I think* – have left souvenirs in that basket."

"So have some raspberries," smiled Lord, regarding the bottom of the basket, which was of the kind used by fruiterers for packing their customers' purchases of fruit. "So it's nearly six months since it left wherever the raspberries came from. That's why it was so nicely packed with paper – to hide uninviting stains, eh? The lady with the black hair, I presume, is a Jane from Chi and the white dog is the very kind they make Beef Extract from in the Jungle. And I'll swear that apple is a good American. The bread, however, seems dull – just stodgy old English dough. Though all good Cheddar comes from the States now, I believe. Well – I suppose I must toddle off and start laying for the lout in the leggings. I'll drop along and see Dr. Dorch tomorrow sometime about that cheque, and let you know what he says. Better keep these hairs, I suppose. Many thanks. Goodnight."

Chapter Eight

Nov.	18.	*Melhuish sent cheque to Dorch*	
	20	*Melhuish recd. letter from Dorch*	*(Q.E.D.)*
		Melhuish kill ed	
	21.		*(Q.E.D.) Woodbine*
			fd. badge
	22.		*Woodbine killed*

The above memorandum, scribbled on the sheet of grey paper which had served as background for the seven hairs – represented the sum of Gore's reflections until bedtime that night. It indicates pretty clearly the line along which his thoughts moved backwards and forwards for something over three hours – and from which they declined to move. While it was true that no other line whatever suggested itself to them in connection with Melhuish's death at the moment, it seemed that something more than just helplessness justified that obstinacy.

The line started, at any rate, from the curious little emblem found in Woodbine's pocket. And it worked backwards – dubiously and by the dimmest of light – to Melhuish. *Prima facie,* the supposition of any possible link between the two men – one a Downs loafer, the other a prosperous and at least locally distinguished physician – seemed absurd. The use by Dorch of the abbreviation Q.E.D. might have been the merest coincidence. The initials on the badge might be intended for any of the six possible permutations of the three letters – D.E.Q., D.Q.E., E.D.Q., E.Q.D., Q.D.E, Q.E.D.

But even so, the odd fact was certain that those three letters *had* been connected, within the space of three days, with two persons in Linwood who had been murdered ruthlessly and with diabolical ingenuity. Murder had been done before in Linwood; that was as true as that a thunderbolt had fallen in Gore's memory in one of its peaceful roads. But, normally, it was and had been for a couple of centuries, a superior upper middle-class place of residence of the utmost respectability, decorum and security. A murder in Linwood was, in fact, a thing no more or less likely than the fall of a thunderbolt. Yet, in three days, two had been committed there.

The coincidence of the connection of the three letters with both was a curious one. But if the initials of the badge were to be read Q.E.D., it was a still more curious coincidence. Before he went to bed Gore sent off a wire to Tolley, his partner, with two requests. One that his car should bring down to Westmouth without delay his man Stephens and a member of his staff named Yeoland; the other that Scotland Yard, with whom unfortunately the firm happened to be at the moment on no very friendly footing, should be consulted as to whether the initials, in any arrangement, had any suspicious significance for it.

In the morning, he decided, he would look up Bullock and take him over the ground covered by Woodbine's tragedy. Of one fact in regard to it he was already aware. From Dr. Dorch's house in Downshill Road to the part of Linwood Downs where Woodbine had died was not more than, at most, three or four minutes' walk.

Again there was the American colouring of some of the details. The lettering of the badge was American at any rate in design. The newspaper which had lined the bottom of the basket was an American paper. The supposed chauffeur had been, if

Bullock was right, an American. Dorch was an American. So, by adoption, was his secretary, Ross. So was his houseman. If Scotland Yard failed to supply any interesting information, it might be well to cable New York's Central Office or Pinkertons' Agency.

It would be interesting to hear what Dorch had to say about that cheque. Also about the badge, which Lord proposed to show him. Gore rather wished that he could have heard the answers in person.

Just why, he wondered, had that furniture van been loading up outside Dorch's house – just then? Some commission for a friend? Rather a large one, then. A quantity of stuff had already been loaded into the van when he had seen it – heavy cases. No furniture – no loose stuff. Other cases had still been coming out.

Why had the van remained outside the gates? That gave the men a longish carry from the house down the drive. Had there been another van loading at the door? One couldn't see from the road, because the drive curved sharply behind a lot of shrubs. Suppose there had been two vans loading – loading quickly. Did Dr. Dorch happen to be moving house – in something like a hurry – just now? But the van had not been of the usual pantechnicon size usual in cases of house-moving; a thirty-hundredweight or two-ton van. And there had been no furniture in its load.

Doctor Dorch.... Doctor Dorch.... Wasn't there something about Dr. Dorch? No. That was Doctor Stork.... The next thing for Gore after that was his early tea next morning, his post, and an intimation that Mr. Yeoland was waiting to see him. The person who made delivery of these details was his man Stephens. Stephens was of opinion that his master's Buick wanted decoking badly; on the way down from town she had refused to do an inch over seventy-five, even for him.

The proposed promenade with Bullock did not take place. Inquiry at a miserable lodging house in an unsavoury lane be-

hind Tenby Road elicited, after a good deal of fencing, the fact
that Bullock was in trouble. Over-indulgence in beer – presumably purchased with those two half-crowns – had ended in
"words" with a bobby and a cell in a police station. For some
days Mr. Bullock would be away from home.

"'What might you have wanted to see him for, Mister?" inquired the lady of the house, evidently scenting further trouble
for her lodger.

Having learnt, however, that it was simply a matter of a short
walk and a couple of shillings, she summoned from the dingy
interior behind her buxom person an almost exact replica of
Bullock named 'Arry, who, they both said, knew as much about
the copping-out of Woodbine as anyone could want to know for
two bob. Accepting this substitute, and an increase of a further
bob in the fee, Gore was led up Tenby Road towards Linwood
Downs, his guide, who had seen many changes, discoursing
volubly along the way. He remembered himself, he stated, when
Tenby Road, that dreary if most respectable procession of sub-
urban residences, had been a pleasant country lane, bordered
by fields with cows and cowslips in them. At the head of the
road where it debouched on to the Downs and forked, left to
Downshill Road, right to Upper Downs Road, he pointed with
pride to a large tree standing on a triangular island of grass
between the parting ways.

"That there's the old Gallus Tree," he said, "wot they used to
'ang the blokes from an' leave them there till they was picked
clean. Me father used to tell me when he was a lad you couldn't
hardly see that tree for the crows after a bloke had been turned
off." He pointed across the road towards a castellated stone
tower, some thirty feet in height, rising from the grass at the edge
of the Down, a little distance in from the road.

"See that ventilator tower, sir? That's where Bullock an'
Woodbine used to meet every morning. And that path you see
going past it and through them bushes, that's the way they
used to go. Always the same way – never any different. Wood-

bine knew every berry on every bush. Eye like a 'awk, 'e 'ad. Sometimes in the summer I used to take a walk up this way with Bullock in the morning, to get a bit of appetite for me breakfis. An' as sure as six o'clock, there we'd see ole Woodbine, leanin' against the tower, waiting for Bullock, with his pipe in his face and 'is two sticks under 'is arm. Always 'ad two – one for walking and one for pickin'. He could pick up a fag end wot'd been smoked down to the wet, without stoppin'. Never missed. Wonnerful clever 'e was with 'is picker. I see him once pick a flea off Bullock's neck with it an' Bullock never felt nothin'."

They crossed the road, and were at once on the Downs, which no fencing of any sort separated from it. Passing the blackened limestone tower from whose top a cloud of evil-smelling smoke was at the moment issuing, they followed the path indicated by 'Arry, which, however, quickly deteriorated into a mere vague track, winding its way in and out to avoid bushes and larger inequalities in the rocky slope up which it led. Once a veritable wilderness – allegedly within 'Arry's memory wild flowers had grown on it in profusion – the Downs, if now somewhat tamed and pruned, possessed still the charm of open country. True, in one direction or another, the chimney pots of the tall houses built along the farther side of the roads which skirted its far-flung borders were nearly always in sight. But the underlying limestone, only a very few inches below the turf, cropped up on all sides in miniature cliffs and precipices, enlarged in many places by long-past quarrying. Beneath the thorn trees were hidden countless little dells and glades in which, on a summer day, the Westmouth citizen and his family might picnic in shady seclusion and believe themselves twenty miles from the smoke and noise of the big city. As 'Arry expressed it, of an August Saturday afternoon you couldn't hardly see the grass for paper bags and kids and nood stockings.

But on a damp, misty November morning, the Downs were quiet enough, and those little nooks beneath the trees appeared uninviting – unless, perhaps, to people interested in treasure trove. A very few minutes brought Gore and his guide to the top of the slope running up at the south end and they came out upon the windswept main plateau of the Downs – almost exactly, as Gore estimated, at the place from which Mr. Gardiner's partner had essayed to pitch his approach shot on to the third green. Both ends of that green were now in sight. But the greater portion of it was cut off by a tall bush, perhaps twelve feet in height and as many in width, into the interior of which a low arched opening led obliquely. 'Arry jerked his grizzled head towards it.

"There y'are, guv'nor. That's where ole Woodbine copped out." He pointed to his left, where a miniature forest of thorns covered the descending face of the slope. "That's where the bloke in the leggin's come out from. Bullock an' me we 'ad a good look round there on the Friday morning, after we 'eard about Woodbine's bein' poisoned. We thought mebbe we'd find somefink. But we didn't, 'cept a blurry ole golf ball with no skin to it."

"Which way did Bullock go when he left this man standing there in front of the bush?" Gore asked.

'Arry pointed to his right, in which direction the Downs ran away into misty distances, intersected by a dead straight stretch of tree-bordered road along which a company of khaki-clad cadets from Linwood College were at the moment marching with élan.

"Over that way, as far as the Centre Road, and then back, same way almost. That's why he couldn't see what become of the bloke in the leggin's, cause, you see, that bush hid him soon as Bullock got over towards the road a bit."

They walked on towards the little bower in which sleep had come to Woodbine for the last time, and looked in. Dank, dark, and mouldily-smelling this morning – but not too dusty a doss-down, as 'Arry said, for a bloke as couldn't pay for a better. Not that he expected many would doss down there for a bit – now. Nor do their cuddlin' there neither.

They moved leftwards to the edge of the slope. And 'Arry indicated the precise spot at which the legginged man had first appeared to Bullock's view. Another rather curious coincidence – then. If one faced at that spot directly towards Downshill Road, the first house on that road was directly opposite one. From that height its upper windows were visible. A direct route down the slope to the road would certainly take one over some roughish ground. But the distance could be covered, Gore calculated, in about two minutes.

He made the experiment, surprising 'Arry, who was bad on his legs, by his rapid descent – and reached the road in exactly two minutes. At the gates of Wavertree stood either the van of the day before or its twin, and behind the van a couple of cases rested on the ground. The men in charge of it were apparently in the house at the moment. Accompanied by 'Arry, Gore crossed the road and, passing at the rear of the van, paused to light a cigarette and cast a casual glance towards the labels of the cases. They were marked, however, with numbers simply. To be delivered by road to their destination, then. He noted the last number in sight – twenty-three.

Some instinct caused him, as his eyes rose from the cases, to look into the interior of the van. It was dark in there, but not too dark for him to recognise, sitting on an already loaded case at the front of the vehicle, in rolled-up shirtsleeves and regarding him intently through markedly unfriendly eyes, Dr. Dorch's manservant. Evidently he was assisting in the packing of the van, and was awaiting the return of the two men who did the carrying.

Not quite as soon as he could have wished, Gore despatched a winning smile into the shadows.

"Oh, er – good morning. Can you tell me if Mr. Ross has heard yet definitely when Dr. Dorch is to return?"

The tall, powerful figure reared itself up from its seat and came slowly to the back of the van, walking on its toes like a big cat. The man stood there, hands in pocket staring for several moments before he spoke. His reply twisted itself out of one corner of his mouth in studied impertinence.

"Early this mornin', ain't yeh?" His slits of eyes moved to 'Arry. " 'Nother dick? No. I ain't heard when the boss is comin' back."

"Perhaps I could see Mr. Ross for a moment?"

A stream of saliva passed Gore's right ear without the alteration of a muscle in the parchment-like mask which looked down at him.

"You could if you was in Liverpool and didn't look where he wasn't. What's the big idea? The Westmouth cops planning fireworks an' a brass band for the boss when he gets in?"

The two stalwart fellows who had arrived at the back of the van with another heavy case, guffawed alike at the question and the impertinence of its tone. Rightly, as it proved, Gore guessed that Lord had already visited Wavertree that morning. Also, it was clear, the manservant believed, from the fact that he had been in Lord's company the day before yesterday, that he and 'Arry were both police detectives. He continued to smile engagingly.

"Don't worry,' he said lightly, with a glance at the case. "England's damp still. Didn't know there was quite all that whisky in it, though."

He was turning away when the corner of his eye caught sight of something that induced him to linger for just a moment longer than he had intended – or than was to prove wise. With a considerable effort the two bearers of the case had lifted it to the level of the floor of the van, where the servant man took sole charge of it and carried it unaided to a place beside the case on which he had been sitting. But it was not merely the enormous strength of the fellow that had attracted Gore's attention. The side of the case had pushed up his shirt-sleeve nearly to the elbow and revealed, tattooed in blue and crimson on his herculean forearm a reproduction of the design of Woodbine's find, half as large again as the badge. For the brief instant for which Gore had stared at it, his interest had, no doubt, been obvious. The bearer of the case twisted his head sideways to discover the reason of his unguarded attention and perceiving that his forearm was uncovered, eased its pressure against the case to allow the shirt sleeve to slip down over it. As he did so his eyes, two oblique black lines, set with two pin points of blazing light, met Gore's again. A second too late Gore smiled genially in return to that glare of menacing question, and turned away. As he passed along the side of the van he noted in large black and gold lettering the owner's name and address. "Winton & Sharp, Furniture Removers, Bushey Lane, Linwood." He noted also that the van had obviously made a long journey very recently on muddy roads.

Very probably then, this was the van which he had seen the day before, about to make another trip. Another long trip. Another fast trip. Otherwise one large van would have made one trip and finished the job. He paid off 'Arry a little way along Downshill Road and made for his hotel as fast as a pair of long legs could carry him.

"There's a brown thirty hundredweight van loading up outside a house called Wavertree in Downshill Road now, Yeoland," he instructed his subaltern. "Downshill Road is the left-hand turn right at the top of Tenby Road, running along the Downs. Get there or thereabouts in the Buick right away. I want to know where that van delivers its load. And I do not want a song made about it. Any information about the other end will be gratefully received. Take Stephens along. You may have to leave the car. Sorry there's a deep depression coming down from Iceland. You may have some way to go. Bless you, my child."

Chapter Nine

WESTMOUTH ITSELF AND THE extensive docks at the mouth of the river forming a port of first importance for transatlantic traffic, its American consul was an American. With this courteous and very efficient gentleman Gore had already had some conversation by telephone. He found him in person no less willing to render any assistance in his power to a visitor who proposed to enter into business relations with his friend Dr. Dorch.

At the time of his own arrival at Westmouth seven years before Dr. Dorch had, he believed, already lived there for four or five years. Five to be exact, upon reflection – since he remembered that Dr. Dorch had once told him that he had left London in 1917 on account of the air raids. Dr. Dorch had invited him to his house – he had dined there, he supposed, two or three times a year during the past seven years. A very charming fellow, Dr. Dorch – clever, amusing, an excellent host, and, he judged from his knowledge of him, an extremely wealthy man. A widower – with an extremely pretty daughter who had been educated in England and had married an Englishman – a doctor named Simpson, who was attached to the Westmouth Infirmary staff. A nice fellow, the son-in-law; but, he believed, not quite the husband his father-in-law would have selected for his only girl.

"I will be quite candid with you, Mr. Curtice," smiled Gore trustingly, "I'm on the lookout for some decent pictures – not old masters, but good modern stuff. Rye found a chap who has some to sell – or rather, has to sell some – and I like the things he's got. But he wants to sell through Dorch. I don't know why, and of course, it's no affair of mine – provided I can rely on Dorch to give me a fair deal. I really know nothing about pictures – I mean from the expert, market point of view – so naturally – well, I thought I'd come along and have a chat with you."

"Delighted to help you. But you need have no anxiety whatever, Colonel Gore. I know that Dorch sometimes undertakes deals of this sort for friends who want to buy or sell pictures and so on. He's a first-rate judge of these things, I've heard – collects all sorts of things himself. You'll be in perfectly reliable hands. His house is full of treasures of all sorts – a kind of museum. If it will help at all, you are very welcome to mention that we've met."

"As a matter of fact, I suppose Dr. Dorch and I have many friends in common in this part of the world."

"You haven't met him yet, then? Oh yes, Dorch has plenty of friends in Linwood. I've always met the most charming people at his house. Probably you know many of them."

He ran off a little list of names, which Gore memorised carefully, and then raised humorous eyebrows above his tortoise-shell glasses.

"In confidence," he said, "my wife, for some reason, took a violent dislike to Dorch from the first moment she saw him. An odd thing – because he's a good-looker and looks someone. But you know what women are. Every time we get an invitation to dine there, there's a battle royal for twenty-four hours. But, as I say, personally I have the highest opinion of him. He's a Doctor of Science, by the way – not of medicine."

"English degree – or American?"

"I'm sorry I can't say. First-rate pianist, too – a most cultured fellow. Can I offer you a cigar? Well – I'm very pleased to be able to speak well of anyone. Goodbye, Colonel."

From Mr. Curtice's office he drove to Victoria Square and saw Pickles for a few moments. Most of the people whose names the consul had mentioned as having been his fellow guests at Dorch's house proved either friends or acquaintances of hers – in most cases, patients of her husband's. Half a dozen of these, people whom she knew pretty intimately, were found on the telephone and would be delighted to see Colonel Gore at varying hours that morning. All lived within easy reach and were seen within the following hour and a half.

In five cases the lady of the house was the person inter-viewed. There was a striking similarity between the five fem-inine reports. In each case a husband was responsible for the acquaintance with Dr. Dorch. Each lady considered Dr. Dorch a quite striking looking person, clever, interesting to talk to, and a first-class performer on the piano. All of them had been impressed by the good taste of his house's equipment and by his *savoir faire* as a host. All of them had found some apparently unexplainable reason for not liking him.

A composite picture drew itself detail by detail. Dr. Dorch was well over average height, noticeably pale of skin, wore a moustache and a small beard, had unusually pale grey eyes was rather more of a dandy in his clothes than was customary for the Linwood male, had no accent and would be taken for an American by anyone who did not know him to be an English-man. He seemed to have travelled all over the world – and was extraordinarily expert at all kinds of tricks with cards and glasses and handkerchiefs and so on. At one time his daughter, Mrs. Simpson (then Miss Dorch), had acted as hostess; that had been for a couple of years after she had left school. Since her marriage, however, it was generally understood that she saw little of her father and rarely visited his house. It was agreed that she was an extremely pretty girl of rather "foreign" appearance, very cold and reserved in manner, a little spoiled by her eyes which had the same rather disagreeable pallor as her father's. One informant believed that Dr. Dorch had lived in London for a considerable time, before he had settled in Linwood.

The sixth person interviewed was a Mr. Willington, an elderly gentleman of leisure and means, very much absorbed in the misperformances of one of his internal organs and reserved to the point of frigidity about everything else. He thought Dorch quite a good fellow. Someone had introduced Dorch to him somewhere, sometime – he thought it was a man called Hilpett, at the Vagabonds' Club. He hadn't seen anything of Dorch for quite two years. Pots of money, he believed. Reason why he had been introduced to Dorch by Hilpett, now that he came to think of it, was that at the time he had been looking for a good second-hand Rolls. Dorch had got him one – at quite a reasonable price. Oh yes – everything had been quite satisfactory, as far as that went. But he had practically given up motoring now – practically given up everything. That damned bladder of his – He was unaffectedly glad to get rid of his visitor.

Armed with a note of introduction from Pickles, Gore called next at the Linwood branch of Lloyds, where Melhuish had kept his bank account. The cheque for £125 payable to Dorch had come through, endorsed duly and bearing the stamp of the Linwood branch of the Metropolitan and Western Counties Bank. The manager of the Lloyds' branch office knew Dr. Dorch slightly in person, very well by repute. So far as he was aware, Dr. Dorch was a perfectly satisfactory person to have dealings of any sort with.

At the Metropolitan and Western Counties' branch office, the manager had the same absolute confidence in Dr. Dorch's reliability. Dr. Dorch he said, had to his knowledge executed commissions of various sorts – some involving extremely large sums – within the past twelve years. A little foible, the manager supposed – pleasure in making a deal – pleasure in the particular kind of thing he was dealing in; certainly due to no need for money; as a matter of fact, he had heard, the commission charged by him was always eminently reasonable.

Everything Gore learned that morning, in fact – with the
exception of the fact that Dorch's manner towards women was
apparently a little too *empressé* for Linwood standards – was
eminently favourable to him. It was clear that he was a feature
in the daily landscape of the place – a man, too, of outstanding appearance, in whom suspicious movement of any kind
would have been conspicuous at once – a man, who for twelve
years now, had lived a perfectly obvious, perfectly respectable,
perfectly prosperous life. Coincidence or no coincidence, it
was impossible to suppose such a person likely to commit any
murder – still more impossible to suppose him capable of the
murder of two people – and of two people so widely separated
socially that any connection between them seemed out of the
question. The idea was, on the face of it, ridiculous.

There was that dangerous-looking gorilla of a manservant of
his – the hands and arms that had made light of that heavy
case could lift a man's weight breast-high, easily enough. But in
heaven's name what motive – what interest could have brought
the ugly brute into any contact with Melhuish beyond the
opening and shutting of his employer's doors for him?

He had a design tattooed on his arm. Why not? The design
was the design of the badge found by Woodbine somewhere on
the Downs. Why not? Quite probably he was the owner – and
loser of the badge – and there its whole significance ended. After
all Woodbine had certainly not been killed because someone
wanted to recover the badge, unless that someone had bungled
his job badly; for the badge had been left in Woodbine's pocket.

It was a dreary, muggy day and the whole business of living –
and dying – seemed a little more futile than usual. The dim light
that had wavered towards Dr. Dorch had faded by lunchtime to
the merest of flickers. Having decided that, when he had done
his little bit, Bullock must be asked to say where precisely on
the Downs Woodbine had found the badge, Gore retired to the
smoking room and read extracts from *Martin Chuzzlewit*, Mrs.

Gaskell, and *The Lady of the House* – the only literature in sight – until he fell asleep.

He woke up to find a stoutish gentleman in plus-fours, in whom he recognised the fellow guest who shared his table in the dining room, regarding him fixedly.

"I was looking at your ears, Colonel," he said with gravity.

"Are they unusually pink?" Gore asked. "That beef was rather underdone, I thought. So sorry."

"Their colour is several shades deeper than the normal healthy red of the human ear, certainly," agreed the gentleman in plus-fours. "But I was looking rather at the shape of your ears."

"Very good of you," Gore smiled. "Er – collecting?"

The other tapped a largish volume, still in its wrapper, which rested in his comfortable lap.

"I'm reading an extraordinarily interesting book about the detection of crime – *The Mark of the Beast*, it's called – extraordinarily interesting. It's written by – someone called Gunter – evidently someone who knows all about it – I should say probably someone actually at Scotland Yard. It deals with the detection of crime – the actual modern scientific methods – extraordinarily interesting. Extraordinarily minute... He gives details of all the processes—" He ran through the pages of the volume quickly. "The Bertillon Method... Fingerprints... marvellous how they can tell one fingerprint out of millions – disguises – the chromoscope – spectrograph – ultra-violet rays..."

"Anything about salt?" Gore asked gently.

"Salt? No. What do they use that for?"

"They don't put it on the tails of the ones they don't catch. Hope my ears aren't worrying you, are they? I'm afraid my left tragus has slight leanings towards bigamy."

"No, no, no," protested his companion. "It's really a most serious matter. Especially for the criminal. Do you know that it says here that the chances of a man who commits a murder escaping – are – I mean is – one in ten thousand."

"Remarkable how many of them take it," commented the audience.

"The scientific mind knows that the exceptional instance is negligible, my dear Colonel."

"Well," sighed Gore, "the unscientific person must only console himself with the thought that it's only the exceptional instance that interests him. By the way – does your Mr. Gunter recommend catching your murderer before you look at his ears or do you just get a nice pair of ears and—"

But the man in plus-fours had closed his book and was moving towards the sound of the tea gong, carrying it against his most salient convexity. He moved slowly, and visibly, as he moved, he polished up a crushing retort.

"There are no exceptional instances," he said from the door. "Even the jest of the unscientific person can be reduced to scientific fact. There is no problem in the universe to which, ultimately, the mind of man will not write Q.E.D."

It was the last straw. Gore went to the pictures.

Chapter Ten

He dined at Victoria Square that evening with Pickles, her brother and his wife, and – in honour of his presence – Simon Wyckham. Afterwards the talk was of that young gentleman chiefly. An interview with her husband's solicitors that afternoon had informed his mother that at all events Master Simon's future was securely provided for. Already she had decided that he was to follow in his father's footsteps and be a doctor. A London doctor. In point of fact, *the* London doctor for something or other. Linwood had too many sad associations now for Pickles. She proposed to sell the house in Victoria Square and settle in London. London was to be Simon Wyckham's city – the sooner the better. There was a good deal of talk about London. Her brother and her sister-in-law, who lived there, were strongly in favour of the proposed migration. Gore, secretly overjoyed, said all the things he would have said if he hadn't been.

His fellow guests, doomed to an early train back to town next morning, left shortly after nine, and for a little space he fenced cautiously with Pickles' questions, saying nothing whatever of his own failure, and stressing the enormous difficulties which the police had to contend with. It was clear, however, that she was bitterly disappointed that he had brought her no news and that she hardly heard his vague platitudes.

"I've found out about that cheque," she said abruptly. "The one Sydney paid to that man with the hideous name—"

"Dorch? Yes?"

She handed him a letter, addressed to Melhuish, which had
arrived that afternoon. The writer was a parson named Pettitt,
who some years before had been attached to Linwood Parish
church, and whose family Melhuish had at that time attended.
Subsequently Mr. Pettitt had gone out to Italy, and had been
appointed chaplain to the English church at Valaccio, where
there was a considerable colony of his fellow countrymen, settled there for economy's sake, since the war. A son, named
Hugh, was at the moment a medical student at Linwood University. It was to this young man that the letter had reference.

*"My DEAR DR. Melhuish, – I find myself utterly at a loss to
thank you for your kindness and promptness in complying with
the request contained in my last letter. I feel sure that you will
realise the pain and anxiety which my son Hugh's conduct has
caused me and my wife and the deep relief with which I received
your letter informing me that you had seen this man Dorch and
that the matter was now closed. I enclose cheque for £65, which
with £60 already sent you, repays our financial obligation to you.
Nothing can ever repay, however, our real debt to you.*

*"It is our trust that this affair, and the misery which it has
caused Hugh for months past, will be a lasting lesson to him. I
have written to him telling him that the money has been repaid
to Dorch and the promissory note cancelled, and asking him to
take the earliest opportunity of seeing you and thanking you for
your good offices in his behalf. Youth is always impatient of rebuke
and advice from its elders. But if you would say a few words of
warning to him, when you see him, and help him to realise what
a terrible punishment might have befallen his folly and what a
severe strain upon my resources this payment of so large a sum has
been, I should be, if that is possible, still further in your debt.*

"Believe me, my dear Doctor,
"Yours very sincerely,
"WILLIAM PETTITT."

"I suppose," commented Pickles, "that it means that Dr. Dorch lent this boy money."

"Something like that," Gore admitted. Personally, he suspected that the matter had not been quite so simple a one as that. If it had been merely a question of a loan by Dorch to this young man, the transaction would have been closed, presumably, by his father's sending Dorch a cheque for £125, apparently the amount due. That Pettitt Senior had chosen to employ Melhuish as intermediary pointed, however, to some difficulty in settling the affair. A rather unpleasant kind of difficulty suggested itself – one which would account very easily for Dorch's unwillingness to cancel young Pettitt's promissory note. For there had evidently been a promissory note.

Now, why should a man in Dorch's position lend a medical student money on a promissory note? Curious. He was in the act of handing the letter back to Pickles when Clegg appeared to announce that a Mr. Pettitt had called and had asked to see — the butler hesitated, and ended "the Doctor."

Gore put the letter into his pocket and got to his feet. "Time for me to get off, Pickles. I'll see this youth, if you like, about this letter – and perhaps say a few wise words...? Now – don't think people are not trying. I'll look up Lord tomorrow and let you know at once if anything has moved. Goodnight."

"Goodnight, Wyck. It was dear of you to bear being bored by the family. Yes – ring me up at once. I am always waiting for the telephone. It never rings now. It's so odd—"

In the waiting room Gore found a tall, rather weedy youth, with good eyes, a pimpled face, and a weak chin. It was clear that in the interval the visitor had been informed by Clegg that the house had no longer a master. He was in a state of acute embarrassment, and assented hurriedly to Gore's proposal that they should talk as they walked – for some little distance, in the same direction.

In the darkness he clothed himself rapidly in the elaborate casualness of the hobbledehoy of today. He never read anything

but the racing and sporting news whenever he did read a newspaper, he said; so he hadn't the foggiest idea that old Melhuish
had passed over. Decent old chap. He had put the entire Pettitt
family through measles once. Bit stiff in the neck, what. He was
sorry the poor old chap had pegged out. How had it happened?

Gore told him briefly, and then steered the conversation
unexpectedly towards his father's letter to Dr. Melhuish. The
youth's garment of splendid carelessness fell from him swiftly. Oh yes – he had wanted to see Dr. Melhuish about that.
Though why the pater had wanted to drag Dr. Melhuish into
it, he couldn't see. He evinced a marked desire to talk about
something else, and all but escaped in a passing bus, with a
hurried "so long."

Without ceremony Gore grabbed his arm.

"Now, look here, young fellow," he said curtly. "You've bled
your father for a hundred and twenty-five quid – and you're
feeling quite happy about everything and quite sure that your
troubles are all over. They're not... quite. The letter which your
father has written to Dr. Melhuish will probably be put into the
hands of the police tonight. It's better that you should realise
that."

"The police?" stammered the boy. "What have the police to
do with it?"

"They'll tell you. And just remember bluff is not going to
help you with a detective officer. How did you come to borrow
money from Dr. Dorch – exactly?"

"What business is that of yours?"

"If you won't tell me – remember – you will probably be in
custody within an hour from now. I have no particular interest
in you. But your father was a friend of Dr. Melhuish's and I'm
willing to do anything that can be done to get you out of a hole.
Come on – let's have it. I know most of it already, you know."

It was, of course, a disgraceful bluff. But at the word "arrest"
visible panic had seized young Pettitt. He made no further resistance and blurted out his wretched story – precisely the story, in

its main details, which Gore had expected to hear – in unhappy little chunks of confession.

Girls and backing horses – that had been the beginning of it. Loans from friends and bills run up at shops had kept things going for a while – but eventually it had been absolutely necessary to get hold of fifty pounds somehow. Nothing doing with the pater – nothing more doing with the friends. A chap he knew at the Medical School – a fellow student named Hawker – had told him then of a firm of moneylenders in Westmouth called Johnson & Co. Hawker had added in confidence the information that Johnson & Co. were really a man called Dorch; and that Dorch was father-in-law to "Fatty" Simpson, one of the Westmouth Infirmary staff, whose clinics Pettitt and Hawker were then attending at that hospital. Hawker had said that he had heard Johnson & Co. were "very decent" about lending money to medicals on that account. In the end young Pettitt had visited Messrs. Johnson & Co's. Offices and signed a promissory note for £75. For this he had received, on his own signature, fifty pounds. That had been about nine months ago.

Of course he had been unable to pay off the note when it had fallen due. Most unfortunately, just then he had met another girl – a married girl this time – and a very expensive one. At the end of three months he had signed a new bill for a hundred pounds, receiving in return nothing whatever except the consolation of knowing that for three months ahead Messrs. Johnson would make no demand upon him. At the end of that three months he had received a peremptory demand for settlement of the promissory note in full.

Scared to death, on his own admission, he had gone to Messrs. Johnson, But they had been perfect brutes. After several visits, however, they had offered a renewal of the loan, provided he would sign a new note for £125 – which must, however, have a second name to it.

He had been desperate at that time. The married girl had been bleeding him "wickedly," and had been threatening to inform her husband of their connection unless he treated her more generously. To make a long story short, he had forged the signature of an aunt who lived near Westmouth – had told Messrs. Johnson a cock-and-bull story to the effect that his aunt had been so furious at being asked for her signature that, although she had given it, she had announced her intention of never having anything more to do with him (this in the hope that it would prevent their communicating with her) and had then lived three months in "Hell." Foreseeing the inevitable smash-up, he had at last written to his father and told him the whole truth of the matter. His father had written to Messrs. Johnson, offering to pay off the bill. They had declined, however, "as there was some irregularity in the signatures," and had requested a personal interview with him and his son "to explain this."

Terrified, Pettitt junior had wired Pettitt senior, to "try to work Dr. Dorch," thinking it possible that Dr. Dorch was an acquaintance of his father's, since the latter had been associated with Linwood for many years. Pettitt senior, had then, obviously, bethought of him of Dr. Melhuish as a possible friend at court; possibly had known or guessed that Dr. Dorch was one of Dr. Melhuish's patients. At any rate, this medicine seemed to have done the trick, since Dorch had handed over the note – apparently without exacting any further payment, a contingency which the young man and his father had both expected and dreaded.

Admittedly, apart from the exorbitant rate of interest, Johnson & Co. had acted perfectly straightforwardly in the transaction. They had held out no inducement to borrow: indeed they had made difficulties about lending from the first. Their offices – they had three or four, in different parts of the city, it seemed – were quite "decent-looking"; Pettitt had never seen any personal Johnson & Co., but the manager who had dealt with him had also been quite a "decent-looking" chap, if he had proved a "bit of a brute" at one stage in the negotiations. There was nothing discreditable in lending money at interest; under one guise or another the world was made up of borrowers and lenders. No doubt a medical student had seemed to Johnson & Co., very likely to do just what this one had done – blew the money and, at the end of three months, say he couldn't repay the loan. So they had made him pay 200 percent. Quite a usual rate with such gentry for small loans on poor security.

Nothing very greatly to Dr. Dorch's detriment in all that. And quite satisfactory proof that Melhuish's connection with the matter had had no personal significance. The flicker of lunchtime threatened to wink out altogether.

Having obtained Messrs. Johnson's address, and warned his companion to keep his mouth shut if he could, Gore got rid of him without difficulty by administering some paternal advice in tabloid form. Young Pettitt was bound for one of the hostels in which the students of the University were lodged; somewhere in the neighbourhood of Linwood College he took very subdued leave of Gore and disappeared round a corner dejectedly.

When he had gone some way, however, revolving within his alarmed soul vain and bitter thoughts, it occurred to him that he had forgotten to impress upon this unaccountable and uncomfortable person named Gore who had suddenly erupted into his affairs, the absolute necessity of keeping Hawker's name out of it – whatever "it" might prove to be for himself. The fact being that he owed Hawker over twenty pounds and that if Hawker was dragged into "it," Hawker would insist on getting his twenty quid – and the fat would be in the fire with the pater all over again. No policemen must go bothering Hawker with questions. He decided to turn about and pursue the uncomfortable Gore and get that point quite clear.

The immediate neighbourhood of Linwood College consists of a network of crossroads somewhat confusing to the stranger. Pettitt, however, had known Linwood all his life, and knew also the direction in which Gore was now moving towards his hotel. He broke into a smart trot, calculating that in four or five minutes he would come up with his quarry somewhere close to the College gates in College Road.

Reaching College Road, he was delayed for several moments by an elderly woman in nursing uniform, who asked to be directed to a bus route. She appeared an exceptionally stupid person, but, for the sake of her uniform, the medical student lingered to give her clear instructions. He ran on then in pursuit of his quarry and came up with him almost exactly where he had expected to do it. But the uncomfortable Gore was no longer a disconcertingly tall and upright person who looked down at one from an unfair advantage. He was lying on the ground half in and half out of the gate of one of the College houses, crumpled up in an unpleasant way and bleeding through his overcoat like the traditional stuck pig.

To do young Pettitt justice, he did what he could without delay. Under a quarter of an hour later Gore was in a nursing home, swathed in bandages, with a fractured skull, two nasty knife wounds in the neighbourhood of his digestion, and a sporting chance of facing his Maker before the morning. This last, however – being an obstinate person with a passion for finishing off jobs – he threw away.

Chapter Eleven

LINWOOD, THE POLICE AUTHORITIES considered, had had quite as many thrills within the past week or so as were good for it. Vague rumours strayed to and fro. No reference to his misadventure had appeared in the local press, however; for although College Road had appeared deserted when Pettitt had arrived upon the scene, a crowd had collected from nowhere before Gore had been carried off in a passing car pressed into ambulance duty. It was not until several days later that Mrs. Melhuish was informed of what had befallen her guest on his homeward way. Young Pettitt had several interviews with police officials before he went to bed that night, and received strict injunctions to preserve absolute silence as to the affair. The gravity of this warning confirmed his suspicion that his companion upon that uncomfortable walk had been himself a detective officer. He obeyed his instructions so implicitly that he shut himself up in his bedroom for the greater part of a week with alleged shingles, and refused to see anyone save a sardonic-visaged person called Lord who persisted in calling at the hostel daily for a prolonged visit.

For ten anxious and impatient days Lord and his superiors waited upon the pleasure of a grievously outraged constitution. But when at last a rather white and limp Colonel Gore was permitted to receive callers, he had but the most meagre information to give the harassed Inspector.

He had just turned into College Road out of Spencer Road, he said, when the thing happened. Before it happened, he could not recall having noticed any person taking an at all suspicious interest in him. He had met, he supposed, at most three or four people after parting from Pettitt. They had, as far as he could remember, appeared just the sort of quiet people one would expect to meet at that hour in that quiet place. Some amorous couples, an elderly nurse, two elderly ladies with a small boy; he could recall no others.

On his left hand, when he turned that corner, had been the College houses, facing the College itself and its grounds and playing field across the road. It had been at the second gate that the attack had been made on him. As he had turned the corner he had noticed – in the most casual way, merely – a somewhat elderly man with an umbrella (it had just begun to drizzle slightly) – coming towards him at the inner edge of the footpath. As they had both arrived at the gate in question, the owner of the umbrella had turned outwards across the path and, to avoid the umbrella, he himself had naturally turned inwards somewhat. This had brought him close up to the gate. Just as he was passing it, something had come round his neck sideways and tightened with a savage jerk. He had felt himself lose his balance and fall backwards and sideways – and that was the last thing he remembered. Whether the man with the umbrella had had any share in the attack or not, he was quite unable to say. His head had been pulled backwards and upwards. Everything had disappeared in an orange blaze. The carrier of the umbrella had held it before him and his face and figure to the knees had been concealed from view. His legs and walk had appeared somewhat elderly and – silhouetted against the wet pavement – slightly knock-kneed.

"Notice any cars pass you just before?" Lord asked.

"Yes. Four or five cars passed me after I left Pettitt – going with me or against me. I saw no car that I can remember in College Road itself. But of course, it was a dark, dismal night, and I wasn't on the lookout for cars. Or knives. By the way, both jabs are uppercuts, I hear."

Lord nodded gravely. "Thoughtful sort of beggar, whoever he was. He opened your overcoat carefully before he got busy with his snickersnee. We've had everything in Westmouth that even looks foreign checked up, of course – just because a knife was used, and used in that way. As it happened, there wasn't a boat in the docks that night with anything black, yellow or brown belonging to it. By the way, we gave our friend Dr. Dorch's housemaid – Peterson – a call. I remembered his face, and your hunch about Dorch. So I paid *that* call myself. However, Mr. Peterson – saucy brute he is, too – says that he was in London that night, and Ross corroborates it. Ross says now, by the way, that Dorch won't get back for some weeks probably. He's gone to New York to settle up something or other urgent. Ross was to have seen him in Liverpool, but when he got there Dorch had sailed. Ross says he has big interests the other side and crosses three or four times a year."

"Ask Ross if he knew anything about anything that called itself Q.E.D. for short?"

"Yes. He didn't."

"Tell him why you asked?"

"I showed him the badge, yes. And I told him about the coincidence of Dorch's having used the abbreviation in a letter I had seen recently. I didn't say, however, where I had seen it, though, of course, he wanted to know. Not very eagerly, however. In fact he appeared utterly bored by me and everything I said. Only thing he seems really interested in is wireless. I found him busy making a short-wave set to get Cleveport... Look here – I'm talking too much, old chap—"

"Not at all. You didn't happen to have a look at Peterson's left forearm, did you?"

Lord stared.

"His left forearm! No, why?"

"Because he's got an exact copy of that badge tattooed on it – Q.E.D. and all. Oh – Scotland Yard can't tell us anything about those initials, I regret to say."

A steely-eyed nurse appeared menacingly and so ended Inspector Lord's first visit, with a new perplexity. When he arrived next day, he found with the patient a quiet youngish man, with a rather intent pair of spectacles, whom Gore introduced as Mr. Yeoland, one of his staff. Yeoland was able to acquit Dr. Dorch's manservant, at any rate, of any personal share in the incident in College Road.

He had followed the two vans – as Gore had surmised, a second van had been loaded in the drive at Wavertree – all the way up the Bath Road to Highgate, where they had arrived shortly after dark and had been unloaded at a large house called Cedar Hill, standing in its own grounds, in the direction of Hampstead Heath. The man Peterson had travelled up on one of the vans, both of which had been parked for the night in a large yard at the side of the house. Yeoland had seen Peterson then leave the place in the company of a man who, from his account, had clearly been Ross. According to his instructions, he had then set to work to discover anything discoverable about the inhabitants of the house – a very simple matter, since within ten minutes he had learned at the nearest post office that the tenant of Cedar Hill was and had been for many years, a Doctor Dorch, who, though not now a permanent resident in it, visited it at frequent intervals. The postmaster understood that a housekeeper and two or three servants looked after the house. A very pleasant gentleman, Dr. Dorch; and received a quantity of correspondence, whether he was at the house or down in Westmouth, where he had his regular residence since the War.

All this appeared perfectly normal and satisfactory – at all events from the postmaster's point of view. Yeoland had gone back with the Buick to pick up Stephens, who had contrived to scrape acquaintance with the drivers of the vans and to learn that they were to return to Westmouth in the morning, starting at the "perishin'" hour of 5 a.m., and carrying Peterson and Mr. Ross as passengers. At 5 a.m. accordingly, Yeoland had seen the two vehicles start upon their homeward way, with Peterson in one cab, and Mr. Ross – presumably – in the other. The Buick had then made for Westmouth, where it had arrived in time for breakfast and the news that "the Colonel" was not likely to take any interest in reports, however urgent, for some little time to come.

"Well – it's very energetic of you to have followed up those vans," said Lord. "But, you know – there's nothing to all this about Dorch, Colonel. Certainly, if you like, I'll see this bloke Peterson again and find out what the war-painting on his arm means – if it means anything. Probably a Jane. Perhaps the very Jane of the black hair. For all I know he may be a married man – and, therefore, of course, above suspicion."

"At any rate, let's hear what he says," urged Gore. "Also keep an eye out for that wire-haired terrier – and anything else of interest. Other servants, for instance. The shover, if there is one. By the way – would it bore you to see Bullock, wherever he's doing his little bit—"

"He's done it. He only got seven days."

"Good. Will you see him and ask him if he can say exactly where Woodbine found that badge. Exactly. And why not make *quite* certain that Peterson wasn't the lout in the leggings? You could wangle it so that Bullock could have a good look at him at any rate, couldn't you?"

Inspector Lord began one of his ironic smiles, but on consideration decided that convalescents, with a tendency to a temperature still, must be soothed by being taken seriously. He would see both Peterson and Bullock that morning and report any result of interest later in the day.

But he could not refrain from a farewell word of self-defence.

"You haven't said it, Colonel. But of course you're thinking – here's this B.F. coming here talking my head off and saying damn all. It's quite right. And the reason why is just that I

haven't got a thing to say. We've located both those chaps –
those two pals of Frensham's. One has been in Holloway for
seven months. The other was playing billiards in a pub in Birmingham the night Melhuish was done in. *That's* absolutely a
wash-out. And I tell you frankly – it isn't only that I haven't
another idea in my head. I can't even begin to think where to
start looking for one. I'm exactly like a chap with three blank
walls in front of him and a mad bull just behind him. And mad
bulls *don't* give one brilliant ideas.

"But that's not going to persuade me to see a hole in one of
the walls which I know isn't there. I mean – your idea, I take it, is
that, because Peterson or Dorch or Ross, or all of them, or some
of them, thought you were on to them for something, he or they
tried to lay you out permanently. But – that's exactly what he or
they *wouldn't* have done... If they suspected that you were on to
them – *they* knew that you and I were hunting in couple. Do you
think he or they would have given the show away by knocking
you off? Not on your life..."

The Inspector paused, as he collected his hat and stick, and
then turned towards the bed, expectant of at least polite dis-
agreement. Gore's reply, however, was simply a placid:

"Exactly."

"Well, then?"

"Exactly," said the patient again.

And so, human nature being what it is, Inspector Lord left
the nursing home with the uneasy feeling that that last argument of his was perhaps too sound. He made his way thought-
fully towards the Downs and, the morning being a mild one,
sat down on a quiet seat to think things over for the hundredth
thousandth time.

However one looked at them, one thing seemed certain. Unless a homicidal maniac was loose in Linwood, and unless, by an
extraordinary chance, he had selected Gore for his third victim
by mere accident, the attack on Gore had been meant to clear
him right out of someone's way – because of some urgent and

pressing necessity. It was practically impossible not to suppose that that necessity was connected with Gore's present visit to Linwood and its purpose. In plain words Gore had been making himself too busy for someone's comfort by his interest in Melhuish. Or perhaps, by his interest in Woodbine. And, however anxious Inspector Lord was not to be swept off his neat feet by that active imagination of Gore's, it was impossible not to admit that the two people who had had the clearest view of that interest were both members of Dorch's household – Ross, his secretary, and Peterson, his servant. Both these men had seen Gore in the company of a police inspector, and knew of his anxiety to see Dorch – an anxiety farther shown by a second appearance in the neighbourhood of Dorch's house and farther enquiry from Peterson as to Dorch's return. Curious that Dorch should have selected just the time he had selected to go to America.

His connection with Johnson & Co. might be looked into. A rather unexpected sort of connection... suggesting, inevitably, the possibility of others. All those cases, for instance, which had been moved up to London in a hurry... what was in them?

Find out if Winton & Sharp – a most respectable firm – had carried any other stuff for Dorch anywhere.

When *had* Dorch left Linwood, exactly?

Somewhat curious that he should keep on another big house at Highgate. He was a bachelor... a man, evidently, with a good deal of money... yet not just the type of man, socially, it seemed, who kept a London house and... well, one could hardly call a house in Linwood, even detached, a country house.

If there was anything wrong about Dorch... of course, one would have to move cautiously... if that was possible *now*.

No use rushing at Ross and Peterson.

Presently Lord knocked out some cold ashes and made for the nearest city-bound bus line. It seemed to him that he might as well begin with Johnson & Co., the addresses of whose three offices he had obtained from young Pettitt, who, it seemed, had done a good deal of running from one to the other in search of the manager of the business.

On the third floor of a large building in Walbin Street, at the city's business centre, he interviewed a smartly dressed young clerk who was in charge of two spruce offices. This young gentleman could not say where the manager was or when he would be likely to be at any particular place. Ultimately he revealed that the manager's name was Prescott, and that he might possibly be found at one of the firm's other branches. A short journey in a tramcar carried Lord into a district of shabby, populous streets where he found Messrs. Johnson & Co. operating in a markedly different atmosphere. Along a small converted shop four small cubicles faced a greasy counter, beyond which lay a safe, some ledgers, a copying press, and some shelves littered with dusty bundles of papers speared on files. In the cubicle next to that which he entered, a dejected female was protesting her inability to pay a weekly instalment of five shillings and an unmoved masculine one was reminding her that, unless the instalment was paid, the whole amount of the loan – three pounds – became at once due. A shabby, drink-sodden man occupied the cubicle on Lord's other side; his battered old hat kept impatient watch round the edge of the partition upon the manager's coat-tails, the only part of him at the moment visible. After long discussion a day's grace was granted to the cowed client with whom the manager was engaged; he passed along the inside of the counter, glancing quickly at Lord, and entered into a long murmured conversation with the impatient gentleman on the other side, who was apparently in need of ten shillings until the following Saturday. This client disposed of, the manager went to the safe, unlocked it, and then remembered Lord and locked it again. He came back towards the counter, his legs silhouetted against the fire in a tiny grate. They were not violently knock-kneed; but their knees knocked sufficiently markedly to cause Lord to raise his eyes with an adjusted interest to their owner's face. An impassive, intelligent face of a very ordinary English type – the respectable clerk – eyes, perhaps, too close together – like the knees. Elderly, rather – say fifty-two to five. But quite a decently dressed, respectable, responsible looking fellow.

His glasses offered unencouraging inquiry.

"I am Inspector Lord," said that gentleman, pleasantly. "Of the Westmouth Detective Division. I want some information, please, with regard to the business carried on by Messrs. Johnson & Co. Perhaps you have some place where we can talk in private?"

Mr. Prescott appeared not to have heard. Lord had the impression that – probably a stock demonstration – he was pretending to think of something more important. There was quite an appreciable interval before the thin, respectable lips said:

"Certainly. In my room. Just a moment, while I make sure that there is no one waiting for me in there—"

He passed through a low door at the farther end of the office, shutting it behind him. Beyond all doubt Mr. Prescott had been thinking of something else – for some little time past.

"So I said to 'er," went on one of two ladies who had taken possession of the shabby man's cubicle, "as far's that goes, Mrs. Tabbs, I says, I knows nothing, I says, of your 'usban's affairs, I says, an' if he *does* follow the vanmen round and make them dip in their bags for him so's to keep in with 'im, 'e bein the foreman, well, I says, that's 'is affair, I says. And theirs... But when it comes to your daughter Lizzie 'avin' the cheek to say—" The key of the gabbling voice changed abruptly. "Gawd. Wha's that? Gas explosion. Come on, Tilda..."

Lord brushed the two alarmed women aside as he made hurriedly for the door which had closed behind Mr. Prescott. In a tiny room filled with acrid smoke he found the respectable manager on the floor, quite finished with the necessity to think about things.

***

Another visitor arrived at the nursing home that morning. At last – Pickles, very slim and remote in black. She stayed just long enough to see her chrysanthemums arranged about the room and to snub with unexplained severity the pretty nurse in charge of the patient for the moment.

When they were alone again, she surveyed the rather ascetic little apartment with disdainful disapproval.

"How soon can you get out of this awful hole, Wyck? Have they told you yet?"

"Not for a week or so, I'm afraid."

"Will you be fit to travel then? I mean – of course you'll want to get back to London at once."

"I hope that isn't a command. You know that I'm not going until I get to the bottom of this thing."

Her eyes rested on him broodingly.

"Leave it to the police, Wyck. It's their business. No – I won't listen. You must. You've had a terribly narrow escape, you know – once. I shan't have a moment's peace of mind until you've left Linwood. Promise me you'll go back to London just as soon as you can go."

But he shook his bandaged head – very like an obstinate little boy in bed, she reflected.

"Sorry, Witch. I want to see this little puzzle all in pieces. Anyhow, for a whole week, I'm quite safe here, you know. And really quite comfortable – if nursing home hoovahs would *not* walk in the night. The nurses, I must say, are most attentive and most respectful."

She threw him a little malicious glance.

"Devoted, evidently. Do they *all* call you 'Colonel dear' by the way?"

The patient's flesh-tint warmed slightly.

"My dear Pickles, I have now reached the age which young women regard as the beginning of senile decay—"

"Naturally – if you usually call that fluffy-headed little creature who was here just now 'Gingersnap.'"

The occupant of the bed having murmured a feeble protest that everyone did it, his visitor departed. The patient perceived, then, that his room was shockingly bare and uncomfortable looking, considering the number of guineas per week he was to pay for its use. His bed, he realised, was a large hard lump studded with small hard lumps; and even then, the lump was a foot too small every way. He kicked it vindictively for a while. When the fluffy little nurse returned to him with her bright smile and attempted to arrange his pillows, he was peevish with her and quite savage with the pillows.

"Never mind," she smiled sagely. "Perhaps she'll stay longer tomorrow, old sport."

The old sport sat up in bed by intimidating degrees.

He inserted his monocle in his eye and fixed it upon the daunted Gingersnap.

"I shall ring if I want you," he said icily. "And kindly do not slam the door as you go out."

Chapter Twelve

WITHIN A VERY FEW hours the larger bones at least of Prescott's history had been collected and a skeleton put together fairly coherently.

A native of Westmouth and the son of a tinsmith, he had very early begun to support himself by acting as a sort of itinerant bookkeeper to various small businesses in the obscure part of the city from which he had sprung. Even then he had been lending money on a small scale at stiff interest to friends and acquaintances. Some ten years or so before the war he had established himself officially as a registered moneylender under the name "Johnson," transacting his business in a small office – the dingy little den in which his career was to end so abruptly.

It had never been, in those days, apparently, a very secure sort of business, the class of client with whom it dealt being always likely to refuse payment of a loan except under threat of a writ and – even if the threat was carried out – equally likely to prove without a halfpenny in the world. With grim determination, however, the little money-grubber had continued to extract his weekly and monthly interest from little clerks and shop boys and other such chronically hard-up flies as found their way into the spider's dark little parlour. There had been rumours in later years, Inspector Lord learned, that Mr. Johnson was not unwilling to accept payment in the right sort of kind. The police had even begun to suspect that in some cases the "kind" was some other person's property than Mr. Johnson's client of the moment, and that, in point of fact, he was acting as "fence" in a small way. Nothing definite, however, had been brought home to him. And the war had not only distracted attention from him but had also, in due course, raked him into khaki, despatched him to France and subsequently to Mespots, and closed down his business. The spider's parlour had been transformed into a fish and chip shop with a roaring business, and the local bricklayer's missus and draper's assistant borrowed their half crown or five shillings on Tuesday from someone else and paid him back on Saturday with interest at 500 percent. Cheerfully, remembering that Mr. Johnson had always charged just double for these little conveniences.

In 1919 Prescott had reappeared on the scene, however, and had bought out the fish and chips business and endeavoured to run it himself. But, it seemed, he had not been cut out for fish and chips; his manner had lacked the necessary good-fellowship and geniality, and he had acquired in the army vexatious ideas upon the subject of discipline. Very shortly the little shop had been disembowelled once more and fitted with another long counter and a row of cubicles. "Mr. Johnson" had returned to business.

But his connection was gone – to rivals who had succeeded in staying at home. There had been a couple of years of obscure struggle before his affairs had begun to prosper again: Then, however, prosperity had come with abrupt and somewhat imposing splendour. Mr. Johnson had been transformed into Johnson & Co., with handsome offices in the best part of the city, and hardly less handsome ones in the second best part. The original office was still kept on, unimproved. But, as a rule, a subordinate officiated there, Prescott taking his place at irregular intervals – it was believed, in the hope of catching the subordinate napping, for the latter was always banished to one of the other offices for the day of the manager's visit.

A rather different explanation of this last detail was suggested by certain carefully made-up packages found in the safe which Inspector Lord had seen Prescott unlock. Their contents formed a curiously miscellaneous assortment of stolen property, every article of which was ultimately traced to its lawful owner. Magnetos, a collection of postage stamps, a set of cups won by a well-known local golfer, four automatics, a wad of old and valuable lace, a case of meerschaum pipes, several watches, a quantity of valuable leather, tools, a moleskin coat, pictures cut from their frames, brooches, bracelets, a traveller's sample-bag filled with silk stockings. Such was the inventory of the fish that had found their way into Mr. Prescott's net – presumably that day. The subordinate in charge of the place regularly under-went a searching examination, but his statement that he knew nothing whatever of Johnson & Co.'s sideline appeared to be a truthful one. Prescott, it was to be presumed, had been in the habit of arranging with these special customers the day on which he would take his clerk's place. His junior out of the way, he had dealt with them himself in that back room.

The Westmouth Detective Division put in a busy afternoon that day, and before it ended Lord had interviewed a surprising number of people who knew all about Prescott's sideline. It took him some weeks to lay his finger on the particular clients who had visited Prescott that morning, but the greater number of them, as a matter of fact, faced the Inspector's ironic gaze provisionally within twelve hours of Prescott's death. None of these people, it became clear, had the slightest idea that Prescott had had any principal in either of his businesses.

The four clerks, who, it seemed had been changed over at short intervals from one of the three offices to another, were closely questioned. None of them knew anything of any backer behind Prescott, whom they had all regarded as their employer. Their duties had been strictly limited to ordinary clerical work, the preliminary interviewing of clients and the receipt of in-stalments. The final negotiations in reference to proposed loans had always been conducted by Prescott himself. He appeared to have been loathed and feared by his subordinates for his suspicious cunning and his bullying manner. But it was clear that he had been clever enough to prevent any of them from knowing anything very much about him.

The only evidence of a connection with Dorch, then, was the Pettitt-Hawker link. Inspector Lord haled forth the unhappy Pettitt from a tea shop and dragged him off to the Infirmary, where his friend Hawker was at the moment acting as clinical clerk.

At first Hawker – a laconic young Hercules of six-foot odd, and a three-quarters of fame – denied point-blank that he knew anything about Johnson & Co. Confronted with Pettitt, however – to his visible annoyance – he was induced to modify this statement somewhat. He had met Miss Dorch – now Mrs. Simpson – at several dances before her marriage and had "got to know her pretty well." After her marriage he had been asked to her husband's house several times for tennis and so forth. One day – some time in the early summer of the preceding year – in a moment, apparently of especial confidence, Mrs. Simpson had confided to him that one reason why she had left her father's house and married – somewhat hastily – a man a good deal older than herself had been that she had quarrelled with her father because she had discovered that he was in the habit of lending money as a business. She had given him no details, and he couldn't recall now exactly what she had said. But he believed that she had mentioned that her father was mixed up with someone called Johnson in this money-lending stunt.

"I'm quite vague about it, really," said Hawker. "What I gathered, I think, was that her father carried on this game at his own house on the quiet as well, and that Mrs. Simpson had had a lot of rows with him about it. Of course, she simply hated the idea. That's really all I know about it, I may say that as I've never borrowed a red cent from anyone in my life, personally—"

"Noble youth," smiled Inspector Lord. "In a better world you will, I trust, be rewarded. I'm sorry to say that I shall have to check up this confidence of yours with Mrs. Simpson. However, I'll do it as tactfully as I can."

"Don't worry, old chap," smiled Hawker. "I'm getting on the phone to her myself right away."

The Simpsons lived not very far from Victoria Square, and, though it was now nearly seven o'clock, Lord decided to run the risk of postponing their dinner hour. It seemed wiser to interview the mistress of the house alone, although its master was at home, and he waited for a quarter of an hour while a merrily-chattering bridge party dispersed slowly. The pretty, somewhat exotic young woman who appeared at length informed him at once that she had been in conversation a very few minutes before with Mr. Hawker and that she was acquainted with the reason of his visit.

"But my husband is in. You must see him. He'll be frightfully bored if I keep this thrill all to myself."

Before Lord could detain her, she had flitted from the room, to return a few moments later with one of the fattest men the Inspector had ever seen in his life.

"Now – got your little notebook ready, and your little pencil licked?" enquired Mrs. Simpson. "You rely on your memory? Lucky man, I wish Mr. Hawker's friends could rely on his. Very well then. Whereas on a very hot day at the end of last May – I'm not keeping on with the poetry. Don't be alarmed. Whereas on the aforesaid day Bunny, otherwise Marmion Henry Hawker, was taking tea along with me on the tennis court at 43 Halwell Road, Linwood, and whereas we happened to be discussing my beloved and respected papa – heaven knows why. And whereas I said to him that one of the reasons why I had ruined my life by marrying—" she pointed to her husband, "this —was because I wanted to get hold of someone before everyone knew that I was a moneylender's daughter. I said that, although father did it on a big scale and called it finance, really he was no better than those awful bloodsuckers whose names one saw in the paper – their advertisements I mean – Jews who called themselves by English names like Johnson and Thompson. And whereas I said that, the aforesaid Bunny got it all messed up as he gets everything. And well, there you are. Do tell us what it's all about."

"As a matter of fact," smiled Dr. Simpson, "there *is* a money-lender named Johnson in Westmouth."

"There *was*," amended Lord. "He killed himself this morning."

"What luck for all the poor idiots who owed him money," commented Mrs. Simpson.

"The reason I happen to know of the gentleman's existence," went on Simpson, "is that the beggar had the impertinence to write to me some months ago asking me if I could give him some information concerning one of the students attending the Infirmary."

"May I ask the student's name?"

"A boy named Pettitt. Of course I took no notice of the letter. So he has killed himself, has he? My respected father-in-law *will* be pleased to hear that he's supposed to have been Mr. Johnson's partner. I'm almost inclined to ring him up and tell him – if he hasn't heard it already. We never talk to one another unless we have something really nasty to say."

"You're going to miss *this* opportunity, Doctor," laughed the visitor, "Dr. Dorch is away at the moment."

"Oh, he's always away," yawned Mrs. Simpson.

"Where is he now?"

"New York. By the way, Mrs. Simpson, may I ask if you are an American?"

"Born there, I believe. But I don't remember a thing about it. Father's a good American still, though. He's always running over for a deep breath of liberty."

"You have lived most of your life in England, then?"

"Yes."

"Here – in Linwood?"

"Oh, no. Practically altogether at school somewhere or other, I have lived very little at home – either here or while my father was living at Highgate."

"But you lived with your father, I understand, for a couple of years after leaving school – just before your marriage?"

"Oh, yes. Quite the two deadliest years of my life."

"You became aware then that your father was in the habit of – er – making loans of money?"

"Yes. I needn't say that I was perfectly staggered. I knew that father had tons and tons of money. Why he should want to make more by lending it out at interest – like a Jew – I couldn't conceive. I had some frightful rows with him about it. In the end I told him that unless it stopped, I should leave him and go on the pictures or join the Salvation Army or something frightful. He just said 'Please yourself.' So I did the worst thing I could think of. I married that."

"That" beamed placidly. It was evident that he, at least, had no regrets for Mrs. Simpson's decision.

Asked to be a little more precise as to these financial activities of her father, Mrs. Simpson had very little more to tell. After some time she had grown curious as to the nature of the prolonged interviews which her father used to hold in his study with people who had come to the house ostensibly to dine or play bridge. At that time, she explained demurely, her father's secretary, Mr. Ross, had been "rather keen about her." With this leverage, she had succeeded in discovering from him the explanation of these long confidential conversations which had attracted her attention. She had learned that Dr. Dorch lent at times very large sums; Mr. Ross had once shown her a cheque for £11,000 which he had told her was a loan to someone she knew well. He had covered up the name of the payee, so that she was unable to say who that borrower had been. But Mr. Ross had told her that that was nothing; that her father could write a cheque for six figures and not miss it.

"And the mean old pig won't even give me a Baby for my birthday," she concluded. But her dejection vanished as quickly as it had come. She jumped up, put her arms round the fat man's neck and kissed a large bald place on the top of his fat head.

"Never mind, my dear – I've got the biggest figure in the world for my very own."

Upon this scene of conjugal felicity Inspector Lord bestowed a paternal smile, and then took his leave.

Big George, the University clock, was striking eight in the distance when Peterson opened the hall door of Wavertree and informed him that Mr. Ross was at home and disengaged. He found the secretary busy with his new wireless set in a sanctum at the back of the house and accepted some excellent whisky and the best cigar he had ever smoked.

"I heard from Dr. Dorch this morning," Ross said, when he had made his guest quite comfortable." He expects to get back on the *Calaminia* on Christmas Eve. As I expected, he is very greatly shocked by the news of Dr. Melhuish's death. By the way – as regards that cheque of Dr. Melhuish's – I asked him about that. He writes – well, I had better show you his letter."

He left the Inspector for a few moments and returned with a long communication typed on a large quarto sheet of notepaper bearing the heading "The DORCH-MAYER Corporation, 78-80 Fetterman Buildings, West Thirty-fourth Street, N.Y."

"DEAR Ross, – Your news about Dr. Melhuish's death has given me the greatest shock of my life. You give no particulars, so of course the thing just seems impossible to me. I'm planning to go back on the Calaminia and get home on Christmas Eve. I'm very anxious to hear details of this terrible business. Let me know in your next letter how it happened.

About that cheque of poor Melhuish's. He asked me to try to get back a promissory note which a young fellow in whom he was interested had given Johnson & Co. The amount due was the figure you mention – £125. For some reason or other Johnson & Co.

thought one of the signatures to the bill was fishy and were inclined to make a fuss. Melhuish thought I might know Johnson & Co. – as a matter of fact, I didn't, though I knew the name, of course, and knew that a man called Prescott ran the business. However, I managed to get the bill out of them and Dr. Melhuish's cheque to me closed the transaction.

"How is Duggie? I hope that paw of his has healed up.

"I note that you've seen Cartwright about closing account at Linwood branch in January. But I suppose it will be February before we get settled down at Highgate. I'm looking forward to it, however. I've thought for a long time back that Linwood was a bad place for neuritis. You can move up the books any time, as they're packed. The rest had better go in one piece.

"I'm enclosing cheque for £2,500 for Maudesley, and £100 for current expenses. I note what you say about Phillips and about the Bentley for Sir John Winsley. But they must wait until I get back. "Snow to the shins here.

"Yours sincerely,
"ALOYSIUS DORCH."

"Duggie," Ross explained, "is Dr. Dorch's Pekinese. A loathsome little brute – but he adores it."

"Dr. Dorch is thinking of going to live at Highgate again, then?"

"Yes. He has been trying to make up his mind to leave Linwood for the last couple of years or so. He's a martyr to neuritis. However, as a matter of fact, Linwood has never agreed with him, I think, so we shall run up to Highgate early in the New Year. Indeed I've begun to move already."

"I gather from this letter," said Lord, handing it back, "that Dr. Dorch had no business relations – I mean, regular business relations – with this man Prescott?"

Ross stared. "Business relations? Good heavens, no. I see that this evening's paper reports that Prescott committed suicide this morning, by the way."

Lord nodded. "Dr. Dorch is in the habit of lending money?"

"Oh, yes. But, I need hardly say, in very special cases only – and to a very special sort of person. This Mr. Maudesley, for instance, whom he mentions in his letter – this is, of course, strictly between ourselves, Inspector – is the principal backer of Westmouth Cinemas – a syndicate with about a hundred thousand one way or another behind them. Mr. Phillips is, of course, the owner of Lady Silky – I don't know if you're interested in racing at all?"

"Sufficiently to lose a Bradbury occasionally," smiled Lord. "So I may take it that Dr. Dorch had no connection of any sort with Prescott?"

"Absolutely. I know very little about Prescott, personally. But my impression is that he was in quite a small way of business – I mean comparatively. May I ask what suggested that Dr. Dorch was associated with him? The fact that he had arranged this matter for Dr. Melhuish's friend?"

"Well – yes – chiefly. So Dr. Dorch gets back the day before Christmas. When did he leave Linwood, by the way?"

"On November 20th."

"November 20th. That was the night Dr. Melhuish was killed, as a matter of fact. But I suppose Dr. Dorch had left Linwood before the news got about?"

"No. He went up to London by the night mail – the 12.5. However, he dined with a friend – Mr. Hope – that evening – which, I suppose explains his not having heard anything about it. Hullo, you little beast – there you are, are you?"

A Pekinese of burnished gold and supernatural insolence had sauntered into the room slowly. Having regarded Ross and the visitor with profound contempt it turned and walked slowly out again.

"Poor little beggar," commented Ross. "He has eaten practically nothing since his master went away. Every night he goes solemnly upstairs and coils himself up on Dr. Dorch's bed."

More and more foolish had Inspector Lord's present line of inquiry begun to appear to him. The Pekinese somehow reduced it to absurdity. He rose to his feet.

"This man, Peterson – your butler, here – had he been long in Dr. Dorch's employment?"

"Something like twenty years, I believe. Why?"

"Have you ever happened to see his left forearm uncovered?"

Again Ross stared. "I expect so."

"He's got some tattooing on it, hasn't he?"

Ross reflected. "I can't say that I've ever noticed that. However – why not let us see his left forearm, if it is of any interest."

He rang, and the sinister-looking manservant came into the room on his toes.

"Let's see your left forearm, Peterson," smiled Ross.

"Sure," grinned the man, placidly.

He bared half of a gigantic arm thickly covered with black hair. High up, Lord saw a large gaily-coloured edition of the design which had so intrigued the imaginative Colonel.

"What's that?" he asked, regarding it at close quarters. "Your best girl's initials?"

Peterson grinned.

"I'll say she was some lil girl, Inspector, that one. There was never any other after her had to teach me anything. Care to see her picture? I got it still. An' it's all of thirty years since me an' lil Dorcas rubbed noses last."

"No, no," laughed Lord. "Dorcas, was she? What were her other names?"

"Dorcas Edna Quinney. Super-blonde model – one speed and reverse – no brakes. Second from the left in the Mulligan Guards Troupe she was then – the smartest bunch of kickers on Broadway. Gee, it makes me feel old to think how long ago it is since I was a sucker, on four dollars a week, and Mother's hopes."

Unmoved by these touching reminiscences, Lord took the silver badge from his pocket and compared it with the larger edition of its rather intricate ornamentation.

"What's the rest of it mean," he asked, desiring to have complete refutation of the imaginative Colonel's suspicions. "Anything?"

"Scenic Operators' Guild. I was a stagehand then at the old Pallaseum. That was the Guild badge, them jigsaws round the letters. Funny thing the way me an' lil Dorcas came to—"

Ross smiled dismissal.

"All right, Peterson. We'll take it it was funny."

Peterson reclothed his arm.

"Say, Inspector. I reckon you know that's my property you've put back in your pocket. Where'd you pick it up, anyway. I've missed it weeks back."

"Yours, is it? Well – I'll see you get it back," Lord promised, deciding to leave the question as to its finding unanswered. Peterson seemed disposed to renew his demand for its return but a gesture from Ross dismissed him from the room. Having lingered to dispose of another drink, Lord took his departure. In the hall, the Pekinese, having come slowly forth from a room opening into it, took another disdainful view of him, recognised him for a thing seen before, then turned and disappeared in boredom.

"Keep any other dogs?" Lord asked.

"No, thank heavens," replied the secretary fervently.

"That one cuts four hours out of my day, as it is."

Peterson, waiting by the door, held out a faded photograph of a showy-looking young woman in the comparatively decorous costume of the showgirl of the nineties. At its foot, in faded ink was written:

"D. E. Q. to her Big Boy. 1898. Atlantic City."

"Lend me this," smiled the Inspector. "I want to show it to a friend of mine. I'll let you have it back day after tomorrow."

"Sure," grinned Peterson. "I guess your friend'll want windows in both eyes to see a better looker in his own little art gallery."

He opened the door, and Inspector Lord passed out, buttoning his overcoat about his ears as an icy wind met him. The night was an unusually black one, and he realised with disagreeable vividness before he reached the gates of the little curving drive that the one light which had gleamed even faintly in the darkness had proved the most authentic of will-o'-the-wisps.

However – it would be mildly amusing to see the dear old Colonel's face tomorrow, as he gazed on lil Dorcas's opulent loveliness.

Chapter Thirteen

A GOOD DEAL OF the point of that little joke was blunted for Inspector Lord, however, by two causes.

The first was that he received that night a definite intimation from his immediate chief to the effect that, unless he could do something useful, at once with the Suspension Bridge affair, Scotland Yard would be asked to do it.

Lord was an ambitious, still young, man – before the war a solicitor without clients, during it a gunner officer, after it for some little time a police constable – with an eye fixed steadily upon London and a future worthy of his ability. That ability – envious tongues of course had called it luck – had been proved and rewarded by rapid promotion. But for the past twelve months or so his star had been a little clouded. Quite unjustly, of course, also, the failure of the Crown to secure a conviction in the notorious Mendip murder case had been attributed by his superiors in the first instance to his mishandling of the case, in conjunction with Inspector Shadgold and – most irregularly and improperly – under the suggestion and influence of an unofficial person named Gore. The transfer of this present case from his hands to those of a man from the Yard would probably, he foresaw, strike a fatal blow to his chances of further advancement. Not for many years had any tragedy aroused such popular indignation all over the West of England; the limelight of the Western Press had been flooding the Westmouth Detective Division balefully for over a fortnight. Fortune had given him, he felt, the opportunity of his lifetime. Was it to be snatched from him before he could use it – on the pretext that he couldn't?

Irritated and dejected by this imminent calamity, some of his resentment inevitably concentrated itself on the ludicrous collapse of the theory with which he had allowed himself, in despite of his common sense, to become infected. Once already this imaginer and suggester of vain things, of whom in his ruffled heart he thought that morning as "Ruddy-Gore," had persuaded him to make a ruddy ass of himself. Better keep away from him and that too hypnotic monocle of his, and carry on, on... well, anyhow, *not* on tripe and moonshine.

Still... he had promised to let the beggar know the result of his inquiries. Results—

Of course – there was no getting away from it. Ruddy-Gore *must* have been getting too close to *something* for someone's ease of mind. That was the deuce of it. The beggar must have stumbled on *something*—

Well, anyhow, one could just drop in at the Home, say 'Nothing doing' and 'How goes' and come away again.

The other point-duller was Colonel Gore's reception of his visitor. He smiled with maddening geniality while he listened to what Lord had to tell him – in the end, somehow, it worked out at a good deal more than its teller had intended – and when he had heard it, he lay back on his pillows and grinned. Grinned like a dog – noiselessly and with bared teeth.

"Funny, isn't it?" snorted Lord bitterly. "Sorry I forgot to ask if Dorch's cook always dropped black hairs or whether she was a piebald. Anyhow – that puts the tin hat on the Johnson & Co. theory, I think. *And* on the Dorch theory generally."

He had reserved the photograph of "lil Dorcas" for a climax, and he produced it now.

"This may interest you. The lady's full names were Dorcas Edna Quinney. She was a professional dancer, I gather, in a well-known troupe."

The convalescent gazed upon Miss Quinney's charms through a placidly critical monocle. Then he thrust out a hand to his bed-table, picked up a telegram to which was pinned a pencilled slip, and tossed it to Lord. The telegram was in code, but the slip gave a transcript.

"Patterson says now Pinkertons state Q.E.D. name used by minor N.Y. gang operated nineties headquarters. The Windmill Chrystie Street run by Quinton, Monk Eastman, Aloysius Droch or Dorch, went out of business when Eastman severed, Eastman killed 1920. Quinton real estate agent Cincinatti, Dorch went to England ends cabling N.Y. for further information Tolley."

"I expect Inspector Patterson knows what he's talking about. No mention of Dorcas Edna, you see," commented Gore.

Lord re-read the transcript with feelings extraordinarily mixed. The realisation that he had been told the tale and had swallowed it without a blink filled him with humiliation. But he was wise enough to forget his personal emotions for the moment. He knew the great Chief Inspector Patterson of the Yard well enough by repute to feel very certain that the information at which he was staring was absolutely accurate. Hope sprang in his breast, new-born. Even if the horns of that mad bull were perilously close behind – there was a door in one of those walls, after all. He tried to make his tone as casual as possible.

"Interesting, Colonel. But the 'nineties are a long way off. However, we'll look into Dr. Dorch & Co. a little more closely. When did you get this?"

"Yesterday afternoon."

"So that you may get a further report any old time. I should like to see it, if I may. Unless you'd prefer that I got into touch with Patterson and New York myself—"

Gore grinned again silently. "Just as you please, my dear chap. Of course I'll show you anything I get with pleasure. Only, for the Lord's sake – be careful." He tapped the telegram warningly. "All this gives us for the present is the fact that Dorch was mixed up with a New York gang thirty years ago. Also Peterson, presumably. Of course – a 'gang' may mean anything. However, as I'm sure you know, Monk Eastman was rather a celebrity in his day. Not in the nineties, perhaps, so much as later. Still, to have been in business with him, at any time, must have been an honour – and must have demanded special talent. If I might make a suggestion... suppose you look up Dr. Dorch's past history carefully before you show any further sign of being interested in his present. You want him to feel quite happy and comfortable, for a bit, don't you. And, if he's in New York – you want him to come back from it – to start with. If you're not a little careful... he mayn't."

"If he's in New York?" repeated the Inspector. "Why do you say 'if'?"

"Well – they had that photograph all ready for you. I rather suspect they got that letter all ready for you, too. It's such a nice, explaining sort of letter, from your account of it. That touch about moving the books separately, for instance... in case anyone named Inspector Lord should have wondered what was in all those cases that were sent off in such a hurry a couple of weeks ago. And then, such care to prepare Inspector Lord for Dr. Dorch's leaving Linwood – in case Inspector Lord should be surprised if he found Wavertree shut up. Bank account to be closed – neuritis to disappear. That homely, affecting inquiry for the poor little doggie's paw. That so very clear explanation of why Dr. Dorch was able to oblige Dr. Melhuish by wangling his young friend's promissory note out of Johnson & Co. Rather too clear, the whole letter, it seems to me. If there's one place Dorch isn't now, I'll swear it's New York, for instance. Of course, I'm a suspicious sort of person. Still... it's too damn slick, Lord. You know it is."

And somehow, such was the persuasive force of that infernal monocle, Inspector Lord saw at that moment clearly that it *was too damn* slick.

"There's no getting away from it," he admitted. "Ross forced that letter on me. And Peterson forced the photograph, I see that now."

"Just as well perhaps," suggested Gore consolingly, "as things have turned out. Much better, in point of fact. Have you seen Bullock, by the way?"

"Yes. But he won't talk to a policeman now. Sulky over his last little bit of trouble. Not that it matters a tinker's oath where the badge was found. Peterson has admitted that it's his; that's what we want to know. His description of the man in leggings – doesn't seem to me to fit Peterson at all. I mean, anyone who clapped eyes on Peterson for five seconds would be able to say at once 'Chinese,' and nothing else. Besides, he's a great big brute. But Bullock has said from the start that the chap in leggings had nothing unusual in any way about his mug, except his mouth. But of course – any time we want to, we can give Bullock a chance to check up on Peterson."

"Quite," agreed Gore.

"Well, why not let us want to now," reflected Lord.

"There's any amount of cover on the slope of the Downs opposite Dorch's house. Peterson *must* go out sometimes. Or better still, why shouldn't Bullock go along with a rake and ask if they wanted any odd gardening done. Peterson's certain to open the hall door. Bullock can have a good look at him."

"Quite," agreed Gore again. "And Peterson can have a good look at Bullock. If they've met before, that will be very useful – for Peterson. However, I think we may take it that they haven't and that Peterson was not the man in the leggings."

"Why do you think that?"

Gore explained that, having thought carefully over every incident which had immediately preceded his adventure in College Road, it had occurred to him to wonder what had become of his friend 'Arry when their morning promenade had ended with a parting not – unfortunately – very far from the gates of Wavertree and the van which had been loading up outside

them. He had deputed his *aide* Yeoland to interview 'Arry on the
subject. And 'Arry had confirmed the shrewd suspicion which
had suggested this step.

It transpired that, after leaving Gore, he had strolled back in
the direction of the van and, as he passed it, had been stopped
by Peterson, who had given him a couple of shillings and questioned him closely as to the "tall guy" from which he had just
parted. Two bob was two bob to 'Arry, and there had seemed
no reason why he should not tell the simple truth concerning
the pleasant gentleman with whom he had been taking a little
walk on the Downs. Yeoland had expended five shillings upon
an account, as nearly verbatim as 'Arry could make it, of what
he had said and what Peterson had said. And a portion of that
conversation had dealt exclusively with the personal appearance
of Bullock, whom it was quite clear Peterson had never seen, but
in whom he was markedly interested.

Now Bullock, while in no wise a distinguished-looking person, had a nose which, once seen, could fade from no memory – a nose, enlarged and corrugated by the countless pints
of close on seventy years, always a warm crimson, on a cold
November morning assuredly a flaming scarlet. If Bullock had
been able to speak to the man in the leggings, the man in the
leggings had seen Bullock's nose. But 'Arry's description of it
had clearly touched no familiar chord in Peterson's memory. He
had requested other clues to Bullock's identification. And so –
presumably – Peterson had never seen Bullock – *then*. It was
very possible, however, that in the interval since his chat with
'Arry he had given himself that pleasure.

"No," said Gore musingly, "I don't hope that Bullock can tell
us anything about Peterson. What I want to get from him is the
place where Woodbine told him he found the badge."

"Can't see that it matters. We know Peterson lost it."

"*Do* we?"

"He admitted himself that the badge was his, and that he had
lost it a bit back."

"Just so. That's why I think it isn't his and that someone else lost it."

"Oh, well – you've got to believe *something*, Colonel."

"Not in this world," replied the occupant of the bed cheerfully. "You see Bullock again and get that bit of information out of him, at any rate. I suppose you'll also see these people the letter spoke of. But *they'll* be O.K. They'll tell you, if you force them to, that they've been in negotiation with a perfectly respectable and reliable person called Dorch for the loan of money for perfectly respectable purposes. Be careful. They're safe to let Ross know a policeman has been worrying them, and kick up a fuss over it."

"We must take *some* risk," urged Lord.

"Quite. I think you'll have to chance Mr. Hope, whoever *he* is – the friend with whom Dorch dined that night. Because I suppose you'll try to check up Dorch for that night, somehow."

Lord took a long time to reply.

"What motive could Dorch possibly have had for getting Melhuish murdered? Because I don't suppose you suggest that he murdered him with his own hands, do you?"

"Certainly not his own hands unaided... no. What motive? Well... I admit that I can only answer that question by another. What motive had anyone for murdering Woodbine? What motive had anyone... in Linwood... for trying to murder me? None that I can conceive... except one that answers all three questions. Melhuish, and Woodbine and I knew something... or we each knew part of something which we oughtn't to have known. I take it you've dug up Woodbine's social circle fairly thoroughly?"

"Yes. No killers in it."

"He wasn't killed because he had the badge. But he may have been killed because he knew who owned the badge. But why should it matter whether he knew who owned it? Why should *I* have been supposed to know who owned it? Nobody could have known that I had ever seen the confounded thing. As for

Melhuish – well, the only clue to *that* is that 'old friend of mine.'
What the deuce could Melhuish have known or cared about
badges? Anyhow, I wish you'd see Bullock again and—"

"Inspector Lord," said an icy voice from the door. "You have
now been here an hour and a half. Will you kindly go away –
and do *not* come back today."

The Inspector, much more cheerful than when he had arrived, accepted his dismissal with grace and went out into a
December morning in which he detected now a distinct whisper
of Spring. Before going down to the Central Station to set in
motion an inquiry into Dr. Dorch's history since his arrival in
England, he decided that, under the pretext of an apology for
not returning Peterson's photograph for a couple of days, he
would call at Wavertree, taking Bullock with him, in order to
settle definitely the question as to whether Peterson was the
"man in the leggings." Having collected Bullock under duress,
much to that gentleman's indignation, he led him to Downshill
Road and, a little way from Wavertree's gates, delivered to him
final instructions.

"When the hall door is opened, you'll hear me clearing my
throat. Come along then slowly – pass the gate, looking in –
come back and come in – as if you thought there might be a
dog about. Don't hurry it. Come on right up the steps about
halfway. If Peterson shouts to you to clear out, pay no attention.
Put your hand to your ear as if you were deaf and keep coming
on until you can see him plainly. All the better, the more you
hear of his voice. Ask him then if he wants the drive cleaned up.
Keep on asking him until you're sure. Got it?"

Bullock, fingering his hoe and rake with sullen, unaccustomed awkwardness, nodded, and the Inspector went on
to the gates of the house alone. As he reached them a
tall, fresh-coloured middle-aged man emerged slowly, swing-
ing an umbrella meditatively. Lord took careful stock of his
good-looking but somewhat bloated and dissipated face as they
passed, concluding from the careful smartness of his general

appearance and his air that he was some client of Dorch's, disappointed to have found him away.

The Inspector was aware that Peterson, having recognised him, stood awaiting him at the open hall door. He went up the steps, clearing his throat duly, and while he produced his palaver concerning lil Dorcas's photograph, he heard Bullock's feet come shambling slowly up the drive. His eyes were on Peterson's face and he perceived that the butler had recognised the man with the hoe at a glance.

Peterson made no concealment of the fact. "'Nother half-dollar's worth?" he remarked sardonically. "Say, Inspector, you'll have the Linwood bums running round the Downs in their automobiles, if you keep on. Look at his lovely tools 'n all."

Bullock had come on up the steps slowly and unchallenged. Instead, however, of his arranged lines, he had made up a little palaver of his own. The chance to get some of his own back on the blurry coppers was too tempting. He winked sociably at Peterson and said, deliberately:

"No. That ain't the bloke I saw the morning Woodbine copped out. 'Sno more like him n'r *you're* like a real gent. An' here's yer blurry ole tools for you. You may carry them yourself."

Dropping his disguise. He turned and shambled down the steps again. Whatever his feelings, Lord displayed no resentment although Peterson's yellow mask was twisted in a grin all the more derisive because it made a pretence of suppressing derision.

"What's your staff, here?" he asked casually, picking up the tools.

"Housemaid, parlourmaid, cook an' me indoors. Shover out. All strictly sober, honest and industrious. Like to see them, Inspector?"

Lord nodded, and followed the butler into the hall. "I'll see the shover first. What's his name?"

"Markey"

"American?"

"No. Britisher."

"Fetch him along, will you?"

But a glance at Dr. Dorch's chauffeur was sufficient for the Inspector. The small, perky little fellow whose speech was unmistakable Westshire bore no faintest resemblance, except in the matter of his leg-wear, to Bullock's description of the man in the leggings. After a few questions as to the length of his service in his present place and his previous employment, questions answered straightforwardly, Lord nodded and the butler dismissed his colleague with another grin.

"What's your 'bus?" Lord asked, as the chauffeur reached the door.

"Rolls."

"Colour?"

"Black."

"Right. Let's have the maids. One at a time."

But the two youthful damsels and the responsible-looking middle-aged woman who presented themselves in succession were just typical specimens of their respective species, all three natives of Westmouth, and all three, except for a certain frigidity upon finding that they were being questioned by a policeman, candour itself. Not that the Inspector's inquiries were in the least degree alarming, his idea being simply to "get" the general atmosphere of Dr. Dorch's household. He noticed that the women treated Peterson with marked respect and that the highly respectable cook, who had been in service at Wavertree for nearly ten years, had grafted on to her soft Western dialect a number of flowers culled from the butler's vocabulary. This was, Lord knew, one of the highest tributes the lady could have paid a fellow-servant of alien race. The girls, too, complied with Peterson's signals with smiling readiness. No bully, then, Dr. Dorch's "houseman," despite his unprepossessing looks – no twister. To use his own phraseology, after several years of joint service, these women had nothing on him.

Lord was staring at him meditatively, after the womenfolk had left them, and had just decided that his age was probably somewhere round fifty and his arms the longest pair he had ever seen, when a key turned behind him in the hall door, which opened to admit Ross. The secretary, however, who had obviously been taking the Pekinese for a constitutional, did not for the moment perceive the caller in the rather dark hall. He was preoccupied by an attempt to induce "Duggie," who had lagged behind in the drive, to ascend the steps. When Duggie did at length decide to do so, he was followed into the house by a boisterous wire-haired terrier, which frisked in rings about him in vain endeavour to arouse him to playfulness.

Ross came into the hall in pursuit of this intruder.

"Here – Buster. Go home. Go on – beat it."

Succeeding in driving Buster forth, he shut the hall door and then became aware of Lord.

"Morning, Inspector. Another visit. We are honoured. Darn these infernal dogs – sorry I can't shake hands. I've been carrying Duggie because Duggie found an old fish on the Downs and rolled in it. Of course every dog in Linwood followed us home. What can I do for you?"

"I should like Dr. Dorch's New York address, Mr. Ross. It has slipped my memory."

Ross gave him the address printed at the head of the letter which he had seen the evening before, and stated that Dorch & Mayer were theatrical agents, a business in which Dr. Dorch had retained an interest from the days of his former association with New York's theatrical world.

"When was that?"

"From about 1890 on, until he came to England."

"When was that?"

"In 1907."

"While he lived in London, did he follow any business?"

"Not regularly. As I have told you, he has a weakness for dabbling in all sorts of things. In London – well, he did very much the same things as he does here – perhaps not quite to the same extent. His weakness for little deals has increased a lot of late years."

"Happen to have a good photograph of him?"

"No, I'm sorry. He has always had a violent objection to being photographed, as long as I have known him."

"How long is that, Mr. Ross?"

"Very nearly twenty-five years now."

"When did you yourself come to England?"

"In 1907, with Dr. Dorch."

"Where did he take his degree?"

There was just the slightest fraction of a second's delay before the secretary answered.

"That was before I knew Dr. Dorch, of course. I rather think he was a Princeton man. It has never occurred to me to ask him. But of course I can easily find out for you."

"I should like a specimen of his handwriting."

"Certainly. Won't you come into the study?"

Lord followed his guide into a very comfortably equipped working room, lined with bookcases. While Ross selected from some papers on the writing table a sample of his employer's handwriting, the Inspector's observant eyes ran round the well-filled shelves. Several shelves were filled with volumes dealing with celebrated trials, celebrated criminals, celebrated detectives and works of a similar kind, English and American.

"Takes an interest in criminology, evidently," he remarked as Ross handed him a couple of largely-scrawled sheets.

"It's a craze of his. He buys every crime book that comes out. Reads them in bed always."

Lord reached up and selected an orange-covered volume which had held his gaze for some moments.

"*The Gangs of New York,*" he said musingly, as he turned its pages. "That ought to be interesting."

He stared Ross in the face abruptly, but the face expressed merely polite agreement.

"Mind if I borrow it for a day or so?" he asked coolly, and, taking permission for granted, moved towards the hall door. "Another wet afternoon, I'm afraid. Thank you, Mr. Ross. Goodbye."

Outside the gates of the drive – excluded in the interval, no doubt, by Peterson – the wire-haired terrier still lingered in hope of Duggie's reappearance. Lord, who was fond of dogs, stooped and tickled its ears in passing, automatically. Had he known it, his fingers touched then for an instant a key that was eventually to open the complicated lock which he was trying to pick.

But his thoughts at that precise moment were bent, not upon keys and locks, but upon a hoe and a rake which Peterson, with a final grin, had handed him as he had let him out. These, with care, he ultimately lost in a thorn bush on the Downs.

Chapter Fourteen

ON HIS ARRIVAL AT the Central Station he found the intent-eyed Yeoland awaiting him outside its grim and grimy portals.

"Good-morning, Inspector. The Colonel thought you might be interested by some news he got this morning after you left the Home. One of our men has been up to Liverpool making inquiries. He wired this morning that there's no Dorch on the passenger list of any passenger boat that has left Liverpool for anywhere within the past three weeks. And no one named Dorch – or Ross – has registered at any hotel in Liverpool or the outskirts during that time – that is to say, registered to the knowledge of the office of any hotel there. At the Royal Lancashire Hotel, however, the name Aloysius I. Dorch had been written in by someone at the bottom of one of the three pages covering the date November 28th. But when the hotel people looked it up, they discovered that no one named Dorch had occupied a room, eaten any meal, or paid any bill there on that date... or apparently any other, since August 17th, when Aloysius I. Dorch stayed a night there. He has stayed there four or five times a year for a night for many years back and they know him well by appearance in the office. It's absolutely certain, they say, that he didn't stay there on the date his name is last entered in the register for."

Inspector Lord, a little taken aback by this energy on the part of Messrs. Gore & Tolley's staff, filled in some moments by exchanging greetings with a passing colleague to give himself time to prepare a suitable reception of Mr. Yeoland's remarks.

"I expected as much," he said coolly. "As a matter of fact I was just going to have inquiries made in Liverpool. Righto, Mr.—"

"Yeoland."

"Righto. We'll look into it. By the way, if you see Colonel Gore, you might tell him that, as I expected, Bullock says Peterson is nothing like the man we're looking for. Though, as far as that goes, I wouldn't believe Bullock's death-bed oath."

"Bullock saw Peterson at close quarters?"

"As close as you are to me, Mr. Yeovil."

"Yeoland.... But, I take it, Peterson was not aware that Bullock was trying to identify him?"

"You may take it," said Lord shortly, turning away, "that he was. There's nothing to that idea."

"The Colonel asked me to suggest to you, Inspector, that it might be as well to keep an eye on Bullock."

"Keep an eye on him? Why?"

"Well, he *may* be rather an important witness, you see, if we have any luck."

That "we" really annoyed Inspector Lord. It was quite sufficient that one of Gore & Tolley's young men should have got that information at Liverpool first. But that another of them should presume to give Inspector Lord advice as to keeping eyes on people and use "we's" when he did it, was a bit too much of a good thing.

"I think," he said curtly, "that you can trust us to look after our own business."

He disappeared into the dark entrance-archway of the Station, walking like a man who knew exactly what he was going to do and intended to do it forthwith. But in truth he had at that moment not the faintest idea what he was going to do – except that he was certainly not going to waste a K man on that filthy old loafer, Bullock.

"Of all the confounded... *We*... What next?"

He shut himself up in the tiny dog-box which was called his office, consumed a lunch of bread and cheese without zest and then, lighting a pipe, settled down to an attempt to clear his ideas. Cleared they must be without delay. Twenty-four hours would probably prove the limit of the Chief's patience – forty-eight at the very outside. Something definite must go up to Room Eleven before midday tomorrow.

But – what? Where to pick an end out of the infernal tangle?

Who killed Melhuish? That – and nothing else – was the thing that mattered – the question that must be answered by Inspector Lord.

How had that job got confused with Woodbine's?

Simply because Ruddy-Gore had found those infernal initials in a letter received from Dorch by Melhuish. That letter had been allowed (Ruddy-Gore again) to associate Melhuish's death first with Dorch, then with Woodbine, then with Peterson, and finally, to complete the vicious circle, with Dorch again. Round and round in a ring.... Vicious circle.... Inspector Lord snarled the words aloud.

For now it was perfectly clear that the "Q.E.D." in Dorch's letter to Melhuish had had no significance whatever beyond that given usually to the abbreviation in ordinary conversation. Therefore that letter did *not* link Melhuish with Woodbine's badge. The vicious circle never *had* a beginning – never *could* run round to Dorch again. And therefore, whatever games Dorch & Co. might have been or be up to, those games had nothing whatever to do with Melhuish's death... so far as there was a tittle or jot of evidence to show.

Nothing whatever to link up Dorch suspiciously with Prescott; nothing whatever to show that the Pettitt-Johnson incident had meant more for Dorch than just what his letter to Ross had said. Nothing whatever, in fact, to show that his relations with Melhuish had been anything but just those of patient and physician.

Damn Dorch and his Q.E.D. And damn Ruddy-Gore and his young men. Once and for all, that Q.E.D. snake must be scotched. By-and-by... if necessary, one would look into Dorch & Co.

Woodbine? It wasn't by any means certain that he had been murdered by anyone. But, even if he had, there wasn't a jot or a tittle to show that that thrice-accursed badge had any connection whatever with that someone. It had been Woodbine's business in life to find things on the Downs. He had found that one. And that was all there was to it.

The attack on Gore? Well... *that* might be a different matter. One could keep an open mind about that. The man with the umbrella had not been found... Knock-knees were plentiful enough, God knew. Nothing good enough to link up Prescott with that....

And so – looking at the thing now with a perfectly cleared mind – it mattered not a tuppenny damn whether Dorch had belonged to a New York gang or to Sheffield Wednesday – whether he was now in New York or in Hades – whether his cases had held crime books or someone else's family plate or gooseberry jam or dog biscuits. Dorch must be cut right out. One must begin at the very beginning again with the Melhuish job – undisturbed. No more of Ruddy-Gore's red herrings.

And no more "we's."

Strengthened and consoled by this new vision, Inspector Lord decided to begin again at the beginning with Mrs. Melhuish – and the Melhuish chauffeur. Yet, to his annoyance, as he spruced himself up before a small mirror in preparation for a visit to a lady of whose meditative gaze he was a little doubtful, the thoughts that insisted upon untidying his tidied mind were too connected with the menage at Wavertree. One was that if Ross had sent Dr. Dorch's books up to Highgate in those cases, he had forgotten one whole roomful of them. The other was that the dog which had pursued Duggie into the hall and which

Ross had called by its name, had not only been a white terrier but a wire-haired one.

Certainly, it *was* devilish odd the way things insisted upon fitting themselves into those blind-swipes which, it was to be supposed, Ruddy-Gore called his ideas... By the way, had anything turned up about that fruit basket? Inspector Lord heard through a speaking-tube that it hadn't and very well couldn't be expected to, considering the sort of basket and the raspberry stains. Inspector Lord remarked through the tube acidly that he had given up expecting anything to turn up through it. Then he went out into the November day and decided it was a rotten day.

To his disappointment he was informed at Victoria Square that Mrs. Melhuish had gone down to Tavistock on the preceding day to stay with some cousins. Master Simon, the car and the chauffeur had gone with her. They would probably return before Christmas, but the date was not yet fixed.

The Inspector returned to the Central Station and for a couple of hours was occupied in receiving reports from subordinates and interviewing people with things to say about the late Mr. Prescott that ought to have been of interest, but were not for the moment. And then, a little before four o'clock, as he was dipping with edification into the colourful pages of *The Gangs of New York*, came the dreaded summons.

"Chief would like to see you, sir."

"Well, Lord," asked the peremptory voice that audibly expected an unsatisfactory answer to its question, "... anything to report about this business on the Suspension Bridge?"

"Yes, Sir," replied Inspector Lord's voice, to his dismay. "I think I may say we've got a line. But it wants careful handling or it's going to snap and give us a lot of trouble."

His superior, agreeably surprised, sat back in his chair almost amicably. "What's the line?"

"The man I told you I thought had been mixed up with Prescott and Dorch. I think we've got enough to bring him in, at any rate. But we've got to find him first. I suspect he's gone to earth."

"You said yesterday he was in New York."

"Perhaps. Probably not."

The Chief Inspector's rusty head jerked towards a chair. "Let's hear what you've got."

And so Inspector Lord's voice proceeded to describe that vicious circle aloud – describe it with a calm, concise conviction which in the end convinced himself. His Chief listened with absorbed attention, the grimness of his mouth softening gradually to pouts and even small whistles of satisfaction.

"Damn smart, Lord," was his verdict. "If you can put this over—" He left the sequel to Inspector Lord's imagination. "It's spotting those initials in that letter of Dorch's to Melhuish that gets me. Damn smart that, I must say."

Lord was as honest as any healthy-minded man feels called on to be, and his conscience really *did* desire to say that someone else had done that bit of spotting. But only too clearly did his imagination picture the results which would follow upon the mere mention in Room Eleven of the name Gore. The memory of the Mendip Case was still accursed in that room. It was rumoured that the Chief had had a window in his own house, which happened to have a view of the Mendips, built up. The Inspector smiled hurriedly and modestly.

"Rather a lucky shot, that, Sir."

Would that white dog strike the Chief as damn smart also, he wondered for a moment. But ultimately he decided not to risk it, and went downstairs empowered to set in motion the mighty man-hunting machine. Having despatched a long cable to the Pinkerton Agency in New York, his first step was to provide the machine with something to get on with. A taxi carried him to the Simpsons' house where, to its mistress's alarm, he succeeded in obtaining what he wanted without explanation. Within a few hours every police station in the country would receive a detailed word-picture of Dr. Aloysius I. Dorch, followed, not many hours later by copies of the "*Morning Report*" and "*Printed Information*" containing further particulars and reproductions of his photograph.

Bitterly now did the Inspector reproach himself for having exposed his hand that morning by the Bullock fiasco. It had been foolish, too, to allow Ross to see that his explanations had not been accepted without reservations – foolish to yield to the temptation to shake him up – foolish to have selected that particular book from the two thousand or so that filled the study's shelves. The Chief had said at once that Wavertree must be left alone for the present; he had been told nothing of that ill-advised gesture nor of Bullock's essay in sleuthing.

Wavertree, however, was now to be kept under observation night and day, two men being assigned to each spell of this duty, as Ross and Peterson would probably require independent shadowing. Having arranged that this vigil should begin forthwith, Lord called shortly before seven o'clock at Mr. Hope's handsome house, which was situated at Bishop's Leaze across the Downs. In the surprised gentleman into whose presence he was ushered by a maid whom privately he considered rather too pretty and too flighty a bit of goods for a bachelor establishment, he recognised at once the caller whom he had seen leaving Wavertree that morning.

A little preliminary inquiry had already informed him that Mr. Hope was one of the partners in a well-known firm of Westmouth solicitors; forty-two years of age; well-to-do; unmarried; a keen sportsman if not a very keen or brilliant lawyer; and a very sociable and popular person. All these things, indeed, were written large upon Mr. Hope's personality even if – seen without a hat – his somewhat florid good looks were a little marred by a long, still imperfectly healed, scar on his forehead, where his ruddy skin disappeared into his sleek blondish hair. He stared at Lord with a smile whose geniality did not conceal the shrewd speculation of his rather bloodshot hazel eyes.

"You are acquainted with Dr. Dorch, I believe," Lord asked, when he had introduced himself.

"Dr. Dorch? Oh, yes."

"Intimately acquainted?"

"Intimately? Well, yes – pretty intimately."

"Socially?"

"Socially, yes."

"And in business matters?"

"Business matters? No."

Not a babbler precisely, Mr. Hope. And a little disposed to repeat questions in his port-wine voice before he answered them.

"You are aware, perhaps, that Dr. Dorch is in the habit of lending money?"

The other laughed with the fruity heartiness of the sport.

"We're all foolish enough to do that at times, aren't we?"

"In Dr. Dorch's case, I understand, the loans are made in the way of business – at interest. Large sums at times. Are you aware of that?"

"I believe I have heard something of the kind. Yes. In fact, I remember now hearing that he had lent money to back some business enterprises in Westmouth. Certainly I know of one case in which he advanced a large sum *without* interest. He lent nine thousand to the Board of the Women and Children's Hospital to cover the erection of some additional wards a few years ago."

A new light on the many-faceted Dorch. Lord made a note to check up this transaction.

"How long have you known him?"

"How long? I should say, four or five years."

"You have been to his house, I presume?"

"Oh, yes."

"To dine and so on?"

"Yes. Bridge, mostly."

"The people you met there were, I suppose, like yourself, social acquaintants of Dr. Dorch's?"

"You mean – were they people who borrowed money from Dorch? I haven't the faintest idea."

"Have you yourself at any time borrowed money from him?"

"I? No. I'm answering the question. But I want to know why it's asked. This is a very extraordinary proceeding, you know – coming here to catechise me about Dr. Dorch this way—"

Lord smiled his smile.

"It's a very extraordinary world, Mr. Hope. However, you've said 'no' to my question." He waited, but received no qualification to the 'no.' "Have you ever heard of a firm of moneylenders in Westmouth called Johnson & Co.?"

"Johnson & Co. Yes. I believe I have heard the name. As a matter of fact, wasn't there something in the papers...?"

"Quite. Can you recall having heard anything at any time that gave you any idea that Dr. Dorch was connected with Johnson & Co. – or with a man called Prescott who managed the business?"

"No."

"You never heard Dr. Dorch mention his name – or the name Johnson & Co.?"

"Not that I can recall."

"Dr. Dorch dined here with you on the night of November 20th?"

A lot of people dined with Mr. Hope, it seemed. He had to reflect for some moments before he answered.

"He dined here one night two or three weeks ago. I can get the actual date—"

"I know it was November 20th. He dined with, you alone?"

"Alone? Yes."

"At what hour?"

"I dine at eight always."

"So that he arrived here say about ten to eight?"

"I expect so, yes."

"And left here?"

"Left? I should say some time round half-past eleven."

There was no hesitation about the last two replies. At any rate Dr. Dorch had not been on the Suspension Bridge at nine o'clock that night, if the replies were to be relied on.

"Can you recall whether he said anything about going up to London that night after he left you, by the night mail?"

"Yes. He told me he intended to do so."

"Did you notice anything at all unusual about his manner that evening?"

"Unusual? No."

"Did he make any reference to an intention to go to New York – or to any place in America?"

"No. Not that I remember. But I was told at his house this morning that he had gone to New York a couple of days after that."

"If he left here at 11.30, that gave him very little spare time for the 12.5, didn't it? It was an unusually foggy night. He could only just have managed to reach Chapel Fields Terminus in time."

"Only just is plenty to spare. Anyhow he caught his train, I believe."

"How did he leave here? On foot?"

"No. Car."

"His car?"

"No. Mine. It left him back at his house. He wanted to pick up a bag. He had a taxi waiting there to take him on to Chapel Fields, he told me."

"You know Mr. Ross, Dr. Dorch's secretary?"

"Ross? Slightly. Very slightly."

"Is he a man in whom Dr. Dorch has implicit confidence?"

"Good God, man, how do I know? Ask Dorch."

"I thought you might have known."

"No. This is all devilish mysterious, you know. What's up? Old Dorch hasn't done a bunk, has he?"

"Now what put that into your head?" Inspector Lord asked encouragingly.

"Your infernal questions. Now, look here, my dear man – I've got several useful things to do before dinner."

"I won't interfere with them, then, Mr. Hope. Much obliged. Still more obliged if you'll regard this little conversation of ours as confidential."

"Well," laughed the other good-humouredly, "as it's the damnedest silliest conversation I've ever taken a hand in, I shall be very happy to think that no one is ever going to hear about it. Goodbye. I suppose, by the way, that you *are* a Detective Inspector, and not a bloke after my umbrellas? Can I offer you a drink? No? Beastly weather, isn't it. Bye."

On his way back to the city the Inspector's conscience decided that it would be only kind to drop in on the Colonel for a moment and tell him that things had got a move on. With some difficulty he obtained permission to see the patient at an illegal hour and found him dining in a richly coloured dressing gown by his fireside. The Colonel's greeting was lacking somewhat in the bright gaiety of his principal garment.

"Hullo," he said through a mouthful of chicken. "It's you, is it? Well, you've made a nice old mess of it, I hear."

"Mess?" echoed Lord stiffly.

Gore pointed to his inadequate but at the moment neatly-made bed, and the Inspector picked up a telegram which lay on its virginal counterpane. The sending office, he saw, was Marlborough; the hour of despatch 6.50.

"Bullock lost here returning Yeoland."

"Marlborough," frowned Lord glumly. "What the deuce took Bullock to Marlborough? Looks as if they had nobbled him."

Only the vicious grinding of a knife and fork answered him. But he brightened a little.

"Well.. if they have, so much the better. That gives them right away. We'll get Bullock back all right. And quick."

"You think so?" enquired Gore with elaborate politeness. "Oh, well, then, that's all right, of course. Go to it, bright boy. Sorry I can't offer you some dinner. But there isn't nearly enough for one. If you'll look under the bed, though, you'll find a suitcase, and if you open it, you'll see something that isn't allowed to perforate innerds, but is good for people who have dropped bricks."

This time Lord did not decline consolation.

"Yeoland followed him to Marlborough, then?" he asked as, having wedged the door against surprise, he manufactured himself a drink.

Gore explained that, understanding from Yeoland that Inspector Lord had seemed indisposed to keep an eye on Bullock, he had decided that someone else must do it. Feeling pretty certain that an attempt would be made, and made quickly now that Bullock's value was known, to get him out of the way, he had put both Yeoland and his man Stephens on the job – the former to keep in touch with Stephens with the Buick in case of a sudden breakaway. This anticipated emergency had evidently arisen. Yeoland's awaited return must explain how Bullock had got lost.

"Heading for London, then, probably," commented Lord. "Possibly for that house of Dorch's at Highgate. Pity I didn't know about this sooner, Colonel. I'd have had the Highgate house watched."

"That's being done, of course," remarked Gore quietly. "Two of our London men started for Highgate ten minutes after I got that wire. They wouldn't know Bullock – but they'll tell us if a car rolls up there between eight and eight-thirty. Not that I think for a moment it will."

"Why not?"

"Because I think we're expected to expect that it will."

Mr. Yeoland, somewhat crestfallen, was admitted in time to hear this cryptic utterance of his employer's. His failure, he reported, had been due to a travelling circus of outrageous length which had completely blocked the narrow exit from Marlborough at the London side for nearly ten minutes. The car containing Bullock had just got through in time; the Buick had been just too late. It had seemed useless to pursue any farther when the jam had at last been broken up; both cars had been doing over sixty most of the way from Bath, and the chances of pulling up a start of ten miles or so had appeared negligible. So Yeoland had sent off his wire and returned to Westmouth.

"Who got him?" Gore asked.

"Two men. Stephens saw one of them. I've brought him along. It was too dark to make out anything of the chap who drove the car."

Stephens – sometime sergeant in the Westshires – was brought up to tell his story. He had watched Bullock's lodgings until a little after five, when Bullock had come out and proceeded along Tenby Road towards the city. When he had gone a little way – Stephens following him, and the Buick following Stephens – a shortish man leading a small dog on a lead, also going citywards, had crossed the road, overtaken Bullock and addressed him. After a little talk Bullock had taken over charge of the dog and had turned about as if to go back along Tenby Road towards the Downs. The stoutish man, however, had signalled to the driver of a car which passed just then, coming from the direction of the city. It had stopped, and after another brief conversation, Bullock and the shortish man had got into it with the dog and had been driven away. Yeoland had picked up Stephens and followed, into Westmouth and out of it, on to Bath, and ultimately to Marlborough. From the way in which the car had been driven and its attempts to induce the Buick to pass out, they believed that its driver had been aware that he was being followed, even before Bath had been reached.

The impression left on Stephens' mind was that Bullock had been asked to take the dog somewhere – that the car had been stopped by arrangement just as he had consented – and that somehow he had been induced to get into it – probably by the prospect of a drink a good hour before opening time.

"If so, he had it in the car, Sir."

"Very likely," agreed Gore. "With something to do him real good in it. Hydrate of chloral. I believe, is what our brothers across the ocean favour for quick results. Get the number of the car? Not that it matters, probably."

"HW 5449, Sir. Sunbeam saloon. Black and cream lining."

"Notice anything else about the short man?"

"A bit knock-kneed, Sir. About forty, I'd say. Stiff little chap – stuck out his chest and his elbows. And his ears stuck out. Wore one of them scutty puce coats and Oxford bags and a grey Homburg. Deetroosy nose, Sir, what you'd call. But it was dark of course, Sir."

"You couldn't see the driver of the car?"

"No. But I heard him, Sir. He was a Yank."

Gore perceived that he had forgotten a small piece of cabinet pudding. He ate it delicately.

"I wonder if Bullock has met an old acquaintance. All right, Yeoland. It can't be helped. Get something to eat and come back here."

"Me, too, Sir," Stephens asked.

"Yes. It's unlikely – but you may have to run up the Bath road again. Better fill up."

"Very good, Sir. She is filled up."

Inspector Lord had finished his drink. But he hung on unobtrusively until a nurse had removed the paraphernalia of the late meal.

"I should like to hear if anything comes through from your people at Highgate, Colonel. They'd phone, perhaps?"

"If they had anything to say. But they won't have. Bullock hasn't gone to Highgate. Ross knows that's the first place he'd be looked for."

"There's something in that," Lord admitted. "Know anything about this house at Highgate?"

"Something. It's called Cedar Hill. A big place – a Russian Grand-Duke lived there before Dorch took it on in 1909. About three acres of gardens and grounds. Since Dorch came to live down here in 1917 it has been looked after by a housekeeper named Marvin and his wife. Very nice quiet, respectable people – keep themselves to themselves. Telephone Number 6366. Two entrances; house lies between two roads. Housekeeper has a small saloon and a box-body. Dr. Dorch goes up there frequently."

"HW 5449," the Inspector noted. "I'll find out the owner of the number straight away – though, as you say, it's probably a fake or a stolen car. Perhaps you could get a phone message through to me at Central Station if you hear from Highgate?"

"Depends whether my night nurse's corns are inflamed tonight or not. Very good of you to look me up, Inspector. Hope you'll get Bullock back intact."

There was the faintest underlining of the "you." Inspector Lord decided not to notice it.

"Oh, we'll get him," he said, "– intact or tact."

Ruddy-Gore's grey eyes followed him to the door.

"I say, old chap, he asked dubiously, "you're not by any chance thinking of running round to tell Ross how much we miss poor Bullock, are you?"

Some embarrassment stiffened Lord's smile. For with that idea, in point of fact, his fancy had been toying.

"Hardly," be said. "Well – glad to see you on your legs again, Colonel. You won't forget that telephone message. Goodnight."

Chapter Fifteen

THE REPORT FROM HIGHGATE, however, when it arrived next morning, was absolutely negative. Up to 6 a.m. no car had arrived there; the house appeared to be unoccupied; this would be verified later. By the time that this information reached Inspector Lord he had acquired from Mr. Asbury's book a good deal of information about New York's underworld which was quite new to him. Also he had received from the Pinkerton Agency a report of his own.

"Dorch-Mayer Corporation established over twenty years, reputable theatrical and variety agency, founded by Aloysius I. Dorch; still retains controlling interest. Ignatius L. Dorch, son, and Hermann Mayer, cousin, partners.

A. I. Dorch last visited offices August 23rd; nothing known of intention to come to New York in November. Registered Imperial Central Hotel for night Dec. 3. No trace of landing or movement after leaving hotel Dec. 4.

Personal. – Aloysius Ignatius (Droch) Dorch, born 1869, Rochester, N.Y., father musician. Originally schoolmaster Rochester, sentenced two years for criminal assault assistant schoolmistress 1891. Went N.Y., became associated with Monk Eastman and Cyrus H. (Cosher) Quinton. Ran notorious joint, The Windmill, Chrystie Street, organised Q.E.D. gang afterwards merged in Eastmans. Subsequently ran well-known New Atlantic Restaurant, Broadway and 27th, and other joints (Hell

Fire Club, 6th Avenue and 30th Street; The Locotaxy, 27th and 6th Avenue, notorious creep joint). Prominent inward politics under Tammany régime; reputed to have cleared $1,000,000 in various ways, some straight. Married 1900 Doll Pilgrim (Olga Chinska) variety star. Went England 1907. Visits U.S.A. frequently.

Believed to have engineered the Hartmann forgeries 1906 and other similar frauds. Always used straight business as cover. Generous subscriber to charities. Changed name to Dorch 1893 after imprisonment.

Ross not known by name or description given as associate of Dorch this side. If left-handed, right eye dark blue, left dark brown, may be Hartmann, sentenced twenty years for forgery and various bank robberies 1906. This man believed to have acted under Dorch's control. (See above.)

Peterson, from description, probably Snap Peters, well-known thug and strong-arm man of Q.E.D.'s and afterwards Eastmans. For some years professional strong man variety stage. Several sentences homicide – all quashed Dorch's pull. Speciality, spine-snapping. Dangerous."

Now when Inspector Lord read this very expensive cable, his imagination was still under the influence of a strong literary stimulant. All through the watches of the night – for he had waited on at the Central Station in expectation of a message from the Colonel – he had saturated his mind with the heady atmosphere of New York's Eastside. His whole scheme of values had altered; humdrum Westmouth, with its occasional, clumsy burglary or beery wife-basher or non-stop manslaughterer, had faded; he was living for the moment in a world that lived for crime and for nothing else – crime organised to commercial enterprise, crime that valued human life not at all and a policeman deplorably little. All night long he had walked dark, sinister streets, where every furtive moving figure carried a gat or a blackjack, or strayed along no less perilous ways where every pair of eyes that glittered in the blaze of the lights held the cold furtive vigilance of the crook on business, and at any moment the roar of the traffic might be stabbed by the crash of a bomb or the crackle of automatics. Aloysius I. Dorch had walked those streets once; so had Snap Peters; so, probably had the smooth-tongued Ross. The uneasiness which Lord had felt concerning Bullock since his visit to the nursing home the evening before crystallised itself into a need for urgent action. Bullock must be found before something happened to him... if it hadn't happened to him already. All very fine for the Chief to talk about giving those beggars at Wavertree a little more rope. They had had enough. It was quite time to take in the slack with a jerk.

With this opinion his Chief, in view of the Pinkerton cable agreed, when he arrived at nine o'clock. Bullock's joyride was just a little too curious, following on his failure as a jobbing gardener. In the Chief's opinion, that Pekinese clinched the matter.

In addition to the two plainclothes men on watch near Wavertree (they had nothing to report, Lord learned in passing) a uniformed man was in prominent view close to its gates when the Inspector ascended its steps. From the expression of the maid who opened the door and who recognised him with a nervous blink, he divined at once that his appearance had sharpened an uneasiness already felt.

"Mr. Ross in?"

"No, Sir."

"When do you expect him back?"

The girl hesitated. "Well, we don't know, Sir. We expected him back to lunch yesterday. But he didn't come. Nor he didn't come back to dinner. Nor he hasn't been back at all since he went out yesterday morning. It's funny it is, him being so regular and fussy about his meals at the exact minute."

Sudden suspicion flashed across Lord's heart.

"Is Peterson in?"

"No, Sir. Mr. Peterson went out yesterday morning, too. He hasn't been back since neither."

Behind her smart black-and-white Duggie appeared, emerging from the study. He fixed upon Lord a tearful gaze of contempt and withdrew again in disgust.

"Did that dog go out yesterday?" the caller asked sharply.

"Duggie? Yes, Sir. He went out for his walk in the morning with Mr. Ross."

"I know that. In the afternoon – did he go out again?"

"No, Sir. There was no one to take him out in the afternoon. He was just out in the garden by himself."

"Now, my girl, I want to know about this exactly. At what time did Mr. Ross go out?"

"We don't know, Sir. No one knew he had gone out. It wasn't until lunchtime we found he was out."

"And Peterson – when did you see him last?"

"Some time after you were here, Sir, yesterday morning. None of us saw him after that. About half-past eleven it was I saw him going into the study. That was the last time I saw him."

Lord swore mentally. The Colonel had been only too right; he *had* made a mess of it.

"The dog? Get this accurately now. Where was it all the afternoon? Not in the garden the whole time?"

"No, Sir. There's a door left open in the greenhouse at the back. Duggie goes in and out that way. He was about the house and in and out of the garden. The housemaid put him to bed in Dr. Dorch's room at ten o'clock."

"Did you see him in the house or in the garden after four o'clock?"

"Oh, yes, Sir. I saw him in the study in Dr. Dorch's chair when I went in there at six to look after the fire."

"Sure?"

"Oh yes, Sir."

"See him between four and six?"

The maid reflected.

"I may have, Sir, I couldn't be sure."

"Get up the other two women."

The housemaid, however, had been "off" yesterday afternoon until ten o'clock. The cook had not left her own domain all day.

The parlourmaid, on the other hand, stuck to her guns and was clearly a truthful young woman. If Duggie had been at Wavertree at six o'clock, clearly he couldn't have been in a Sunbeam car travelling towards Marlborough at sixty miles an hour. Another dog to look for – the third.

Of course, Duggie *could* have been got back to Wavertree – if one of the occupants of the Sunbeam had contrived to get out of it unnoticed by Yeoland and Stephens. Or, if the Sunbeam had passed anywhere near Wavertree, the Pekinese might have been put out and left to find its way home alone. The first pair of plainclothes men had gone on duty at Wavertree after half-past six. No use asking them if they had seen it. Having warned the two men now on duty to keep a sharp lookout, the Inspector made hurriedly for the Central Station and set the telephone at work. Wires and wireless awoke for some hours to feverish interest in two hitherto quite un-famous persons named Ross and Peterson. And in the little pub behind Tenby Road which Bullock "used" twice a day, its patrons were gratified by hearing a loudspeaker proclaim before midday closing hour that he, too, was in request.

Before he went back to Wavertree, Inspector Lord had received a report from the Highgate police. Cedar Hill had been found closed-up and empty; no one in the neighbourhood had seen or heard anything of the Marvins for several days past. The house had been "inspected" – for the sergeant in charge of the proceedings had not obtained a search warrant – but nothing in the least suspicious had been found. Everything, the report stated, indicated that careful preparations had been made for closing up the place for a considerable period; the furniture had been sheeted; all doors locked and shutters barred; all water jugs emptied. Some at least of the cases – seventeen of them – which had been brought up from Westmouth had been found in an outhouse, empty. They had been packed with straw, which had seemed to the sergeant an unlikely precaution if they had merely contained books. He had searched the straw carefully and had found in one case a gold pin set with diamonds and emeralds, obviously of considerable value, in another, three lower-case types of an ornate kind. The car and the box-body had been found in the garage with emptied radiators. Some of the cases appeared to have been carried up to the second floor and unpacked in a small apartment at the back of the house which was virtually a strong room and contained two large safes of the most modern design. Some remains of straw packing discovered in the carpet had led the sergeant to this belief. The safes had not yet been opened. No letters or papers which could throw any light whatever upon anything, save the expenses of the housekeeper's weekly accounts with local tradespeople, had been found. The house contained no books except some old issues of American and English illustrated journals.

At Wavertree the water jugs had not been emptied, it was true, and every door, including that of the safe stood open. But a clean sweep had evidently been made here, too, of every scrap of paper that could afford the smallest clue to the interests or private affairs of any person – save one. In the safe, pinned together, Lord found three promissory notes, two for £1,500 each, the third for £3,500, all three bearing the signature Hector Hope and all three due on November 22nd. With what motive they had been left for certain finding, Lord was for the moment too busy to decide.

Some marks upon the flooring of a room opening off Dr. Dorch's study attracted his attention. Eight bedplates had evidently been bolted to the flooring for a considerable time and only very recently been removed. The servants could throw no light upon this matter; the room had always been kept locked, even when Dr. Dorch or Mr. Ross had been working in it. The day before the cases had gone off to London Peterson and Mr.

Ross had been very busy in there, packing. Examination revealed that the floor had been strengthened by two cross girders; something of considerable weight, which had once rested on those bedplates, had been removed to Highgate – and subsequently elsewhere.

Disappointed by the barrenness of his search, Lord called at the nursing home to endeavour to clear up the mystery of Duggie's appearance in the study at six o'clock. He found the patient resting after his first walk outdoors while he watched with a vigilant eye a nurse who was learning how to insert trousers in a trouser press. The lesson over and the pupil departed, the visitor unburdened himself of his tidings as of a thing expected. The beggars had twenty-four hours start. But it wouldn't help them much. If they had got out of England, they would find themselves back in it very quickly. If he could get warrants, of course – it would speed up things a bit, perhaps. But "they" were making a silly fuss about warrants— "no good grounds." As if the thing wasn't as clear as a pikestaff...

And so on, for some time.

"At any rate," he concluded, "even if we've nothing definite in the Melhuish business – we've quite enough to take them inside over Woodbine's job. The moment they knew what Bullock could say, they got hold of him and cleared out. That's good enough for anyone but a fatheaded—"

"That is –," said Gore without enthusiasm. "Ross and Peterson cleared out. If they *have* cleared out. And Ross and Peterson nobbled Bullock – if the dog Stephens saw was the Wavertree Pekinese. But – was it?"

"Quite. I wanted to see Yeoland and Stephens about that, to find out whether they could have dropped the dog or the dog and the short man, anywhere in Linwood."

"Yeoland will be along before lunch. But, anyhow, the point is – Dorch is out of the whole Woodbine job, if our information is correct. If he went to London on the night of the 20th – I say, *if* – it's hardly likely that he came back here to lay poison for

Woodbine on the 22nd, is it? If he registered at a New York hotel on Dec. 3rd, he must have left England not later than November 29th. But, even suppose he cleared out to the States straight away – say on the 21st or 22nd – it's hardly likely that he'd have started back here on December 6th or sooner to see Bullock out of the way. Of course – he *could* have done these things. And we know something of his record. But I don't think so.

"Then there's that badge. Someone lost that on the Downs, along the path that runs down to the head of Tenby Road and Downshill Road – almost certainly on the night of November 20th. Or, at any rate, some time after darkness fell that evening. Now, the only person I'm certain does *not* own that badge is Peterson – because he said he did. Why did he say that? Because of course he didn't want us to know that it belonged to someone else. Who was that someone else... amongst the people we know to have been connected with this Q.E.D. stunt? Not Ross. If there was any risk for Ross in being the owner of it, Peterson wouldn't have claimed ownership. Besides, we don't know that Ross ever had anything to do with the Q.E.D.'s. If Pinkertons are right, he came at a post-gang period in Dorch's career in the States. Well – from the knowledge we have – there's only one person it does seem to belong to—"

"The man in the leggings?"

"We've nothing to link *him* with Q.E.D. No, I think it belongs to Dorch himself. And I'm wondering why Ross and Peterson didn't say so. It's a free country – a chap may carry the whole alphabet on his tie-pin if he wants to. Or is Peterson such a devoted henchman that he felt called upon to conceal a possible clue to his boss's past history? Perhaps. I wonder. By the way – if Mr. Ross *does* happen to have once used the name Hartmann – mightn't it be just as well to make sure that everything is quite satisfactory as regards Dr. Dorch's bank account? It's over three weeks since Dorch disappeared from view, you see."

The trend of the Colonel's thoughts was obvious. Too obvious. For twenty-four hours Inspector Lord's colours had been nailed to the beam from which Aloysius Ignatius Dorch was to swing for at least procuring the murder of Dr. Melhuish and Woodbine. And here was Ruddy-Gore most annoyingly suggesting, not only that he had had nothing to do with either, but that...

"You mean?" he asked sharply. "You mean that you think Ross and Peterson are on their own?"

"Well – it's this now, isn't it? Either Dorch bolted or he didn't. If he didn't – that's that. If he did, why did he? Is there really a solitary damn thing to show? There isn't. But suppose he bolted for good reasons – either he told Ross why or he didn't. If he didn't, what would Ross have done? Ross would have said 'There's something wrong' and either he would have told you that Dorch had bolted or, he would have bolted himself. He wouldn't just have sat tight. If Dorch did tell him why, and if Ross knew there was trouble coming to Wavertree, would he have sat tight for Dorch's sake? Not unless God made a mistake about his face. Again, either he'd have told you that Dorch had bolted and possibly why, or he'd have cleared out himself. But he did neither. He sat tight. Why? Because no one was to believe for a moment that Dorch had done a bunk, and because Ross thought it quite unlikely that any trouble was coming down Downshill Road. That is, he thought so until yesterday, or perhaps a little before. But anyhow yesterday he stopped thinking it. So he bolted. And Brudder Peterson did likewise. There are gaps in it, I admit. But that's the way I feel about it just now. I think Dorch is right out of the frame. I don't think he bolted. On the whole I'm inclined to wonder just now whether he ever left England – ever left London – perhaps... now, shut your eyes; it's going to taste nasty – perhaps ever left Linwood."

"*What?*" snarled Inspector Lord, opening his eyes instead. "Then, where the hell is he now?"

Gore shrugged, and did nothing else. So the Inspector performed some syncopated movements about the room, his hand thrusting away from him the baneful aura that emanated from the reclining figure upon the bed.

"Certainly, I admit that I don't take any stock in that registering at the hotel in New York. He *would* have gone to look up his son sometime in ten days if he was in New York really. But hell…"

Mr. Yeoland presented himself at that moment and stifled the Inspector's almost passionate explosion of protest. In reply to the query as to what exactly had happened after the Sunbeam car had picked up Bullock and the shortish man until it had cleared Westmouth, he replied, however, succinctly, "Nothing."

"Sure the dog got into the car?" Lord asked.

"Yes"

"Sure it didn't get out of it?"

"Yes."

"Then that lets the Wavertree Peke out. And *that*—"

"Wait a moment," interrupted Gore. "The Sunbeam came up Tenby Road to meet Bullock and the short man and Stephens. When did it turn back towards the city?"

"It had stopped just opposite College Avenue. When Bullock and the short man and the dog got into it, it turned left out of Tenby Road into College Avenue; then left into College Road and then on into Westmouth."

"Where were you with the Buick before the Sunbeam moved off out of Tenby Road?"

"About fifty or sixty yards back along Tenby Road, towards the Downs end."

"How much start did you give the Sunbeam?"

"Just enough to let it get well ahead, but not out of sight. As we turned the corner into College Avenue, the Sunbeam was turning out of College Avenue into College Road."

"But for a little time – say a minute or two – the Sunbeam was out of your sight, going along College Avenue – while you were still in Tenby Road, picking up Stephens?"

"That is so," Yeoland agreed. "A minute – or a minute and a half. Not longer. If the Sunbeam had stopped in College Avenue – or even slackened speed, it couldn't have reached the College Road end of the Avenue by the time we turned into the Avenue. As a matter of fact, I was a little surprised to find that it had got so far ahead, when I turned the corner. I knew then I had a shifter in front of me."

"The short man *might* have chanced his arm and jumped – with the dog – then. There's a right hand turning out of College Avenue about half way along it – Elmtree Road. It comes out into Downshill Road just below Wavertree. If he did jump out, he *could* have cleared off up that road before you came along?"

"Why should he have got in, if he was going to get out a hundred yards away?" Lord objected. "He couldn't have doped Bullock in that time. When Bullock saw him jumping out – with the dog – he'd have – well, Bullock's a bit too ancient to do any movie stunts out of cars doing 60 m.p.h. – but any rate he'd have stuck his head out and made a row of some sort, for certain. Because he'd have guessed there was some game on. But he didn't. He seems to have gone on, anyway as far as Marlborough, as quiet as a lamb."

Gore nodded. "Quite. And so, probably, he never did go on to Marlborough. Nor did the short man and Duggie. Nor did the Sunbeam that picked them up in Tenby Road. I'll bet the whole outfit turned up Elmtree Road, Yeoland, and left you to follow something else. Of course you saw the number of the car you *did* follow to Marlborough, some time?"

"Oh, yes. In Bath I had to keep right on its tail. The number was HW 5449 all right."

"Black with cream linings?"

"Well. I won't swear to exact colours, seen at night, Colonel. But it *looked* like the car we saw in Tenby Road."

"Well, then," said the gentleman on the bed definitely, "there were two Sunbeams on the job – two alike enough *for* the job. One to get Bullock – one to kid us that he'd been taken to Highgate. Of course they knew Bullock would be watched, he had to be pinched right under our noses. Speaking without prejudice, I think they did the job very neatly."

"Too clever," objected Lord gloomily, both hands this time repelling that insidious aura. "Too clever altogether. Too complicated – too elaborate. Hell – two Sunbeams – exactly the same. Think Ross took a walk round Westmouth before breakfast and found two Sunbeams lying about... exactly the same? Just roped them together and took them home and pinned fake registration numbers on them so as no one would *ever* think they'd been pinched. This is Westmouth, Colonel – not Hollywood."

"Ungrateful Inspector," reproved the Colonel. "Not a word of thanks for explaining why Duggie was safely at home at six o'clock. And giving you something to hand your Old Man – even if you can't swallow it yourself. But – as regards Sunbeam cars, you know – how certain are you, Yeoland that *any* car you saw was a Sunbeam?"

"Stephens was not six feet from her radiator at one time, trying to see the driver's face. He saw the badge distinctly."

"Good. Well, now, Inspector – I have here some little information I had collected for myself before you went to call on Mr. Hope. I am indebted to Mr. Yeoland for the collection. I find looking at his memorandum, that Mr. Hope has two cars, a Sunbeam and a Chrysler. And, curiously, the number of his Sunbeam is HW 5449. Also, curiously, its colour is dark green with cream linings, and it is a saloon. Now – suppose Mr. Ross did take that walk before breakfast. We know one place where, for a practical certainty, *he* knew he might find a Sunbeam saloon lying about. One isn't two, I agree. Still... one's getting on, isn't it?"

Mr. Yeoland took off his spectacles and wiped them with some dejection. "I'd forgotten that number," he murmured. "I think I had better go back to the land and resume manure-tossing."

But one of the Colonel's coquettish socks waved him back to the chair from which he had risen.

"You *could* discover where in Linwood and the neighbourhood another Sunbeam saloon was lying about yesterday afternoon, couldn't you?" Gore suggested, with a winning smile for the Inspector's enticement. "Or perhaps you'd prefer that Mr. Yeoland called at the Registration —"

"I'll see to it," said Lord sharply. "I think the idea of two cars is unnecessarily complicated... still... I'll look into the local Sunbeams. Of course – it's something to know that that blasted dog *could* have got back to Wavertree before six. It's queer if Hope's car was used in the stunt. *And* his number. Looks to me as if Hope's pretty well mixed up with this little lot. I found something funny at Wavertree this morning – three signatures of his on three bills for six thousand five hundred altogether – due..."

The Inspector paused. That fatal aura surged and eddied about him – stifling, irresistible.

"By God—" he ejaculated. "Those bills were due on November 22nd – six thousand five hundred. And Dorch dined with him on November 20th – at his house and – that bang on the forehead – how did he get that?"

He gazed, like Cortez, silent, if not upon a peak, upon the Colonel's socks which reposed gracefully on the rail at the foot of his bed.

The steely-eyed sister appeared, preceding a subordinate bearing Colonel Gore's lunch. Inspector Lord grabbed up his belongings. "I'll let you know anything I hear, Colonel," he promised and disappeared. On each landing of the stairs, as he descended, he said,

"By God—"

Yeoland remained to watch his employer eat a hearty meal consisting of four square inches of minced brown glue, four of boiled white ditto, a digestive biscuit and a napkin. Afterwards, however, the suitcase was taken from beneath the bed and the Colonel, having absorbed a very small one, spoke for the first time since the Inspector's departure.

He said:

"Give me my trousers, old chap."

Despite the protests of the Matron in person, in ten minutes the Buick was bearing him towards Mr. Hope's residence and he was explaining to Yeoland why. Arrived outside a pair of imposing gate-pillars, he alighted and walked up the drive, one hand flicking a little conspicuously an envelope which the other held.

Obviously an envelope to be delivered at Mr. Hope's hall door. Instead, however, of ascending the balustraded steps, the Colonel passed on along the flank of the house until he found himself in a tiled yard backed by a capacious garage. In the garage he saw two cars, a Chrysler two-seater roadster and a Sunbeam saloon, dark green with cream linings, registration number HW 5449. He paused and gazed about him, expectant of a chauffeur's appearance – but no chauffeur appeared. He then entered the garage and, with intervals of precaution, examined the interior of the saloon car very carefully. The fact that the upholstery of the driver's seat had been obviously washed in three places, in a not very successful attempt to remove three largish rusty stains, interested him a good deal. A further examination of the cushions with the aid of a lens revealed a number of golden-brown hairs adhering to them – phenomena which reappeared also on the floor mats.

Leaving the garage, he strayed mildly for some moments at the rear of the house and was finally detected by that too-pretty and too-flighty young woman of whom Inspector Lord had disapproved. He advanced the envelope winningly. He had been asked to leave it for Inspector Lord; was Inspector Lord there just then? Learning that he had been there a short time before, but had been told that he would find Mr. Hope at his office in the city and had gone away, the Colonel said oh, then, he would try to catch the Inspector at Mr. Hope's office. Mr. Hope was an old friend of his. How *was* he, by the way? Quite fit? Splendid. He had managed to give himself rather a nasty bang on the head a few days before, hadn't he?

The maid tittered.

"The Inspector wanted to know all about that, too, when he was here just now. Such questions as he asked – love a duck... I suppose you're a detective too, aren't you?"

The grey eye behind the monocle winked without displacing it, and where the envelope had been was now a nice new Bradbury. In five minutes Gore was back at the Buick with what he considered a pretty good quid's worth.

"It was Hope's Sunbeam Duggie had his joyride in, all right, and now if Inspector Lord isn't discussing car cushions with Hope at his office, we shall find him at the Crescent Café, I expect, talking Egyptian. We'll look in there first."

Chapter Sixteen

STATEMENTS TAKEN BY INSPECTOR Lord, 12/12/29.

MARGARET PATCHER, 25. I am a professional dancer. I use the name Suleika Hazadji professionally and have appeared under it in London and the provinces for two years. At present I am fulfilling an engagement of two months at the Crescent Cafe in Westmouth dancing in the afternoon. I came to know Mr. Hope at the café some weeks ago; he introduced himself to me. I have been about with him once or twice, motoring and at dances. On the afternoon of November 20th he asked me to dine at his house and bring my partner Nilotis Darabi with me, as there would be another gentleman there. We went to his house and were introduced to a Dr. Dorch, an elderly man, very quiet and very amusing. I heard him say during dinner that he was going up to town by the night mail so that he couldn't stay late. He and Mr. Hope seemed very friendly until Mr. Hope took too much to drink and got fresh with us ladies. Dr. Dorch tried to stop him, but Mr. Hope lost his temper and there was a row all round. We two ladies cleared off and left them at it. I don't think Mr. Hope knew what he was doing at the end. He was silly drunk and hardly able to stand steady. Dr. Dorch drank very little. Two maids waited. We went to the house in Mr. Hope's car, driven by himself. We left it on our flat feet.

ELIZABETH DUGGAN, 24. (professionally known as Nilotis Darabi), corroborated Margaret Patcher's statement.

Mr. Hope had been absolutely blotto when she had seen him that night.

HECTOR HOPE, 42, solicitor. (First Statement.) Dr. Dorch dined alone with me at my house on the evening of November 20th. Two ladies of my acquaintance came in during dinner and stayed for some little time. They went away about eleven. About half-past eleven I drove Dr. Dorch home to his own house. He was to catch the 12.5 to London, he said, and had to pick up a bag. He intended to change on the train. He said a taxi would be waiting at his house to take him down to Chapel Fields station. The night was very foggy. I cannot recall having seen a taxi waiting outside his house, but it may have been in his drive. I did not go up the drive; Dr. Dorch got out at the gates. I drove back home then. Possibly I had taken a little more than was wise at dinner; as I was getting out of the car, I managed to bump my head severely against the jamb of the door and cut it badly. I sat down in the car and tried to stop the bleeding with my handkerchief. I must have fallen asleep while I was doing that. When I woke up, I found it was after six o'clock next morning. As I felt rather seedy and stiff, and as I didn't want to wake up the house, having no key with me, I went on the Downs and walked about for a while. At seven o'clock I went back to my house. I did not see Dr. Dorch after he got out of my car at his house and went in through his own gates. I had no quarrel with him. If I had had, I should hardly have driven him home. The two ladies went home alone. I have no chauffeur at present; the last man I had, Tempett, was unsatisfactory. I dismissed him, I think, the next morning for gross impertinence. He was an Englishman, but had been in New York for some years, he said, and he always put on an American accent and used American slang. He was recommended to me, I believe, by Dr. Dorch."

(Second Statement.) I have at various times during the past few years borrowed money from Dr. Dorch. The three promissory notes shown me bear my signature; they fell due on November 22ndand have not been redeemed by me. My object in

inviting Dorch to dine with me on November 20th was to try
to induce him to renew the three notes, as, at the moment it was
not convenient to pay them off. I did not, however, have an opportunity of discussing this matter with him, as he came late and
had to leave in a hurry to catch his train, and it was impossible to
discuss business matters before ladies. The two ladies who came
to dinner were two professional dancers, engaged at the Crescent Café. If they say that I was drunk and that I insulted them,
I have no recollection of anything of the kind, but I believe that
I was in fact drunk when they left. After they had gone Dorch
made some remark about them which offended me and we had
I think an argument upon the point. But I do not remember
that there was anything like a serious quarrel. I remember that
I had to drive very slowly to his house, on account of the fog. I
might not have seen a taxi even if it was waiting outside his gates.
At the gates he got out and said goodnight. I was trying to start
up, as my engine had stopped. He opened the door he had got
out by – he had sat in the back seat right behind me – and got
in again. I was bending forward towards the starter. The next
thing I remember is waking up about six o'clock next morning
and finding myself in the car in my own garage. The doors of
the garage were shut. My forehead was bleeding and there was
blood on the cushions. I felt very dizzy and unwell, but as I had
no key, I didn't want to wake up the servants so early. It came
into my head that I would walk over towards Dorch's house and
see Ross and try to get some explanation of Dorch's attacking
me. I walked nearly to his house, but in the end decided not
to make a fuss, and went home again. I called at Dr. Dorch's
house afterwards, but have never seen him since. When he came
back to the car again and opened the door, he said nothing.
I think I thought he had left something in the car. I did not
speak to him or look round that I remember. I borrowed that
money from Dorch to speculate with, on his advice; I had done
so before, usually with successful results, but, of course, not
always. I bought Amalgamated Domestic Enterprises for a rise

two days before the Cantwell group crashed. I am solvent. I did not strike Dorch at any time that night. I have no idea where he is at present, beyond Ross's statement that he is in New York. My chauffeur, Tempett, did not accompany us in the car that night. I did not see him after I left my own house at half-past eleven with Dorch until after breakfast next morning when he gave notice. He was a good driver and fitter, but impertinent. He had been with me for some months only. He lived over the garage at my house.

I have never heard of any association calling itself Q.E.D. I knew the late Dr. Melhuish slightly. I was not a patient of his. I cannot recall having seen him for many weeks back. I know nothing of Dr. Dorch's secretary, Ross, or his butler, except that I have seen them at Dr. Dorch's house. I know nothing of a man called Whigham or Woodbine, nor of a man called Bullock.

I have two cars. One is a Sunbeam saloon HW 5449. I am not aware whether it was out at any time on Wednesday December 11th. If it was it was out without my knowledge or permission. On that day I was at my office until five o'clock, when I went to the Linwood Club. I remained there until half-past eight to dine. I then went to Major Heath's house in Selkirk Place and played bridge until after eleven o'clock.

HESTER QUIMP, 19. I am parlourmaid at Mr. Hope's house. I remember the night of November 20th, when Dr. Dorch dined at the house. Two ladies came to dinner. Mr. Hope was not sober at the end of dinner and the two ladies got annoyed with him and went away. Dr. Dorch tried to keep Mr. Hope quiet. I heard them arguing after the ladies went. I heard Mr. Hope say "I'll do what I like in my own house, you blasted old bloodsucker." I heard a noise as if a glass had been thrown after that and smashed against something. Dr Dorch and Mr. Hope seemed friendly, however, when they were going off in the car. Mr. Hope abused Tempett, the chauffeur, for being slow in bringing the car round.

I thought I heard the car come back about half an hour after they left. But I was in bed then and didn't get up to look. The next time I saw Mr. Hope was at seven next morning, when I opened the hall door to him. He was in evening dress, and his forehead was bleeding a little. There was blood all over his face. He didn't seem to know quite what he was doing. He said "Has the milk come, my dear, or am I first?" and went up to have his bath.

I never heard Tempett speak of anyone named Peterson. I know that he went sometimes to Dr. Dorch's house with messages for Mr. Hope. He was a cheeky fellow, always trying to be funny. He spoke like an American, I think. I did not see him anywhere near the garage or the house on yesterday last, Wednesday December 11th. I have never seen him after he left the morning after the row with Mr. Hope. Before Mr. Hope came in that morning, Tempett went to the garage and found both cars there. He got some hot water to wash some stains off the cushions of one of them. He did not tell me that the stains were blood.

(Three other maid-servants at Mr. Hope's house corroborated the greater part of Hester Quimp's statement, but added nothing to it.)

BEATRICE LACKWORTHY, 51. I have been employed as cook at Dr. Dorch's house for, I think, something over ten years. I have always found him a very kind and considerate gentleman in every way; also Mr. Ross, his secretary. I have nothing to complain of about the butler Peterson, except the way he looks at you sometimes.

I knew a man called Tempett used to come to the house sometimes with messages from Mr. Hope. I have seen Peterson and Mr. Ross talking to him, as well as Dr. Dorch. The last time I remember seeing him at the house was on the afternoon of the day Dr. Dorch went away, about four o'clock. Dr. Dorch was in when he came. I heard Tempett talking to Peterson outside the basement door. He usually came to that door. I did not hear what they were talking about.

I remember that day clearly, on account of the fog being bad all day and having the lights on in the kitchen from when we got up until when we went to bed. Dr. Dorch did not go out that day until he went out to dine with, I believe, Mr. Hope. His neuritis was bad, Peterson said, and he was busy in his study as he was going up to London that night. I am quite sure he did not go out all day. From the kitchen I can see everyone going up or down the hall doorsteps. He was in for lunch and tea. If he had gone out, Alicia, the parlourmaid, would have told me.

About five o'clock Peterson came downstairs and told us that, as the Doctor was dining out, we could all take the evening off from seven o'clock and go to the play. He handed each of us a ticket for the stalls at Prince's Theatre, and said Dr. Dorch had told him to get them for us. Dr. Dorch often gave one or other of the maids a ticket or money to go to the play or the pictures. But we'd never all three of us had them given us on the same night before. We left the house about seven and went to wait for the theatre to open. I was taken a bit poorly waiting in the fog and the cold, so I decided not to go in with the two girls, and went to see my sister. As she was out, I went back home and let myself in with the key of the side door. I was surprised to find no one in the house, because I expected Peterson would have stayed in to take care of it and not have left it empty of everyone. It was about half-past eight when I got to the house. I had some tea and went to my room and got into bed. I didn't go to sleep because my head was bad and feverish. I had only a nightlight in my room. About ten o'clock I heard someone moving upstairs; I heard Mr. Ross's little cough so I knew it was him and that he had come in. A few minutes after I heard Peterson coming in by the side door. He stopped outside my door and called out, "Hullo, Beatrice. Gone to roost?" I didn't like him talking to me when I was in bed, so I just said, "Goodnight, Mr. Peterson." My alarm clock was beside the nightlight. I remember the time well he and Mr. Ross came in. It was just after ten. The two other girls came in at a quarter-past eleven they had left early because the play was no good. They went off to bed. If they hadn't come away early, they couldn't have got home until twelve. We never did from Prince's. About a quarter of an hour after they came in, I heard a car stop outside the house on the road. And about ten minutes after I heard another stopping out there too. Then they both drove away after a little while, first one, and about ten minutes after, the other went away. I did not hear any voices or any other noise except the cars. It would be half-past eleven or so when the first car stopped; say twenty to twelve when the second one stopped. One went away very soon – a couple of minutes after the second one stopped – and then say about ten to twelve the other went away. I did not hear Mr. Ross or Peterson leave the house after I heard them come in. They could have left it without my hearing them. I did not hear either of them moving about upstairs again that night after Peterson said goodnight to me on his way upstairs. Peterson slept on the first floor, next to Dr. Dorch's dressing room. I did not hear Dr. Dorch come in. He might have come in without my hearing him. I saw his suitcase in the hall when I came home after the theatre. I knew he was to call for it on his way to the train.

ALICIA TRIPP and LILY BLACKADDER, housemaid and parlourmaid respectively at Wavertree corroborated Beatrice Lackworthy's statement in some details. Neither, however, had heard any car stop outside the house nor any other noise outside it or inside it after they had gone to their bedrooms. Lily Blackadder had often come on Mr. Ross and Peterson both talking to Tempett. She had never seen Mr. Hope having "what you'd call a conversation" with either of them. Neither maid had heard Dr. Dorch come in. There was no suitcase in the hall next morning at 6.30.

P.C. B.130. I passed along Downshill Road at 11.30 on the night of November 20th. Outside Wavertree I saw a car waiting. I took it for a private car. I did not note the colour or make or number. The driver was pumping up a tyre as I passed. I next passed along Downshill Road at 2.10 a.m.

The Wavertree parlourmaid stated that Dr. Dorch seldom used taxis, even when he went out late at night, but sometimes did so. In such cases the local branch office of the Westmouth Tramway Company, which supplied the principal taxi service, was rung up. Inquiry at the company's office, however, showed that no such call had been received there at any time on November 20th for Dr. Dorch's house. Inspector Lord ordered at once a thorough combing of all hackney vehicles plying for hire as well as of the public taxis.

"If Dorch didn't go out that day until a little before eight," the Colonel reflected, "and if he lost that badge, and if he lost it that day – he must have lost it after a little before eight."

"Obviously."

"How did he go to Hope's house?"

"His own car."

"Then he lost the badge on his way back from Hope's. But Hope says he drove Dorch to his own gates. Then how did Dorch lose the badge on the Downs?"

Inspector Lord, it seemed, had no reply for that question. Neither had the Colonel himself, it seemed, for the moment.

Again the wires were busy – this time with Roger Tempett, last seen apparently, by the flighty Hester Quimp, whom he had endeavoured, unsuccessfully, to embrace at the moment of his departure with the small suitcase containing his belongings. No tidings of any of the missing had, however, been received up to midnight that night.

Some additional information had come to Inspector Lord by that time. The safes at Cedar Hill had been opened and found empty. This was a disappointment. On the other hand Mrs. Simpson had been thoroughly alarmed by her portable's inquiries and had at last rung up the Central Station to ask that Inspector Lord might go out to her house. This confession

which she made to him there an hour later consoled him a good
deal for the draw-blank at Highgate.

It was quite true, she told him, that she had known – through
Mr. Ross – that her father had been associated with Johnson &
Co., and that a man called Prescott had been simply managing
that business for him. It was quite, true that she had told Mr.
Hawker about this. The reason why she had denied knowledge
of it on the occasion of the Inspector's first visit, had been that
just before his arrival, Mr. Ross had rung her up and warned her
that she must on no account repeat anything that he had told
her in confidence about her father's business affairs – especially
about his connection with Johnson & Co. He had impressed
upon her also the unpleasantness for herself and her husband
which would follow upon its becoming generally known that
there had been that connection. And so – extremely foolishly
but extremely skilfully as Lord admitted – she had to use her
own phrase, "muddled it up and bluffed him off."

She still denied having ever known anything of her father's
history in America or of having ever heard or seen the initials
Q.E.D. used with any but their usual significance. She had never
known her father possess a badge, silver or otherwise. She was
greatly surprised to hear that her father had left Linwood on
November 20th, because, having written to him on November
15th asking him for some money for her husband's hospital,
which was in need of funds, she had received on November 22nd
a cheque for £25, with one of his usual curt notes. Lord read the
note:

"DEAR ELEANOR,
"Cheque herewith. Hope you and Percy are well.
"Affectionately, ALOYSIUS I. DORCH."

The cheque had been payable to the Registrar of the Infirmary ("Trust Father," Mrs. Simpson commented on this pre-

caution) and had been forwarded to him by Dr. Simpson's hand, the day after its receipt.

"I'll keep this note if I may," Lord said pocketing it.

"But what is all this fuss about?" Mrs. Simpson urged. "Surely you can tell me, yes or no, whether there is something wrong?"

"Something very wrong, I'm afraid, Mrs. Simpson. That's all I can say. I'm sorry – but there it is."

From Mrs. Simpson's he drove posthaste to the Linwood branch of the Metropolitan & Western Counties Bank, and had a longish interview with the manager and the chief cashier. Dr. Dorch's account there had not actually been closed formally, he was informed, though notice had been received from him, personally, early in November of his intention to close it – probably in January – when he intended to leave Linwood to reside at Highgate again permanently. A balance of £982 still stood to his credit. As a rule his credit balance had been greatly larger – usually around £5,000, sometimes much more than that. In November and December, however, he had drawn large sums against his account and paid none into it. Lord obtained a list of the cheques drawn since November 1st. Their total reached the imposing figure £12,359 16s. 6d. divided over twelve cheques, dated as follows

Nov. 2   £74   J. T. Maudesley
Nov. 5   £225   Self
Nov. 5   £183 17 0   J. T. Maudesley
Nov. 10   £610   Self
Nov. 13   £2120 15 0   Self
Nov. 18   £963   10 4   Self
Nov. 20   £3792 16 8   J. T. Maudesley
Nov. 20   £1100   Self
Nov. 20   £564 17 6   Self
Nov. 21   £25   Registrar, Westmouth Royal Infirmary
Dec. 10   £100   Ross
Dec. 11   £2600   J. T. Maudesley

All cancelled drafts had been returned by request to Dr. Dorch with his balanced account on November 26th. The two cancelled drafts of December had been returned to Ross personally on the morning of the preceding day.

J. T. Maudesley, the manager believed, was a financier and company promoter. He had had an account at the branch for over two years. The cheques to self had been cashed in each case by Ross. There was nothing unusual in this procedure. It had always been Dr. Dorch's habit to cash large cheques – sometimes half a dozen in one week. The usual course had been that Dr. Dorch wrote a day or two in advance advising the manager that a cheque for such an amount would be presented by Mr. Ross for cashing on such a date. This course had been followed in the case of each of the "self" cheques cashed in November and December. Lord asked to see the advising letters, and after prolonged examination of them by the manager, the chief cashier and himself, took them away with him, together with some similar letters of various dates since the preceding January – and other specimens of Dorch's signature, including some executed by Dorch himself incontestably and under the eyes of one or other of the cashiers.

"I am aware," said the manager, "that Dr. Dorch is in the habit of lending money, and has done so ever since he opened an account with us in 1917. Businessmen in Westmouth are rather sensitive; a cheque of Dorch's going into a man's account might attract a clerk's attention and so start awkward rumours; so many of Dr. Dorch's clients, I understood, preferred cash down. I once handed Ross £16,000 in notes, myself, some years ago. I have known him now for twelve years. He is the last person in the world I should ever have thought of distrusting, personally."

"Yes, yes," nodded Lord sympathetically, and, with difficulty keeping his smile from too blatant exultation, hurried off to set the wires busy once more. Late in the day to stop all those big notes, whose numbers had been duly listed for him; no doubt they had all been got rid of long ago. Still in the end, Lord felt pretty confident, the history of every one of them and of every smaller note into which might ultimately divide themselves would be known accurately. It did not take a Ruddy-Gore's "blind swiping" to do a little routine job of that sort.

But there was no bitterness now in Inspector Lord's thoughts of the Colonel's blind swipes. Inch by inch that seemingly absurd figment of Ruddy-Gore's imagination was revealing itself as actual fact; inch by inch the thread woven by that imagination was dragging out into the light the once incredible truth. As Lord sat by the fire in his little office that night – for he knew that no bed would bring him sleep – his heart warmed several times to gratitude, if he could not altogether admit admiration, for the Colonel's methods. This was during intervals when a Chief Inspectorship at the Yard seemed to him not very far off and a Girl – *the* Girl – very much nearer than she had been yesterday.

He was swallowing some boiling tea a little before seven next morning when he was called to the phone.

"That you, Lord?" asked the Colonel's voice. "I thought I might find you thereabouts. Look here – I've got an idea. Had it all night and didn't blink a wink. Can you pick me up here right now? Bring along a taxi. You can? Stout fellow."

In the hall of the Home, when he arrived there, the Inspector found the Matron, two Sisters, and a chorus of nurses endeavouring to dissuade the Colonel from going out on an icy cold morning before breakfast.

"Ever since you came here, Colonel Gore," said the Matron "you have set all regulations at defiance. I have put up with it – foolishly. But this is really too much. If you go out now without my permission, I must ask, you to leave the Home. I am responsible..."

To the horror even of Inspector Lord, the Colonel placed a finger and a thumb against the worthy lady's plump cheek, pinched it, patted her on the shoulder, and escaped down the steps into the taxi with surprising agility, giving the driver a brief direction as he did so.

"Where are we going?" demanded Lord, as the vehicle sped up Tenby Road, whose lamps still struggled with the dawn sickly.

"Walk on the Downs," Gore replied, and whistled excruciatingly for the rest of the brief drive. It ended at the Gallows Tree, the taxi waiting beneath its black and dripping boughs, the two fares crossing the road to the beginning of that path which Woodbine had followed so many mornings.

There Gore halted, gave his companion a cigarette and lighted two. "See anything?" he asked then, and added by way of encouragement, "of interest?"

Inspector Lord looked. If day had come, night had not yet gone and the limited view before him was vague and gloomy. The sky, the slope that ran up to it, and the bushes on the slope were all the same sad slaty black and all to his eye equally devoid of interest. His gaze came back along the narrow twisting path and rested for a moment on the small tower which rose from the grass beside the path in the immediate foreground.

But the tower, too, was uninteresting – grimy with smoke, glistening with damp. His eyes returned to Gore's finally.

"No," be replied decisively.

"I'll give you a lead. Where did Bullock say Woodbine found that badge? Just about here, wasn't it – in the grass, beside the path? Now...?"

Lord looked again. But this time his eyes went straight to the tower, climbed it, and rested on its castellated summit. At one side of its summit a little turret, a miniature reproduction of itself, jutted up.

As Lord looked at it a cloud of heavy dunnish smoke surged from the top and blotted out the view for some moments, filling the air with its reek. That smoke, Lord knew, rose from the mile-long railway tunnel which, a hundred and twenty feet below, ran beneath Linwood Down from the riverside to Linwood

Down Station, the tower marking the summit of a ventilation shaft.

He turned and looked at Gore again silently. The Colonel nodded gravely.

"Sorry I can't shin up myself," he said. "But it's possible that it may be worth spoiling that nice Burberry of yours." He turned about and pointed to the gates of Wavertree some fifty yards away. "There's one of your men over there. I expect that, if he looks carefully, he'll probably find a rope of just the right length somewhere about Dr. Dorch's residence."

This prediction fulfilled itself accurately, except that the rope found was, in fact, two ropes joined together – one sufficiently light to lasso the small turret with and thus enable the stronger rope attached to it to be hauled up and looped around this support. Lord climbed up and over the castellated coping.

"There's a grating over the shaft," he called down. "Padlocked. No, by Jingo! The padlock's been busted. Half a tick. I'll want you up here, Dickson."

His subordinate climbed up to him, leaving Gore to gaze up towards the now rosy sky expectantly. The two men raised the heavy grating, revealing an iron ladder disappearing perpendicularly into a circular pit of evil-smelling blackness. Barely six feet down the Inspector could, before another rush of rancid smoke blotted it out temporarily, just discern a small greyish disc close to the ladder; but that was clear enough vision. Descending, he found Dr. Dorch roped to the ladder, black with soot, still in evening clothes much disordered, still holding one glove in a gloved hand. His pale, distinguished face was horribly distorted. In half an hour Lord knew definitely that he had been killed with diabolical violence and swiftness, and warrants had been issued for the arrest of Hope, Tempett, Ross and Peterson. One detail of the crime was significant, the victim's back had been broken, though he had probably been dead when that had happened to him.

"Great shooting, my boy," grunted the Chief, patting Lord on the back. "How the devil you ever thought of that shaft, I can't think. Sort of thing you'd stare at for fifty years and never see, much less suspect."

But Lord's conscience had reached its limit. "Well, Sir," he began. When he ended he was alone, and the Embankment and the Girl were very far away again.

Gore went back to breakfast and the Matron's wrath. As he remarked to Yeoland later, given that Dorch had lost the badge just there and that he must be somewhere, why not look for him there? On the whole he appeared depressed by the morning's discovery, now that it had been made. If it had been difficult to link Dorch up with Melhuish's death, it seemed impossible to suppose that Ross and Peterson could ever have had any point of contact with Melhuish whatever. But, it seemed clear now, Ross and Peterson, and not Dorch, *must* somehow have been linked with Melhuish. In the name of Providence, how.

The Matron kept to her word. The Colonel's goods and chattels were packed most cheerfully, by Stephens, and he and they transferred to Mrs. Melhuish's house. For Pickles had insisted that if the patient left his Home while she was away at Tavistock, he must take up his quarters in Victoria Square. Clegg found the guest disquietingly thin and thoughtful, and was privately disposed to regard these appearances as due to things not having joined up quite all right. But the things in Clegg's mind were not the things whose loose ends were furrowing the Colonel's brow.

Chapter Seventeen

WHATEVER DR. DORCH'S SUBMERGED activities had been – and there seemed little doubt now that some of them at least had been unlawful – it was plain that they had been terminated by accomplices more enterprising and more ruthless than himself. Beyond all doubt he had been in the habit of keeping available for immediate use a very large sum of money; no doubt he had found fifty or sixty percent more attractive than the dividends to be obtained from ordinary investment and speculation. Aware, too, of the constant danger from the possibility of his nefarious association with "Johnson & Co." being discovered, there could be no doubt that the greater bulk of his capital had been always kept in a form easily and quickly negotiable, and, if necessary, transferable to a fresh basis of operations unobtrusively and without delay. Large as the total sum of the balance in his current banking account at the time of his death had been, the probability was that a much greater sum in easily negotiable securities had disappeared with Ross and his lieutenants. Ross, of course, had been the mastermind – his, of course, had been the master-hand that had used his position of absolute trust and his superlative skill in forgery to get hold of, certainly, twelve thousand pounds – possibly three times that amount. How long back he had been perpetrating similar frauds and manipulating his employer's account it was impossible to say. But it was simple to suppose that the plundering had begun some time before the final coup, which, if carefully planned, had plainly been carried out in something of a hurry.

The underlying idea had obviously been to obtain a clear period of reasonable length to manipulate Dorch's funds after he had been put out of the way. For that purpose, all that was necessary was that he should continue to be supposed alive. A man, apparently without any real friends, alienated from his only known relatives, his daughter and her husband, he was unlikely to be missed by anyone, or to awaken anyone's anxiety or interest by an absence even of many weeks. As Inspector Lord put it, "the beggar asked for it."

There was nothing to indicate at present for how long Ross had intended to "sit tight." Nor was there sufficient at the moment to explain why, in point of fact, he had sat tight so long, since for several days he must have known that intensive interest was being taken in the master of Wavertree and his affairs. Some urgent reason, Gore felt convinced, must have induced him to remain at his post and to retain at least some of his accomplices at theirs. What reason, it was difficult to surmise. But it was at any rate clear that his plans had gone sorely amiss, somehow.

Tempett had retired from the scene evidently with some precipitation – possibly had got clear away. But Ross and Peterson – the shortish man and his confederate who had driven the Sunbeam which had carried off Bullock (possibly the driver had been the celebrated "man in leggings": Tempett's description, generally, did not tally with Bullocks picture of that individual except in the matter of the American accent) – these four had carried on with Inspector Lord's hands practically upon their shoulders. Some very secure line of retreat must have lain close at hand for them... perhaps carefully prepared long beforehand for just such a final emergency. And yet, Gore thought, that final emergency had not been the one that had been foreseen.

How long had they hoped that the secret of the ventilator tower would remain undiscovered? Perhaps for months – perhaps for years. Perhaps the point had not concerned their desperate defiance greatly, or at all. As a matter of fact, Gore had learned, the shaft was inspected at intervals. But probably Ross had learned that several months elapsed between each inspection as a rule.

A foggy night – an unusually foggy one – had been practically indispensable for carrying out their design. While the hours at which the policeman on duty on the Downshill Road beat passed along it had doubtless been carefully noted, the ventilator tower was plainly in sight, under normal circumstances, from the junction of three much-used roads, Downshill, Tenby and Upper Downs. Even in winter, courting couples were fairly plentiful on the Downs itself up to eleven o'clock; one more persevering specimen, happening to descend that path half an hour or so later than that, might have ruined the whole plan. For it had not been such a simple matter to carry Dorch from, say his own drive, fifty yards across the road to the tower, make preparations for hoisting him to the top, hoist him up, secure him to the ladder, and descend again without being seen by someone. No doubt the feat had been carefully rehearsed and the padlock of the grating filed open beforehand. But at least three people must have been necessary for the job, and it could not have taken less than five minutes at the very least. So that, without doubt, a night of unusual fog had been waited for.

Probably one of Dorch's frequent visits to London or elsewhere had also been waited for. If he had mentioned to even half a dozen people that he intended to go to London, very much the better. But the servants had to be considered carefully – got out of the house until everything was over. The accident that, as a matter of fact, they had all returned to it before the expected time – a quarter to twelve – might well have proved fatal.

If Dorch was to catch the 12.5 on such a night, and to call at Wavertree to pick up a suitcase, it had been easy to calculate the approximate hour of his return to his house from Hope's – half-past eleven at latest. That taxi – of which Dorch had spoken—? *Had* he spoken of a taxi to Hope? Two cars had been heard by the cook, stopping outside the house and subsequently driving away, Hope's and another, which arrived earlier and which the policeman saw at 11.30. Both had been there together for some little time, according to Beatrice Lackworthy. But Hope said he had seen no other car waiting outside Wavertree. If his story of the assault upon himself were true, the driver of the other car must have witnessed it if he was still there. Which car had gone away first – Hope's or the other?

Hope had been very drunk; there could be no doubt of that, unless he was a very skilful actor. Yet, he had been able to drive his car on a night of blinding fog a distance of over a mile... Had he, or had he not been in the plan? That those promissory notes had been left to be found, was quite clearly a plain attempt to point suspicion towards him. Why should Ross have done that, if Hope had been one of his confederates? He would have foreseen that Hope would almost certainly give the whole show away if he found himself in danger? On the whole, Gore doubted that the patron of Egyptian art had had the remotest idea of what had happened after Dorch had said goodnight to him outside the gates of Wavertree.

Well... it was entirely a matter for Lord now and the man-hunting machine. The only interest which the Colonel displayed for the next four days in Dr. Dorch and his friends was, so far as the Inspector could discover, a sudden passion for the society of Duggie – an animal for which Lord himself had contracted an equally passionate hatred. Wavertree having been closed up, and the maids dismissed with warnings to remain within immediate reach, the future of Duggie had become a problem. Mrs. Simpson had refused point-blank to have anything to do with him. None of the servants could bear him. It had been all but decided by Lord that he should be taken to the Dogs' and Cats' Home when an urgent demand was received from the Colonel for the transfer of the unwanted aristocrat to his own care. The purpose hidden beneath this unexpected tenderness of heart on Ruddy-Gore's part was explained when the Inspector discovered that during the subsequent days he spent a large portion of his time in exercising Duggie upon Linwood Downs.

Lord found him one morning rescuing Duggie from an Alsatian which had taken the usual dislike to him.

"Bit of a bore for you, Colonel, what! What's the idea?"

"I'm looking for a dog that loves Duggie," replied the Colonel. "There is one in the world. And I shouldn't have to streak after this — like a — if you had the sense to look at the — collar of that — you saw at Wavertree that morning."

Lord grinned. "It was slow of me, I admit. So that's the idea, is it?" He gazed round the Downs. It was eleven o'clock, the hour at which every dog in Linwood is taken on the Downs. There were perhaps thirty white dogs in close view at the moment – probably some hundreds of them within a more distant one. And it is difficult for a tall, long-legged gentleman to look quite dignified following a Pekinese into the kind of places a Pekinese likes.

But that grin of the Inspector's was to meet with just punishment.

"Well – suppose you find it – and suppose it has an address on its collar – what else do you expect to find at the address?"

"What coloured hair has the Wavertree parlour-maid?" asked the Colonel. "Fox. The housemaid? Mouse. The cook? Old grey horse. I'm looking for a lady with nice glossy black hairs. Short hairs; Eton crop hairs. She's practically my only hope at the moment."

Lord stared. "Only hope? Of what?"

Again the Colonel answered with a question.

"Why didn't Ross clear out days before he did? He must have seen trouble coming. He had practically cleaned out that bank balance by the 28th of November. We know now that J. T. Maudesley was Ross himself. He had everything except that last nine hundred odd, yet he waited on for a whole fortnight. Why? There were no serious signs of trouble for him by November

28th. He had to go *sometime*. The bluff was bound to be called.
Why didn't he go then? Suppose we had called at Wavertree on
that day and been told that Dr. Dorch had wired him telling
him to go to New York – we should have done nothing about
it. We should have had no reason to, then. Why didn't he clear
out while the going was good? Because something kept him
here. What? He wanted to collar a few hundreds more? Or
he thought everything was going to be all right for ever? Or
just sheer bluff and nerve? Or a hitch – something or someone
he was afraid of, if he made a move. Something or someone,
perhaps, with black hairs and, probably, a white dog... for instance. For, my sweet Inspector, you and I know that, out of one
hundred assorted hitches in this life, ninety-nine are females. I
believe Woodbine was a hitch, to start with; because I believe
that somehow Woodbine saw something no one was intended
to see, and they knew he had seen it. I'm even hoping that poor
Melhuish was another hitch, and that he, too, knew something
or saw something or heard something he shouldn't have. But
I'll lay you a gallon of Morny's *Mystérieuse* to the stench of that
horrible cigarette you're smoking that the snag that caught Ross
by the toe in the end was a woman. One of *my* cigarettes, is it?
No matter. It stenches. Of Duggie. Everything does just now.
Duggie found a deceased cat up here this morning. Look here,
Lord, will you do something to oblige me?"

"With pleasure. Unless it's to relieve you of Duggie?"

But Gore had returned, in desperation, to that "old friend"
of which Melhuish's unfinished letter had spoken. The service
with which the Inspector did, as a fact oblige him, on that afternoon and the morning following, was to accompany him upon
a second retracing of Melhuish's morning round on November
20th. On this occasion Lord's tone with the patients interviewed was very much more peremptory and inquisitorial. No
result was produced by eight hours' work, however, save a severe
headache for the Inspector. In the hope of getting rid of this he
consented to accompany Gore upon another perambulation of

Linwood Downs in the company of Duggie, now redolent of carbolic And bearable at least by the Inspector's nose.

It was thus that that grin of his was fitly rewarded. The two men were crawling slowly across a wide expanse of very damp grass in pursuit of Duggie's capricious wanderings, when, out of the grey – for there was no blue that nippy December morning – appeared a white wire-haired terrier charging straight for the little cortege. Reaching Duggie, it checked its career and barking frantically, revolved around his insolent indifference, in frantic rings.

"There," snarled Inspector Lord, "that's the—"

He made a dive for the terrier, but the animal eluded him, and increasing its speed slightly, widened its circles. Determined upon its capture, the Inspector, too, revolved around Gore and Duggie, who had now been secured by his lead.

It was nearly one o'clock, an hour at which the Downs was always comparatively deserted. Yet within less than a minute, five other dogs of various sizes were careering in now far-flung orbits in pursuit of Lord and the wire-haired terrier. Afar off various ladies stood and cried feeble, useless things, or blew whistles. It was impossible to say which owned which dog; no dog paid any attention to any of them. Suddenly from behind a clump of bushes appeared the Alsatian which had assaulted Duggie the morning before. Excited apparently by the sight of a running man, it rushed upon Lord, sprang upon his back playfully, rolled him over, and settled down to a somewhat realistic pantomime of windpipe-extracting. Its owner, a weedy frightened youth in ochre plus-fours, appeared, white-faced, with a formidable dog whip. With this he slashed the Alsatian and Lord impartially for some little time. When at length the Inspector regained his feet, the wire-haired terrier was a distant white spot pursued by a yelping pack of various tints. The Inspector's headache had vanished also; but he had some new aches which made him disinclined for further promenading. Also his hat, his collar, and his natty overcoat were sadly besmirched. He parted from the Colonel somewhat curtly, his eyes fixed upon Duggie with malevolence.

For some little time Gore and Duggie continued their walk. Ultimately they saw the wire-haired terrier rejoin a lady in the dark green uniform of a nurse and disappear towards Upper Downs Road. But Gore had seen the nurse at comparatively short range, while the Alsatian had been busy with Lord; for everyone within sight had converged to the threatened tragedy. Alas, no raven-haired, Eton-cropped young woman was she, but one of those rather gingery ladies whose locks fade in middle age to greyish-rust. He was somewhat shaky on his legs still, and the morning's exercise had been a somewhat extensive one. However, he mustered up his best speed, and presently saw the green uniform and the white dog enter the hall door of a house in Sefton Road, a quiet avenue leading out of Upper Downs Road. The house was one of some size; no doubt the hospital nurse was in attendance upon one of its tenants and undertook the exercise of the family dog on the Downs. One would discover presently if any lady with black hair lived there.

Perhaps unwise to have followed so far in pursuit... with the conspicuous Duggie. As he passed the hall door, which, he saw, was adorned with a small brass plate, a window in a room beside it was opened by the nurse. He saw her eyes rest on Duggie, while her hands, raised above her head, suspended the task of opening the window for some moments. Doubtless, if the white dog knew Duggie, the nurse and probably some of the other occupants of the house knew him too. Much wiser not to look towards its windows – very much wiser not to look towards them intently. And yet, for several moments, the Colonel stared towards them – for at least one, stopped to do it.

When he got back to Victoria Square he found two messages awaiting him. One was a telegram from Pickles saying that she was returning next day. The other was a telephone message from Lord.

"Animal found. At Infirmary. Meet there two-thirty."

Not a dog this time; the Inspector had run a larger quarry to earth. In the private ward to which he had been moved for the occasion, Bullock, still bandaged and splinted, told his story. A blocky little chap in a bowler with a cock-nose, gold in his teeth, and a horseshoe pin in his tie (no American accent this time) had stopped him on Tenby Road about five or a little after on Wednesday, December 11th, and asked him if he wanted to earn a bob. Bullock had wanted. He was handed the lead of a small brown dog and told to take it to a house in Somerset Road. The man in the bowler was in a hurry to meet a pal; he would be much obliged if Bullock would take the dog home for him. Just after he had handed over the dog and the promised bob, a car had come along and he had stopped it and asked the shover to give him a lift down to the City. The shover had consented to do this. The man in the bowler had then suggested that they should leave Bullock and the dog at the house in Somerset Road on their way, Somerset Road being not more than a couple of hundred yards' distant. To this the shover had also agreed. Bullock, the dog, and the man in the bowler had got into the car. It had turned out of Tenby Road into College Avenue, and then out of College Avenue into Elmtree Road, travelling at great speed. Halfway along Elmtree Road it had stopped, and the man in the bowler had asked the shover if he couldn't give them a drink at his garage, which appeared to be close at hand. To this the shover had also agreed.

But Bullock's suspicion had already awakened. At the mention of the word drink, his thoughts had flashed at once to his pal Woodbine. He had noticed that the shover did not turn his face towards the man in the bowler when he spoke to him. He made up his mind that there was some game on, said he didn't want no drink, and tried to get out of the car. The man in the bowler had grabbed him and forced him back into his seat. "I may as well tell you, Bullock," he had said, "that I am a detective officer, and that I shall take you to the Central Police Station on suspicion of being concerned in the death of the man known as

Woodbine." At that, Bullock had, he admitted, got the wind up; he knew only too well what happened to friendless loafers once they fell into the hands of the police – too well what happened to them if they tried to escape from those hands. He had argued with the supposed detective for some little time, pointing out that he had no reason for murdering Woodbine and therefore hadn't nor never had murdered no one nor thought of such a thing, and then the car had moved on. At the end of Elmtree Road it had turned into Downshill Road and stopped again there, outside Wavertree.

"You sit there," the man in the bowler had said, "if you wag a toe, there'll be more trouble coming to you, buddy." He had then got out of the car on to the footpath, pulling the dog after him by its lead. The dog had offered a violent resistance, Bullock had taken a chance, opened the other door, and jumped out. As he did so, two things had happened; the shover had turned his head and Bullock had seen his face and recognised the "man in the leggings." The sight had increased his alarm to panic, and he had plunged headlong against the wing of one of the Westmouth Tramways Company's motor-buses which had happened to pass just at that moment. The next thing he had known was that he was in a cot in the Infirmary with a split head, crushed ribs, two broken legs and a broken arm.

He had never seen the man in the bowler before in his life. But he was absolutely sure about the shover. Since he had re-covered consciousness his sole thought appeared to have been a conviction that he had escaped by the skin of his teeth a fate much worse than a mere collision with a motor-bus. It had not occurred to him as prudent to reveal his present whereabouts to anyone outside the hospital for the moment; and so he had reposed, more or less comfortably, in his cot, and kept his mouth shut. Eventually, however, a bricklayer who had fallen fifty feet or so and had come in for repairs, had arrived in the ward and had promptly recognised him as his wife's sister's husband's mother's uncle. The hospital authorities had communicated with the great-nephew with whom he lived, and the police, who had been calling on the great-nephew with regularity ever since his grand-uncle's disappearance, had thus been led to the Infirmary.

It would be some time before Mr. Bullock found his foot upon Linwood Downs again in the flesh. But in spirit he was taken there by Gore at a second interview which took place next morning. By that time he had been allotted a place in a semi-private ward permanently; he had been placed upon a specially generous diet and clothed with a beautiful suit of pyjamas; a lavish supply of cigarettes and tobacco and illustrated periodicals lay upon his table; more attention had been paid to his comfort within the past twenty-four hours than in all the preceding sixty-nine years of his precarious existence. Believing – not quite accurately – that he owed these amenities to Inspector Lord's influence and generosity, he had laid aside all animosity towards the Westmouth police force. And he beamed upon the Inspector and the pleasant gent who seated themselves beside his bed while he was still digesting the best breakfast he had ever eaten in his life.

"Now, Mr. Bullock," said the pleasant gent, "we want you to throw your memory back to the day when Woodbine found that badge we've asked you so many questions about. It was a Thursday, wasn't it – the Thursday before the Friday he died on. November the 21st – Thursday. Now, it was in the morning, I suppose, that he found it?"

"Yes, sir. He found it first thing when he got on the Downs. About seven he got up that morning. Hardly light it was. I got up on the Downs myself by half-six, but it was too dark and too foggy to see anything. So I hung about and waited for Woodbine a bit along the path."

"It was still very foggy then?"

"Terrible foggy, sir. You couldn't hardly see your own breath before your mouth."

"From where you stopped on the path to wait, then, you could not see very far back along it?"

"No, sir."

"Where along the path did you stop? How far, say, past that ventilator tower?"

"Maybe the throw of a stone past the shaft, sir – up where the first bushes are."

"Could you see the tower?"

"No, sir. I couldn't see as far off as that. I didn't see Woodbine until he was just a couple of yards from me, when he come along up the path."

"Did he tell you then that he had found the badge?"

"Not then, sir. A bit after, when he'd got up on the top and the daylight came. He took it out then and showed it to me, and asked me what I thought it was."

"He told you where he had found it?"

"Yes. In the grass just under the ventilator shaft. He told me he had kicked it with his foot and that was how he found it. Because it wasn't a place he'd ever look for anything, nor me neither."

"Can you remember if anyone passed down the path just before Woodbine joined you?"

"No, sir. No one did."

"Or anywhere near the path?"

"No, sir. I wouldn't have seen them, if they had, unless they were on the path, the fog was that heavy."

"You passed the tower yourself?"

"Yes, sir."

"Did you see anyone near the tower as you passed – anywhere near the tower?"

"Yes, sir. I seen two people. I saw a gent in a dress suit under his top-coat with his face covered with blood and no hat on him. He came down the path and passed me just by the tower and then turned across the grass. I stopped to look after him, on account of the blood on his face and his shirt, but the fog covered him up in a moment, so I went on up the path. Me and Woodbine saw him again after up on the top, going the other way. Drunk we thought he was, or maybe a motor accident. But we didn't pay much notice to him, because we were looking at the silver gadget Woodbine had found then."

"A tallish, stoutish man with a fair moustache?"

"Fattish he was, yes, sir, I don't remember what colour his moustache was. But he had evening dress on, I know, and no hat. I seen the same gentleman, Inspector, that day you took me to the house with the gardening tools. He came out just after you, going in by the gates."

Lord nodded in answer to a glance from the pleasant gent's monocle. That, of course, had been Hope on his early morning way to... to what?

"You saw someone else, you say?"

"Yes, sir, a lady. I know her well by sight, sir. 'Orspital nurse, she is. Wears a green cloak and cap with a long thing at the back. Out every morning before seven she has been these four or five months back, with a little white terrier. Elderly lady, what you'd call – often says good morning to me very pleasant."

Again the monocle gleamed towards Inspector Lord for an instant.

"And you saw her that morning – near the tower?"

"Behind it. She was on the grass, with her little dog."

"What? Playing with the dog?"

"I think so, sir. Throwing a ball for him."

"Quite close to the tower?"

"Just beside it, on the far side from the path, sir."

"She was there when the man without a hat passed down the path by the tower?"

"Yes, sir."

"Did he speak to her?"

"No, sir. He didn't look right nor left nor speak to me nor her. Just went on likes if he was walking in his sleep."

"The lady with the dog could see him?"

"Yes. She stopped playing with the dog to look after him, same as meself."

"Did she speak to you?"

"Yes, sir. She said 'That gentleman's had an accident, I'm afraid,' or something like that. 'Seemingly, by the looks of it,' I said. 'Very foggy this morning isn't it?' she said. 'You won't find many five pound notes this morning, I'm afraid.' I laughed and said 'That's the truth, miss,' and went on up the path to where I told you."

"You left her at the tower?"

"Yes, throwing the ball for the dog."

"When Woodbine came along, did he say anything about having seen her?"

"Yes, sir. He told me he'd seen Nursie – that's what me and him called her between ourselves, seeing her every morning – he said he'd seen her with her dog near the tower as he came by."

"Playing with the dog?"

There was a slight hesitation.

"Yes, sir."

The pleasant gentleman's voice lost a little of its pleasantness, temporarily.

"Now – we want the truth, Bullock. Come on – let's have it. The fact is, the hospital nurse saw Woodbine pick up something, didn't she, and asked him what he had picked up? Isn't that so?"

"Yes, sir."

"And Woodbine of course, said he hadn't picked up anything."

"Yes, sir."

"Believing that what he had picked up was her property and that she had been looking for it?"

"Yes, sir. He seen her looking for something in the grass by the tower – at the far side – down on her hunkers she was."

"Not the dog's ball?"

"*He* didn't think so anyway, sir. Course he ought to have told the lady what he'd picked up and asked her if it was hers, as I suppose now it was."

To Bullock's surprise, Inspector Lord patted him on the shoulders. "This isn't a Sunday School, old man. It's a jolly good job Woodbine did nothing of the sort, I may tell you. So he just said he'd picked up nothing and went on – leaving her still looking?"

"Well – he *thought* she was looking, sir – by the way she trampled about in the grass."

Again the monocle gleamed.

"The grass round the tower?"

"Yes, sir. I saw it meself on me way back that morning. You'd have thought all the elifans an lines and tigers out of the Zoo had been prancing about in it."

"You can't recall exactly what Woodbine told you had happened, can you? She was at one side of the tower, and he came along the path. At the other side. She was down on her hunkers—"

"She stood up when he came out of the fog and threw the ball for the dog, likes she was pretending she wasn't looking for nothing. But he guessed she had been. So he went off the path on to the grass by the tower, on the far side from her, and kicked it up with his foot as he went along. When he saw the little bright thing he kicked up, he stooped down and popped it into his pocket quick. She came round the tower and maybe saw him or guessed he'd found something. Anyway she said 'What's that you picked up?' or 'Did you pick up something?' or something like that. And he said, 'I picked up nothing, miss. Have you lost something?' 'Oh, no,' she said, and went on playing with the dog. He thought she'd said that to prevent his looking anymore, and to get him away. So he went off and left her there. That's the best I can remember of what he told me, sir."

"So that, probably, she didn't really know that he had picked up anything?"

"I couldn't say to that, sir. I'm telling you what Woodbine told me, what I remember of it."

"You say you have seen the lady with the dog frequently, early in the morning – for some months back?"

"Yes, sir, nearly every morning, wet or fine she's out with the dog by seven or before. Since about July, it might be..."

"Where have you met her usually in the morning?"

"Oh, all around, sir. She gives the dog a good walk in the mornings – all over the Downs."

"Ever seen her near the tower before?"

"Well, no, sir, I don't think so. Not so far down as that. Up on the top, mostly, she does be."

"She knows you well by sight, I suppose?"

"Yes, sir. Well."

"And Woodbine?"

"Yes, sir. She used to say good morning to the both of us when we were together."

"Ever see her talking to anyone besides yourselves?"

"No. Can't say as I ever did, sir."

"Ever seen the gentleman in the evening clothes with her on the Downs or anywhere else, before?"

"Not as I knows of, sir."

"Anything in particular you think you'd like? Say for dinner?"

Mr. Bullock reflected profoundly and for so long that the pleasant gent glanced sharply at his face. But it looked quite healthy, considering. Its owner spoke at length, dreamily.

"I'd like tripenunyans an' a glass o' malt an' a jam roly-poly puddin', sir. An' mebbe a bit o' cheddar an' a cup o' cawfee."

"Stout fellow," nodded the pleasant gent. Despite the Inspector's frown he slipped two crackling somethings under the invalid's pillow and departed. At one o'clock, Mr. Bullock's dream was fulfilled to the letter. Subsequently he had others. But they, fortunately, did not come true.

Chapter Eighteen

BY THIS TIME ANOTHER surmise of Gore's had proved itself correct. The list of local Sunbeam saloon owners was a long one, and included several black or green-black or blue-black cars with light linings. Inquiry of the findable owners elicited the fact that none of them could have been followed up the Bath Road to Marlborough on the afternoon of December 11th. But one owner was not findable.

Some five months before a new Sunbeam saloon, dark blue with silver-grey linings, had been purchased by a man named Henry Heberts from a local agent. Its registration number had been HW 5404; Heberts had paid spot cash and had taken delivery of the car himself at the agent's warerooms. Sunbeams are not bought every day off even the busiest of dealers, and the agent and some of his assistants remembered this particular purchaser very well as an American, clean-shaven, strongly-built, with a very intelligent, rather pugnacious face, prominent lips and an addiction to chewing gum. He had not seemed precisely the kind of person who might be expected to purchase a new Sunbeam, and the firm had made some unobtrusive inquiries upon receiving his order. These had not been particularly reassuring, since it had been discovered that he lived over a rather dilapidated if roomy garage in a lane behind Downshill Road where he housed an ancient Daimler – his own property or someone else's did not then transpire. He had stated, when taking delivery of the Sunbeam, however, that he intended to use it for hiring out; as he had paid cash down, the agent had troubled his head no further about his customer's affairs and had heard and seen nothing more of him. Lord had found the garage behind Downshill Road closed up; when entry had been made by breaking in the wicket in the doors, he found the Daimler, some empty tins and cigarette packets, some sheets of a New York illustrated paper, and nothing more. Henry Heberts and his new Sunbeam had gone somewhere else. A detail of some interest was that the wall which bounded the rear of the premises was the wall of Wavertree's garden.

On the afternoon following his second interview with Bullock at the Infirmary, Gore learned something more about Mr. Heberts from the least expected source.

Mrs. Melhuish arrived at Victoria square at teatime, somewhat braced-up by her brief visit to Devonshire, but much put out by her guest's delay in returning to London. So much put out, that she refused to hear anything concerning his own activities and Inspector Lord's during her absence from Linwood. Not that the Colonel evinced any eagerness to discuss them. He ate muffins and drank tea with a voracity which satisfied Clegg that some things at any rate had joined up satisfactorily; his gaiety had a bland and happy innocence which made Simon Wyckham appear old and care-worn; and Duggie (the Colonel was not quite candid with his hostess as to Duggie's previous ownership) filled up the blanks fairly creditably. Duggie had cheered up a good deal now, and fortunately, evinced a passionate affection for the returned mistress of the house. Except that the Colonel was strictly forbidden to allow him under the bedclothes, he was accepted as an established fact.

"But he must go away before I get fond of him," Pickles stipulated. "And anyhow, I've only one thing left to be fond of, now. No. You mustn't smoke *that* pipe, Wyck. It's too vile. Simon has brought you a new one from Tavistock."

Simon Wyckham, wriggling a great deal, extracted his gift from his trouser pocket and presented it to his godfather. The

Colonel – rather overcome by the splendour of meerschaum and amber which gleamed in a case of morocco lined with amber velvet – put away his dishonoured old briar manfully, filled its successor and smoked it with enormous satisfaction.

"How deliciously it makes your tobacco smell," murmured Mrs. Melhuish.

The lights were put out at Simon Wyckham's request, and the three sat before the glow of the fire, chiefly in silence, so that Simon Wyckham might see castles and things in the coals without disturbance. His small back buttressed against Uncle Wyck's legs, he reflected many things. Never once that he could remember had Daddy assisted at one of these after-tea reveries by the firelight which were one of Simon's special small joys. Presently he turned his face to the darkness behind him.

"Uncle Wyck, where is Daddy? Why doesn't he come back?"

"Oh, he'll be along one day soon, old chap. Don't worry."

Simon stroked Duggie's silky back for a space.

"The night he went away," he said, "I was naughty. I didn't kiss him goodnight properly 'cause he wouldn't answer a question. I asked him what was an ordinary G.P. and he put me off with a silly old joke. What is an ordinary G.P. Uncle Wyck?"

Gently Gore explained – but not quite satisfactorily to Simon Wyckham.

"But why did Janet say that he was only an *ordinary* G.P. – or General Pracsher or whatever it means? And she made a face when she said it to the man. Like this."

Simon reproduced what the original performer had clearly intended for a *moue* of disdain. But his godfather did not smile.

"Janet had been talking to a man, had she, Simon – that day – the day of the night when Daddy went away?"

"Yes. A funny man with a big sweet in his mouth. It stuck out like this when he wasn't chewing it."

Again the small face was turned to exhibit this time a bulging cheek. Again he noticed that he had not made his godfather smile.

"What a funny man. Tell us about him, Simon. Where did you and Janet meet him?"

In his own way the child told his little story. When it was ended the Colonel relit the gift pipe and finished it solemnly before he spoke again. When he did, his voice had something of its old parade-ground rasp.

"I want to see this woman, Pickles. Before the child sees her again."

Mrs. Melhuish made a gesture.

"What's the use, Wyck?"

"Get her."

Janet, a somewhat mincing young woman of the "lady-nurse" type was summoned, when every light in the room had been turned on. She was one of those persons from whom it was practically impossible to extract a definite reply to any question; but the Colonel accomplished the impossible. Boiled down, her story proved exactly what Simon Wyckham's had led him to expect it would be.

About two o'clock on November 20th she had taken Simon Wyckham for his customary after-dinner walk. They had gone towards the Downs along the Promenade, at that hour deserted. A handsome car of dark colour had passed them, going the same way, and stopped a little ahead of them. When they had reached it, two men, who had got out of it and were looking at a map, had spoken to her and asked her, first, the way to the Gloucester Road and then if she would like a run round the Downs with her kiddy. She had refused this offer, but had remained talking to them for some time.

She described their appearances in terms which, for Gore, left no doubt whatever as to their identities; the Lotharios of the Promenade had without any doubt been Henry Heberts and the shortish man with the gold-stopped teeth. (Simon Wyckham had been as much impressed by the gold-filled mouth as by the sweet-filled one.)

The conversation had at first been merely gallant. After a little while, however, it had concerned Janet's job and employers. Gore's cross-examination elicited that the nursemaid had, in point of fact, been so closely questioned as to Dr. Melhuish's habits and patients, that she had become suspicious and offended, and had walked on. This, probably, had been just what had been desired of her. For she had plainly given, by that time, the information which was wanted – the names of several patients of Melhuish's across the Suspension Bridge, the hours at which he would probably be found at his own house, and his practice as to using his car for night calls.

It was clear that the woman had felt some misgivings, since her employer's death, as to that incident and its possible significance. Lady-nurses, however, being supposed superior to such wayside philanderings when on duty, she had probably been afraid to say anything about it. At any rate she had not done so, even to her fellow servants. She left the room tearful and frightened, having explained, finally, that remark which had aroused Simon Wyckham's curiosity. One of the men – the man with the chewing-gum – when questioning her about Dr. Melhuish, had asked if he was a specialist and if he would be likely to be called in for a consultation. To that she had replied in the words the child had quoted – once, so tragically.

On that afternoon, then, the trap for poor Melhuish had been planned out. At two o'clock or thereabouts, when Melhuish's morning round had hardly finished. Gore went back doggedly to that "old friend" of his. He knew now who that old friend had been. But he must be certain.

"I'm sorry to worry your household staff this way, Witch," he said, when the séance with Janet had ended. "But if you don't want your shover – Halliday, I think, is his name – if you don't want him for a couple of hours from now on, I should like him. No, I don't want your car. *Nor* your cook. Just Halliday, and tuppence-worth of your telephone."

And so, Halliday, most unwillingly, was taken away from the
kitchen fire and placed in the Buick, which Yeoland had duly
delivered at Victoria Square, and told to reproduce as far as he
could recall and as accurately, the places at which he had stopped
on the morning of November 20th. His interest aroused and
his pocket enriched, he did this to the entire satisfaction of the
Colonel. For, at the end of an hour or so of wandering through
Linwood, he directed Yeoland to a house at the end of Abercorn
Road. Now Abercorn Road was a very short thoroughfare at
right angles to Sefton Road. Yeoland got out and, reconnoitring
cautiously, discovered that that house into which the green uniform and white dog had disappeared possessed two hall doors,
one opening into Sefton Road, the other into Abercorn Road.
From the fact that the Sefton Road portion of the house was
in darkness while most of the windows facing Abercorn Road
were lighted up, Gore concluded that the building was probably
divided between two tenants. Also Yeoland reported that a brass
plate at the Sefton Road Hall door bore the inscription:

Mrs. Anna Younger,
Manicure, Pedicure, Massage.

Halliday knew for certain only one house in Abercorn Road
where his master had visited a patient that morning – Number
7, the house outside which the car now stood. But he had possibly visited other houses in that road or others close at hand, as he
had been away from the car for nearly three quarters of an hour.
The chauffeur also recalled that, while he had been waiting for
the Doctor's return a maid, in a state of some excitement, had
come running down the road to the car to ask where the doctor
was. He had pointed to Number 7, and she had gone up to
its door. A little after the doctor had come out of Number 7
with her and gone up Abercorn Road towards Sefton Road.
Owing to the fog Halliday had not seen where they had gone
after passing the car.

"The next stop was at the top of Windermere Road, sir,"
said Halliday, when the car contained its three passengers again.

But the Colonel, to his relief, "Had had enough of that little game," and asked to be driven home again. Mr. Yeoland, having left him there, despatched a wire to Messrs. Gore & Tolley's headquarters, garaged the Buick, and then took up unobtrusive observation upon the house at the corner of Sefton and Abercorn Roads. While the hours passed, three other members of Messrs Gore & Tolley's staff hurried westward by the 6.30 from Paddington. One of them relieved Yeoland shortly after midnight. Inspector Lord, curiously, happened to pass that way shortly afterwards; so, several times during the small hours, did the man on the beat. But neither of them paid any attention to a figure which might quite reasonably have been asked if it was loitering with intent.

After dinner that evening Halliday, at his request, had another little talk with the Colonel. He had been chatting with Glennie, the bridge-keeper, the day before his departure for Tavistock. Glennie had told him for the first time of an additional light which he had noticed on the rear off wing of Dr. Melhuish's car on the night of the crime. Halliday had then recalled that he had seen on that wing next day a small spring clip, gripping the wing tightly. This hitherto unexplained find was now explained. That clip must have held a small flashlight. Therefore, Halliday had reasoned, somebody, must have attached clip and light after he had left his garage that night and taken the car round to wait for Dr. Melhuish. And the reason someone had done that had, it seemed to him, been to enable the people waiting for the car on the Bridge to recognise it in time to stop it. When they had stopped it, they had taken off the flashlight, but had failed to remove the clip, which had a powerful spring.

At Gore's request he reflected deeply and lengthily – with a good deal of scratching – in the attempt to imagine when the clip and light could have been attached to the wing. Only two people, he was of opinion, could have done it.

"Glennie himself, sir – while the car was stopped going on to the bridge, or a hospital nurse that came across the road outside the house while I was waiting for Dr. Melhuish. Lost in the fog she was. The Doctor spoke to her and offered her a lift, but she went off. She could have done it, sir – because she was in the road behind the car. But what would a hospital nurse want to do a thing like that for? Elderly piece, too, she was."

"Quite," replied the Colonel, and no more. But afterwards he spent some time trying to remember whether the nurse whom he had met just before his misadventure in College Road had worn a green uniform. As a result, Inspector Lord had another talk with young Pettitt that evening. Pettitt was quite certain that the nurse who had stopped him had worn a green uniform – of the same colour but of different design from that worn by the Infirmary nurses.

Chapter Nineteen

So MANY OF THE Colonel's predictions had verified themselves within the past few days that Inspector Lord had almost entirely laid aside his distrust of unorthodoxy. He suspected – quite rightly – that the Colonel was still keeping to himself certain reservations with regard to Number 76, Sefton Road, and was a little aggrieved by this supposed reticence. But he consented to a very limited and inconspicuous surveillance of the house by his own subordinates, allowing them to form an outer ring to the intensive watch kept by Messrs. Gore & Tolley's young men. Number 76 was the last house on one side of Sefton Road, at the end nearer to the Downs; at the other side ran only the wall which bounded the back gardens of the houses in Upper Downs Road. By good fortune one of the latter was at the moment vacant, and its windows and its garage, which faced into Sefton Road nearly opposite Number 76, provided useful posts of observation. All correspondence delivered at the house underwent a preliminary examination from Friday, December 20th on; its telephone too received special attention, though these last precautions yielded no result of suspicion, both letters and phone dealing merely with Mrs. Younger's very occasional clients or more often with orders of supplies from the local dealers. It was not until Saturday afternoon that the quantity of food delivered at the house attracted attention. So far as was actually known, now, that portion of the house contained only a single occupant, Mrs. Younger herself. Yet baker, butcher, grocer, and greengrocer arrived at its hall door with filled baskets and left it with all but empty ones. Neither Gore nor Lord had by this time the least doubt that other mouths than Mrs. Younger's were being fed beneath its portion of the roof.

Up to that afternoon no steps had been taken to trace the flurried maid who had come to Dr. Melhuish's car in Abercorn Road on that foggy morning a month before, in search of him. When, however, shortly after darkness had fallen on Saturday, Gore presented himself at the hall door of Number 28 Abercorn Road – the other and larger portion of the corner house – it was opened to him, although he did not then know it, by the maid herself. He was ushered into a cosy sitting room where two ladies received him urbanely and supplied him without hesitation with such information as they possessed as to their next door neighbour, Mrs. Younger.

It was not a great deal. She had occupied the portion of the house in Sefton Road since July, and had already, they believed acquired some small connection professionally. They had never spoken to her, and had seen very little of her, but considered her a very quiet "person," devoted to her little dog – which was occasionally a little noisy – and to her work. In the beginning she had kept a maid; but the maid had disappeared some weeks ago. The ladies raised their eyebrows at the suggestion that Mrs. Younger might have received gentlemen visitors – or gentlemen clients. They did not think so. But if she did, their smiles implied that she was of an age beyond grave suspicion. They had not heard recently any unaccustomed noises through the walls; on the other hand they were both rather deaf as well as somewhat short-sighted. One noise, however, they recalled upon reflection, had attracted their attention at times recently. Mrs. Younger appeared to be taking three baths a day some days, at least two every day. Asked to be precise, they believed they had first noticed these additional activities of next door's bathroom and wastepipe on the Thursday or Friday of the preceding week...

They got up their maids and questioned them. The maids, it appeared, had not only heard the bathroom noises but had formed the conclusion that a male of some sort was living in Number 76 Sefton Road at the moment. From time to time they had heard masculine rumblings through the walls; one night, early in the morning, one of them had been awakened by a man's laugh which, she said, had frozen her blood, so loud and so unexpected had it been at three o'clock in the morning within a few inches of her own startled head. Neither of them, however, had seen any man about the house next door; nor had they ever seen Mrs. Younger speak to any man whatever at any time other than tradesmen's messengers.

Before they left the room, Gore asked their mistresses a question on chance. Had either of them run out in search of a doctor at any time within the past four or five weeks – run down Abercorn Road in a great hurry in search of him – on a very foggy morning.

"Me, sir," replied one girl at once. "Missus sent me out to try and find Dr. Melhuish."

"You found his car in this road, didn't you?"

"Yes, sir. We knew he couldn't be far away, because he'd just only left here."

The ladies explained. Both had been patients of Dr. Melhuish's for many years. On that foggy morning the elder, then inspecting her front garden, had seen Dr. Melhuish pass on foot. Just after he had gone by, the maid from next door – Mrs. Younger's – had rushed up to the garden gate to say that Mrs. Younger had met with an accident and was, she feared, dying. By some means Mrs. Younger had contrived to leave the extinguished pilot jet of her bathroom geyser still on while she was bathing and she had been overcome by the fumes. By the merest accident the maid's suspicions had been aroused and she had gone into the bathroom to find Mrs. Younger lying unconscious with her head under the water.

The maid of 28 Abercorn Road – who was gardening with her mistress – had run off to overtake Dr. Melhuish, and had found him at Number 7. He had hurried to Mrs. Younger's house with her maid, and they supposed, had succeeded in restoring her to consciousness; for she had been seen in Sefton Road in the afternoon of the same day. As poor Dr. Melhuish had never called again, of course, he had never told them any particulars as to Mrs. Younger's mishap.

"But we know that this woman – Mrs. Younger – was certainly not your old friend, or any sort of friend of yours," urged Inspector Lord when he had heard this story at secondhand a very little later. He was about to add that, also, so far as was known, from the account which the Colonel had received, there had been no one in 76 Sefton Road at the time when Melhuish had been summoned there except Mrs. Younger, her maid, and Melhuish himself, a fact for which the maid of Number 28 round the corner had vouched, since she had followed as far as the door of the fume-filled bathroom out of curiosity, before she had gone back to report to her mistresses. But happening to look at the Colonel's face, he was induced to examine it with greater attention.

"That *is* so, isn't it?"

"No," replied the Colonel unexpectedly, "I don't think it is. I say – 'think.' And that's all I'm going to say, for now. But I am inclined to believe that Mrs. Younger and I have met before."

Lord snorted.

"Oh, well – then why the hell didn't you remember that before?" he protested. Then, perceiving the unreasonableness of that, he sat down again. "When did you begin to think it?"

"Day before yesterday."

"Day before yesterday?"

"When I saw her opening one of her windows."

Lord stared. "What the devil did *that* tell you?"

"Well," replied the Colonel slowly, "what does one open windows with?"

"One's hands, I suppose."

"Quite. Well, I saw Mrs. Younger's. She had them raised above her head for quite a long time. I had an excellent view of them,"

"Well – what about them?"

Gore was suddenly affected by an unusual diffidence.

"Er – I thought them unusually large for a not very large lady, that's all."

Amazement beyond speech spread like evening mist across the bright landscape of Inspector Lord's intelligent face. For a full incredulous minute he sat silent, staring. Only too well did he recall a lady with whom he had had some dealings before – a lady whose hands—

"Hell—," he gasped at last.

The Colonel's hand made a warning gesture. "I say – I think," he replied.

"But—," urged Lord, "this Younger woman is fifty if she's a day. I've had several looks at her – close up."

"Not close enough, Lord," said the Colonel. "I *think*."

"I'll swear she isn't a damn good-looking young woman of thirty or thereabouts, anyhow."

"Swear away, my lad. Perjury is the proud prerogative of policemen. Again I say – I think she is, what you say she isn't. Have you seen her without that green cap and veil?"

"No."

"Without those blue glasses?"

"No."

"Without that greyish wig?"

"No – if it is a wig. Of course, I haven't."

"At any rate you've seen that her lips and her skin are made up thickly?"

"Well – but every woman makes up now."

"They don't usually try to make red lips look blue, though – I *think*. Now – you see – Melhuish saw Mrs. Younger... er... uncamouflaged. Her head had been under water. All little adjuncts like powder and blue spectacles and greyish wigs, and so on had presumably been removed. Though – of course – it is possible that the lady bathes in blue spectacles. I'm only thinking. But – if he did – and if *he* recognised her as a lady whom he had done his best to hang not so very long ago – the certainty is, I *think*, that the first person he would have told about the encounter would have been... me. I *think*. Because, you see, it was I who introduced him to the lady originally – and who encouraged him to help as far as possible, to hang her."

Lord, pacing the room, turned and nodded. "That's – *if...*" he stipulated. "I can't believe it. Then – why – ? You think Melhuish's having seen her and recognised her might have—?"

"Yes. If it interfered with some little plan she had in mind. If, for instance, she was somehow concerned with a gentleman called Ross in a plan to blot out Dr. Dorch... I'm only thinking. I can't even suggest any special reason why she should want to help to blot Dorch out. But I think there must have been one. I think she must have realised that Melhuish's having recognised her would put the tin hat on the plan, and that he must be silenced before he told anyone about it. Especially me. For the lady we're talking of is a very intelligent person. She would guess, just as quickly as I should, that Melhuish would certainly let me know that he had come across her again. You've got to consider what Gretta Higgins' history is – what her reputation is... even if she was acquitted by twelve idiots and a case of senile decay in a wig. If her pals heard that Melhuish had spotted her in the neighbourhood of Dorch – Dorch who was to be blotted out in a few hours from then. . . for it was a lovely foggy day... and the night, was going to be just the right sort of night for the job – don't *you* think they would have come to a decision about Melhuish very promptly? And they did. They got busy at once. It was after twelve when Melhuish saw Mrs. Younger in her bath; it was only a little after two when they waylaid Melhuish's nursemaid on the Promenade."

For a long time Lord brooded over this in the uncertain glare of new light.

"Suppose you're right," he said at length. "Suppose Melhuish did recognise her and that she knew he had done so. Why should that have mattered so much to her that Melhuish had to be killed? She was acquitted. . . Unpleasant, perhaps, for her – if she had made a fresh start – to have it become known who she really was – a woman tried for her own brother's murder – a woman suspected of having murdered two other people at least. Unpleasant – yes, but not in the least dangerous. Suppose she *was* working with Ross – helping some way and for some reason in a plan to blot Dorch out and collar his stuff. Suppose that that plan had been discovered, as it has been for all practical purposes – I mean, Ross & Co's. share in it – what would there have been to connect Mrs. Younger with them. . . Even if Mrs. Younger was known to be who you say she is? Nothing. Then why did it matter. Why should she want Melhuish murdered. Why should Ross & Co. be willing to murder him for her? Even she – and even they – would hardly commit a risky murder without a very urgent reason?"

"There was one," replied the Colonel – smoking, alas, his old pipe now, "I think. If Melhuish had had time to spread the glad tidings of my old friend's reappearance, my old friend would have had to come out into the daylight and, probably, clear out of Linwood, quick. Now, if she was interested in Dorch's blotting out for some reason – and she always had a good reason for everything she did, we know – it would be very awkward for her to have to do that. She didn't want to come to the top – she didn't want to clear out. She was to get something from Dorch's blotting out – and she wanted to stay. . . under the bushel. So Melhuish had to be silenced at once. She had the leverage to get it done. She knew what Ross & Co. were up to. She probably said to them – if I have to drop out of this little lot – I'll see that you drop out of it. If Melhuish talks, that idiot Inspector Lord or that thing called Gore, will come

nosing round 76 Sefton Road. Well – if they come – I shall
have something to tell them about your little goings on. And
so, I think, Melhuish was silenced for her. Remember too, that
she's a deucedly fascinating young woman. If Ross was under
her thumb that way also – of course she was all the more likely
to get what she wanted done – and done at once. As it was, I
think."

"Well—," began Inspector Lord, more than half convinced.

A clerk appeared. "Wanted in number eleven, sir. Urgent."

When the Inspector returned a quarter of an hour later it
was to tell the Colonel that he was off to Marseilles, where the
Sûreté believed it had run Ross to earth. Although his Chief still
fought shy of meeting Colonel Gore in the flesh, that gentleman
would find that his wants would be attended to, in reason. With
promptitude – if any should arise beyond his own resources to
satisfy. It was Lord's first trip abroad officially. He was a little
flurried, a little over-eager, the Colonel feared, to believe the
tidings from Marseilles, in an optimism that was the reaction
from the failure of the past few days to reveal the whereabouts of
any of the wanted. The two men parted with a "Good hunting"
and without farther discussion of Mrs. Younger's possibilities.

As Gore walked up to Linwood from the city that evening,
the shops were gay with their Christmas displays, the footpaths
crowded with Christmas shoppers, the country carts, their loads
now depleted, still selling holly and ivy and mistletoe on pitches
permitted them by long usage. The faces that passed – proud
fathers and mothers and uncles and aunts, eager-eyed laughing schoolchildren, decorative young Westmouth nuts with still
more decorative Westmouth flappers – were the faces of a world
from which evil had, for at least a few days, vanished completely. Inevitably, by stark contrast, another face flitted before his
eyes as he walked – a face of angelic loveliness, as Pickles had
described it – the face of the wickedest human being he had
encountered so far. Odd Christmas thoughts those must be that
lurked beneath the drab wig of the mistress of 76 Sefton Road.

Though he was quite prepared to believe, for that matter, that her rooms were already gay with green and scarlet, and that some at least of those numerous parcels delivered in to those unbecoming hands of hers had contained mince-pies and the ingredients of plum pudding.

Recalling Lord's parting words, Gore stopped on his homeward way to ring up the Central Station, and after some delay heard the Chief Inspector's curt voice at the other end. There was a noticeable silence after he had announced his own name, and one side of the conversation remained frigid until its end. But the Chief Inspector was as good as his word and undertook to find out what could be found out of a certain lady's history subsequent to her trial.

"But remember, Colonel," he concluded, "we've nothing on this woman – even if you *are* right. She can wear whiskers and a Mother Abbess' full-dress kit if she wants to. That has nothing to do with us. We've got to find the goods on her, before we'll do a thing – you quite understand that, don't you?"

Gore said he did, thanks very much, and went along to visit his outposts in Sefton Road. But they had absolutely nothing to report of novelty. As usual Mrs. Younger had gone out several times that day as usual upon each occasion she had carried a small attache case, into which, it seemed, she was in the habit of putting her latch key, for on her return it was always taken from the case to open the door. At different hours three ladies had arrived at the house, stayed on an average forty-five minutes and gone away again. As usual everyone of them had been followed, her name and address ascertained, and inquiry made concerning her of local tradespeople and the police. No one in the least suspicious – so far as could be discovered had visited Mrs. Younger since her house had been under surveillance.

"About time someone of that sort did," was the Colonel's comment

A gesture from Yeoland warned him to retreat a little deeper into the dimness of the garage in which they stood. He wheeled about and saw, by the light of the streetlamp at the corner of Abercorn Road, a uniformed figure come out through the gate which a few yards of tiled walk separated from the hall door of Number 76. It was moving now fleetly towards Upper Downs Road, and, yielding to an impulse which he knew entirely imprudent, he followed some fifty yards behind, on the other side of the road. Still more imprudently, when the uniform climbed into a bus at the top of Sefton Road, he sprinted for its steps and, having no other choice, for the vehicle was crowded, seated himself directly facing Mrs. Younger. She had been greeted by two smartly-dressed young women who were his neighbours, and a discussion of the weather was already in full swing. From that the conversation veered to the aches and pains of a lady whose name emerged variously as "your aunt," and "Henrietta." This endured until the two young women got out, by which time every visible inch of Mrs. Younger had been discreetly considered by the gentleman sitting facing her at a distance of perhaps two yards from his monocle to her formidable blue spectacles.

Of her eyes, ears and hands – for she wore very strong, thick gauntlets – he could see nothing. Her voice he failed entirely to recognise as any he had heard before; on the other hand she had something in her mouth – a lozenge of some sort – which perhaps accounted for a certain effect of toothlessness. Her skin was thickly powdered; he could discern no wild-rose tints beneath but at the corners of the daintily-fashioned nose and tips there were no lines to match the incipient grey of such hair as was visible. If the face was more oval than most, it was less so than he remembered a certain face as being. But again the cap and veil and the high, stiff linen collar might account for that difference. Mrs. Younger was bulkier in every way than that old friend of his had been. He watched her carefully – but no vivacious, expressive gesture rewarded him; no hint of lilt, no Irish softening of English sharpness coloured her quiet, stupid mumble. If he was looking at disguise, it was the cleverest he had ever seen. In the end the blue glasses irritated him by their impenetrability. He turned his head impatiently to look out into the darkness in an effort to discover where the bus was at the moment. In the mirror of the window he saw Mrs. Younger's bluish lips part a little and caught the gleam of tiny, pearly teeth.

It was she. Laughing at him. She *would*. Often enough had he watched that roguish little smile during those days last February... amused by the rope that dangled above her little white neck... amused like a baby by a bubble....

"You feel that draught, I'm afraid?" he asked, leaning forward politely.

She turned to glance up to the row of ventilators above her head, and for a moment one ear was partially visible. Well – no camouflage could do anything with *that*, anyhow.

Gravely, he closed the ventilator, and was thanked by a formal bow. At the Philharmonic Rooms he got out, and following the bus in a taxi, saw her alight presently and enter a certain well-known toyshop where the gee-gees and bunny rabbits of his own youth had been purchased, alas, too long ago. While he acquired for his godson a wonderful fire station equipped with six engines that not only went but squirted real water at desire, he saw her buy an enormous flaxen-haired doll. This she bore away to a Linwood-bound bus, delivered it at a house not far from her own, and then returned to 76 Sefton Road. For his benefit, that Christmas purchase, Gore wondered? Perhaps not. A rather complicated person, this old friend of his.

Would that meeting in the bus get her on the run? Well – if it didn't, say, within forty-eight hours, a little more strenuous persuasion must be used.

No hope that carelessness would leave a window off the latch. No back door to Number 76. No chance at all of visiting it unobtrusively during Mrs. Younger's absence....

A very skilled person of Messrs. Gore & Tolley's acquaintance came down from town and opened the hall door lock without difficulty. Inside it was a second door, glass as to its upper hall.

This, also, he opened with a childlike smile. It was, however, bolted on the inner side, and there the investigation ended for the moment. Not just yet had Ruddy-Gore hardened his heart to open illegally. The skilled person unfortunately had for very many years; he was found that night in the kitchen of a Linwood resident eating plum-pudding some days too early, and retired to a place where his talents were not available to the general public.

This was inconsiderate; for his services were to have been invoked not on the following day, which was a Sabbath, but on its successor; the day before Christmas Eve. Various considerations combined to produce this urgency – not the least pressing being that on that Monday morning, Mrs. Melhuish whose plans for Christmas had until then remained uncertain, announced that she and Simon Wyckham would spend it at her mother's house near Wotton in Gloucestershire, whither they would accordingly depart early on Christmas Eve. Christmas Eve being next day, the Colonel concluded that his visit might last until that afternoon, but not, with satisfaction to his hostess, any longer. He had no desire to make another change of quarters in Linwood. What he had to do there, must be done today.

As Pickles gave him his third cup of tea at breakfast on that Monday morning, her long eyes scrutinised his face with more attention than they usually vouchsafed to it.

"*Now* what is it?" she demanded, "you've got that detestable hard look in your face this morning again. I think I'm beginning to dislike your face rather, Wyck. It... it seems to me to have lost any... any..." She cast about for her word. ". . . any spirituality it ever had."

"Good God!" exclaimed the Colonel in dismay. "I've never liked it myself – but I never knew that it was as bad as that. Spirituality.... If I had dreamed of it, I should have grown a beard long ago. Bearded faces are invariably gross. Sorry I look hard, though. The reason I expect is that I've got something hard to do. I want to ask you to do something for me."

"You are not to give me a Christmas present, Wyck—"

"No, that isn't it. Do you know any woman who has a corn and no brain and who can drive her own car?"

"Several, probably. Why?"

"I want you to pick out the most stupid specimen you can think of. I want you to get her to ring up a Mrs. Younger – I'll give you her number. She's a foot-and-hand disease doctor, who lives in Sefton Road. I want her to make an appointment with Mrs. Younger for 4.45 or thereabouts this afternoon – after dark it must be – Mrs. Younger to go to her house to kill her corn or whatever she does to 'em. Whatever hour is agreed on, I want you to get her to call at Mrs. Younger's place half an hour before it, and tell Mrs. Younger that she wants the job done a little earlier, as she has to do something else afterwards – so she has run over to pick Mrs. Younger up. She will then drive Mrs. Younger to her house, wherever it is. You'll let me know as soon as it's fixed up, who she is and where she lives. Think you'd like to do that for me, Witch?"

Mrs. Melhuish reflected.

"This is, of course – the old story?"

He nodded. "The end of one, I hope. It really doesn't matter about the corn. But she must be a perfect idiot and look it. The better the car the better."

Mrs. Melhuish reflected.

"*I* have a corn," she said at length; "as you are aware, I can drive. The other qualification is obvious."

He too reflected. "Ever heard of Mrs. Younger?"

"Never."

"You'd have to give someone else's name over the phone."

"Naturally."

"Well—"

Her eyebrows frowned, as he considered her offer,

"Will you tell me what this means?"

"No."

"Is there any danger... I mean for you?"

"I hope not."

"If there is... I won't do it. I won't ask anyone to do it. Give me your word."

"No danger whatever, Witch – except of failure."

"Very well. What's her number?"

"2616."

Her long fingers rested on his brown fist.

"Solemn Injun, Wyck?"

"Cross me heart, Pickles."

Chapter Twenty

By MIDDAY GORE HAD learned that Lord's trip to Marseilles had proved fruitless, the detained man having been identified as an absconding Belgian notary. The Inspector was on his homeward way, unconsoled by tidings of any greater cheer from Westmouth. Hope, the only capture, stuck to his second story doggedly; of the other suspects no trace was discoverable so far.

The couple who had crossed the Suspension Bridge while Melhuish's car had been proceeding towards its western end, had at length come forward. They had passed, on the north footway of the bridge, either three or four men, neither of them was sure as to the number. Two had been standing talking at the west end; one had been walking slowly towards the east end; they thought a fourth had been walking towards the west end. They had noticed nothing of the appearance of any of them, but they had seen a car, stationary at the west end of the bridge. They believed that its lights had been off, but recalled that its engine had been running.

Some small additional news had come in from London. Seventeen empty cases had been found at Highgate; accepting Gore's estimate of the total number as somewhere round forty, this had left a balance of over twenty unaccounted for. Concentration on Cedar Hill and its late master had unearthed the fact that amongst his activities both during his Highgate period and subsequently until his death, had been a secondhand furniture shop in the Edgware Road and another in Kingston.

Both these establishments had been visited and found shut up and abandoned. In the Kingston shop the remaining cases had been discovered, eight filled with costly furs; the remainder with the disassembled parts of a small printing machine of American make and the most modern efficiency. A large quantity of papers had been burnt at this place, evidently in haste from various still legible fragments it was clear that the printing machine had been used for the manufacture of fake documents of various kinds. Inquiry had elicited that both businesses had been carried on in a quite usual and straightforward way; neither shop had ever evinced any sign of being anything but a respectably struggling enterprise of the kind that, by the hundred in London, drags on its unobtrusive existence to an eventual putting-up of the shutters. The furs were still under investigation; there was small doubt that they were stolen property.

The Westmouth Chief Inspector was a little helpless over the phone that morning with regard to these new developments.

"Must have had a large organisation," he grunted. "Must have been twenty or thirty of them, at least, in the game. Where the devil are they now? You *can't* hide twenty or thirty people in England. The country has been scoured for them – it's sick of the photographs in the papers – and the S.O.S.'s every ten minutes. I'll swear they haven't got out of England unless they've swum. Where *are* they?"

"Well – as you know, Chief," murmured the Colonel, "I never make suggestions."

"Haven't noticed it. What's this one?"

"Suppose you or I were running a little syndicate of this sort – in England. And suppose we wanted to have a nice dry safe hole to nip into if the rain came... Now what *would* be a nice dry sort of hole quiet – comfortable – perfectly safe?"

"*I'*m not suggesting."

"What about one of those nice, comfortable homes for mental cases – say in some quiet picturesque place miles away from everything unpleasant like Chief Inspectors and so on. No decent-minded person would dream of paying any attention to you and your inmates – would they? 'Lunacy Inspectors? Yes... of course. But how often? And how very easily satisfied, with a little forethought. As I say, I hate suggesting but—"

There was a silence.

"Something in that," grunted the Chief. "Rather obvious, isn't it?"

"Quite. Like ventilator chimneys."

"Um. How's the engine working now? All right?"

"Fine, thanks."

"Good. I'll pass in that suggestion you didn't make I think. Bye bye."

After lunch Stephens arrived to pack his master's belongings, and to receive instructions as to his share in the afternoon's programme. Simon Wyckham was resting in preparation for a pre-Christmas party; his mother was, presumably busy with preparations for her Christmas visit and remained invisible until four o'clock, when she appeared dressed for the road.

Every eventuality had been discussed and arranged for. But for the first time in his life Gore detected signs of nervousness in the restless impatience with which she awaited the appearance of her car. At that last moment nervousness had taken possession of him, too. Was he asking this witch whom he valued more than all the rest of all the worlds, to run too great a risk? Was it not only too probable that his old friend had had the curiosity to discover what Dr. Melhuish's wife was like? Suppose she had – suppose she recognised her client. True, the brief interview would take place in darkness – for Mrs. Younger, it had been observed, never afforded herself the extravagance of a light in her hall, even when the bell summoned her to her hall door. Still... a sudden vision of a definitely seen bottle of sulphuric acid paralysed all other perceptions for a moment. But in that moment, with a little smile and a nod, Pickles had flitted from the room. The car was moving away before he reached it. In any case, he felt sure, she would never have allowed him to use any other woman.

Stephens slid up with the Buick, and the Colonel did a fast mile and reached Sefton Road well ahead of his confederate. From the garage, he and Yeoland watched her arrival at Number 76 and the complete success of her interview with Mrs. Younger. The latter had evidently been upon the point of starting to keep her appointment, and held her attache case in her hand when she opened the hall door. For a moment she disappeared again into her house, then came out and followed Mrs. Melhuish into her car. It drove then, not to Victoria Square, but to a quiet road off the Promenade, where the Buick had already arrived a minute or so before. Beside the two cars, two figures only were in sight along the length of the rather gloomy little backwater, a policeman and Stephens. The policeman stood at the end of the road, doing what policemen do in repose. Stephens stood halfway between him and the Buick. Mrs. Melhuish's car stopped just where he stood. If its passenger saw him, she saw a respectable-looking middle-aged man lighting his pipe.

The passenger, being the nearer to the curb, got out first – stepping practically into the respectable man's arms. He uttered an exclamation, snatched her attache case from her hand, threw it into Mrs. Melhuish's,car, and then imprisoning Mrs. Younger with one arm, without ceremony removed her nurses cap and her wig.

Mrs. Melhuish, too, uttered an exclamation. For the face which her headlights revealed, distorted with murderous rage, was the face of that angelic creature whom she had watched for three days of the preceding February. She said, "Great Scott!" and then she let in her clutch with a bang and rushed away from the unseemly and now noisy scrimmage which was taking place on the footpath. For the policeman had moved up hurriedly to join in it, and the Colonel, warily in remembrance of recent interior disturbances, was putting in some useful work on a pair of viciously kicking feet. But the affair was over in a very few minutes, and the Buick once more in pursuit of Mrs. Melhuish.

Both cars drew up with screaming brakes outside Number 76 simultaneously. Gore jumped out, received the latch key which Mrs. Melhuish had taken from the attache case, opened the hall door and disappeared into the black void of the outer hall. The attache case resting open in her lap, Pickles sat rigid, her ears strained for the expected smash of glass. Across the road, in the darkness of the garage four other pairs of ears, too, waited for that sound. But it did not come; presumably this time the Colonel had found the inner unbolted.

A dog barked twice, but without enthusiasm. But for that sound, the moments crept by in silence. Four figures had emerged from the garage now and stood clustered on the opposite footpath, peering dubiously towards the lightless house. A mail van stormed down Sefton Road; its lamps revealed for a moment four tense, vigilant faces.

Without consciousness of the fact, Pickles had taken off her gloves and rolled them into a tight, hard little ball. It escaped from her fingers and fell into the attache case; she switched on her dash light, when her groping hand touched something cold and sharp-edged, and saw, resting on a wash-leather bag of some size, a wicked-looking little automatic. She knew nothing of the special peculiarities of automatics, and it did not occur to her to ascertain whether the safety catch of this one was on or off nor had she the faintest idea whether the thing was loaded or how it might be discovered whether it was or not. For her the outstanding resultant impression of the moment was that chance had provided her with a weapon which ought to obviate any risks which might threaten her fellow adventurer. It seemed to her high time that some noise of some sort should issue from that dark-faced building into which he had vanished. After some further moments of intent listening, she sprang out of the car and hurried into the house. The four figures across the road moved quickly in pursuit, and overtook her in the outer hall.

"Anything wrong, Mrs. Melhuish?" Yeoland asked.

"No. I haven't heard anything. But don't you think we ought to see?"

Yeoland pushed on ahead into an inner hall off which opened two doors leading to two empty rooms. While he and his companions – two of them plainclothes men – investigated these, Mrs. Melhuish flitted up the stairs, halted on a landing and called.

"Are you there, Wyck?"

A faint sound – no louder than a sigh – roared like thunder in her ears. In a flash she was up a second short flight, flung open two doors; flung open a third and burst into a back room where, on a floor covered with mattresses, she saw two figures struggling with a ferocity so grotesque and so animal-like that for an instant she stood in amazed horror, listening to a parody of her own voice trying to cry the word "Help."

But only for an instant. One face she could see, a grinning yellow horror, whose eyes were blotted out by gouts of blood. The other was hidden from her view, bent backwards over the knees of the upper man. But it was very clear to her that something was to be done quickly. She stumbled forward over the mattresses, pointed the automatic at the expanse of black-clad back presented to her, shut her eyes, and pulled the trigger frantically three times.

Yeoland's hands snatched the weapon from hers, before she could fire again. Already his companions were busy with one of the combatants; the other required no attention for the moment. They stretched the limp and unconscious Colonel out close to the door of the room – for it possessed no window – and investigated him anxiously. But one of Mrs. Melhuish's shots had been fired, probably, just in time. The Colonel's spine was still intact, though he had received a terrible beating up and was practically unrecognisable.

Peterson had two bullets in one shoulder and one through a lung. Also one of his eyes would never see again. He recovered consciousness in time to pay a tribute to Mrs. Melhuish before he went away to another place.

"I'm real sorry I was busy when you dropped in, Mabel," he grinned. "You can't shoot, but you're some bad fairy, just the same. S'long, Baby."

***

The first thing the Colonel saw when he opened his eyes was a pair of green ones. He said nothing. The second was the array of mattresses covering the floor. He smiled then slowly.

"Waste of money," he remarked, "if you laugh in your sleep."

The third was a wash-leather bag whose contents Yeoland poured out in a little cascade silently. The Colonel picked up one of the thirty-seven uncut stones.

"Tanquered's stones," he said, "who had them?"

"The woman – in her attache case."

This time the smile came much quicker and stayed.

"The goods," said the Colonel, "Q.E.D."

Chapter
Twenty-One

ROSS – ALIAS EUGENE Hartmann – was arrested in Grimsby
that afternoon. He had arrived there just half an hour before in a
trawler which had found him clinging to the wreckage of a small
plane somewhere in the North Sea. Two of his confederates
who had been his fellow passengers – Heberts, "the man in
the leggings" and Manifold, the shortish man who had stopped
Bullock in Tenby Road – had presumably been drowned.

It was on information supplied by Ross that the Hampshire
Constabulary raided, in the small hours of the following morning, a rest home for mental patients – uncertified – kept by a
Dr. Manifold near Bramley on the outskirts of the New Forest.
There they found the Marvins – late the caretakers of "Cedar
Hill" and two men named Polden and Caulfield, subsequently
known to have managed Dr. Dorch's secondhand furniture
businesses in the Edgware Road and at Kingston respectively.
Tempett (one of many names) late Mr. Hope's chauffeur, was
arrested in Chicago some weeks later – the only member of
the confederacy who had succeeded in reaching the rendezvous
where, had all gone well, the confederates were to have gathered
together for the sharing of the spoils. One by one a number
of subordinates employed at the two secondhand shops were
rounded up; in nearly every case, however, it transpired that

these people had been quite unaware of the subterranean traffic carried on in stolen goods under cover of two perfectly respectable furniture businesses.

It was from Ross's lips that Inspector Lord and Gore heard the first connected story of the conspiracy for the obliteration of Dorch. Peterson and Tempett, loyal to the code of the gangster, preserved absolute silence regarding the affair until they died – grinning and chewing. The Marvins knew nothing of it; Polden and Caulfield, also former Q.E.D.'s, knew very little and had had no direct share in the actual working-out of Ross's plans. Miss Higgins also remained silent until the end, her sole real concern from the moment of her arrest until that of her death being her dog Buster, for whom at her request, Inspector Lord had found a home.

Released in 1911 at the end of five years' imprisonment, Ross – he had then first adopted this name – had come to England in 1912, not, as he had told Inspector Lord, in 1907 with Dorch. While in prison, however, he had been in constant communication with the latter through the machinery of the underworld, and immediately took the place which had been kept open for him in Dorch's operations on this side of the Atlantic.

Although the latter's original intention, having made a large clean-up out of the Hartmann forgeries and rendered his native country too hot for comfort, had possibly been to retire into the security of honesty, the innate twist in his own make-up, and the dangerous pressure of the associates who had migrated to England with him, had proved almost at once too strong for him. When Ross had rejoined him in London, early in 1912, he was already involved in a network of illegal enterprise which; as always in his career, had concerned itself with equal zest with the robbery of thousands of pounds' worth of jewels, and a petty long-firm fraud whose total plunder did not exceed, perhaps, a couple of hundred pounds. Obsessed as always by a mania for the acquisition of money, by any but straightforward means, he still retained his marked ability to look after his own safety and to keep what the risks of other people had secured for him. According to Ross, at the time of his own arrival in England, Heberts, Manifold, Peterson and Tempett, had already begun to discuss amongst themselves the project of getting rid of their leader and securing possession of a sum which they had estimated at that time as close on £600,000. (The total figure of the funds known to have belonged to Dorch at his death and subsequently recovered in the United States, whither by a complicated series of manipulations they had been transferred by Ross, amounted to a little over £500,000.) Into this still vague plan Ross had very shortly been initiated. England, however, presenting difficulties with regard to such schemes unfamiliar to citizens of a new world less cramped and less timid, the project had hung fire – been brought up again from time to time, but always postponed until a stronger and more impetuous spirit had joined itself to the conspirators' councils.

Miss Gretta Higgins' acquaintance with Dorch had begun in 1927. Her brother "Tanquered" was at that time casting about for a safe agent to help in disposing of the stolen stones which he had brought away from South Africa with him, and through some source he had learned that Dr. Dorch might prove a suitable ally. Although, in fact, his negotiations with that gentleman had come to nothing, his sister had from the first taken pains to make herself agreeable to the somewhat mysterious person who paid several visits to Tanquered's house on the Mendips. Mrs. Tanquered also owned a house in Linwood, and from time to time ran up there for a week or a fortnight of greater amusement than the lonely Mendips offered. On these occasions Miss Higgins made it a point to renew the very favourable impression which, from the first, her charms had produced upon Dr. Dorch. Already, without doubt, she had foreseen that she might need to make use of the services which her brother had decided to decline. And, in effect, twenty-four hours after the tragic death of her brother in the tap of the Bower of Bliss Inn, the stones taken from his belt by her were in Dr. Dorch's hands – for safe keeping, and, in due time, disposal. Beyond all doubt Dorch had always known the means by which his lovely client had possessed herself of them; equally beyond all doubt he had made up his mind that any proceeds resulting from their sale would go, not to Miss Higgins, but to Aloysius I. Dorch. And when, not very long after her trial and acquittal in February 1929, she had paid a further visit to Linwood and applied to him for the return of the diamonds, he had made his point of view perfectly clear to her; amorous in a cold-blooded, unimpassioned way, he had never allowed his love affairs to interfere with business of more permanent profit.

He had believed, foolishly as it proved, that she was powerless to enforce any claim to the diamonds. He paid the price of that miscalculation with his life. There was another admirer of Miss Higgins beneath the roof of Wavertree, more impassioned than its master. By the end of April, 1929, her alliance with Ross had been definitely concluded; backed up by Peterson and Heberts, the two more desperate spirits of the central male quartet, Ross had been persuaded by his newly-acquired mistress to consent to his employer's murder. The actual method had by that time been discussed in detail, and the date fixed provisionally for November – a November fog being essential for the undertaking.

Heberts came down to Westmouth and rented a garage behind Wavertree. Tempett also came to Linwood and was obtained, through Dorch's own recommendation at Ross's suggestion, the position of chauffeur to Mr. Hope. A couple of months later a Mrs. Younger installed herself in Sefton Road with a brass plate on her hall door. No share in the actual execution of the plan had been allotted to her; but apparently she had been very determined – against the wishes of Peterson and Heberts – to remain as close as possible to the safe in which her thirty-seven stones were kept locked up at Wavertree. These, Ross had stipulated, were to be handed over to her, if things went well. Things did not go, in the end, quite well; but they were duly handed over to her. How long they would have remained in her possession, but for that unfinished letter of Dr. Melhuish's perhaps only Peterson could have said.

November came at last and the plan still seemed dead easy. There were fogs and to spare; and on the 16th, Ross learned that Dorch would go to London on the night of the 20th. If very foggy, that night was definitely decided upon. Everything seemed quite ready, when the 20th brought the densest fog remembered in Linwood for many years. And then, unfortunately, Mrs. Younger, finding her bath that morning hot enough, turned off the gas from her geyser but forgot to turn off the pilot jet which had somehow contrived to extinguish itself. Her bath was usually an affair of half an hour of luxurious steaming. At the end of that time she was unconscious, and, but for her maid, would have drowned. Instead, a perhaps more serious misfortune occurred to her; Dr. Melhuish walked into her little bathroom and recognised at a glance the very lovely and angelic-looking creature who lay in the bath which the maid had had the presence of mind to empty before rushing off for assistance.

For Ross, Peterson & Co., the recognition would have meant nothing – if it had not seemed to Miss Higgins that it meant a great deal to her. Her conviction had been that Melhuish would almost at once let "that brute Gore" know of the meeting in the bathroom; if the brute Gore learned that she was living in Linwood camouflaged as a manicurist and masseuse, he would certainly take steps to discover why – probably communicate with that other brute Inspector Lord. For her, these possibilities led only to one of two possible results – either Melhuish's mouth must be closed at once and forever, or she must leave Linwood – and her thirty-seven stones. She made it very clear that the second alternative was out of the question; she knew too much to allow of its being forced upon her; the obliteration of Dorch must be proceeded with, because Ross had already compromised himself by frauds upon his employer's funds, certain to be discovered within a few weeks by the vigilant Dorch;

hurriedly the obliteration of Melhuish also was discussed and arranged for. The lovely Miss Higgins' impatience could hardly await the safe dinner hour of her victim; she feared that his interest in her might have induced him to write to the brute Gore in the course of that afternoon.

Another complication had arisen – Hope's invitation to Dorch for dinner that evening. But, as it proved, this difficulty really facilitated matters in the end, since Hope had elected to drive his guest home; had he deputed that job to his chauffeur it might have been difficult to clear Tempett. Dorch was killed in his own drive. Tempett had attended to Hope, drove him back to his game, and left him there shut up in his car, still unconscious. By midnight that night it had seemed to the conspirators that all had gone extremely well. It was arranged that at daybreak next morning Mrs. Younger should exercise her dog in the neighbourhood of the ventilation shaft, and make quite certain that no tell-tale traces had been left behind in the darkness.

But on that foggy morning Fate again proved unkind to Mrs. Younger, and brought Woodbine out of the fog to find her down on her "hunkers" groping about in the grass for any possible fallen property of her confederates or of their victim. Not only that, but, seeing him, as she believed, stoop and pick up something close to the ventilator tower, she had the imprudence to question him as to what he had picked up. He had hardly disappeared from her sight again before she realised the danger to which that meeting might expose her. And with the directness which was the keynote to her character, she rang up Ross immediately upon reaching her house, told him what had occurred, and laid before him, cut and dried, a plan for the obliteration of Woodbine. She knew the man well by sight, and was aware of his early morning roamings, for she herself was in the habit of exercising Buster on the Downs about seven o'clock. Before she telephoned Ross that morning, she had already found the basket in which the bait for Woodbine was to be laid.

Ross refused, he stated, to have anything whatever to do with this project, which seemed to him both unnecessary and highly dangerous. Peterson also opposed it strenuously. Miss Higgins, however, insisted and in the end Heberts was entrusted with the concealment of the basket in one of Woodbine's certain places of call.

Woodbine did what had been hoped of him – and once again all seemed very well. The visit of Inspector Lord, in Gore's company, to Wavertree was a thunderbolt dropped from a sky that had seemed of perfect serenity and benignity.

Tempett bolted at once. Peterson and Manifold desired strongly to follow his example; Ross and Heberts, stronger of brain and nerve, saw also more clearly the danger of a sudden stampede. From that morning on there bad been endless dispute sharpened by the growing distrust which every member of the gang entertained for his fellow scoundrels. Every preparation was made for evacuation; but the quartet stood fast for a while longer, principally because Mrs. Younger refused to leave Linwood in a hurry, and Ross refused to leave it as long as she remained. The thirty seven stones had not yet been handed over to her, the other three men having refused to permit Ross to do this. Ultimately Ross, divining that danger was close at hand, met Mrs. Younger by appointment in a tramcar and handed her the diamonds in a confectioner's paper bag under the eyes of twenty uninterested passengers. But even then she refused to attract attention to herself by a hasty flitting from Linwood. The writing on the wall became abruptly too distinct for farther delay, after the failure to kidnap Bullock. Ross, Heberts and Manifold agreed that it was high time to make a break. For this everything was in readiness. For nearly a year Ross had been a member of the West and South Flying Club, whose principal headquarters were situated on the outskirts of Westmouth. Both he and Manifold had made themselves fairly expert pilots, and the two machines which Ross had acquired had been kept in hourly readiness for the past ten days. Peterson, however, refused to accompany the others to Spain – their immediate objective. There had been a violent quarrel with Ross upon the discovery that the latter had fulfilled his promise to Miss Higgins. Not only had Peterson little faith in aeroplane excursions across the Channel conducted by amateur pilots, he was most determined not to lose sight of Miss Higgins and her thirty seven stones, the only tangible result of the plot now left within sight and reach. A very few minutes after Ross left Wavertree to join his two loyal adherents at Fillways Aerodrome, Peterson strolled across the edge of the Downs, turned down Sefton Road, and installed himself as Mrs. Younger's most unwelcome guest. Such, at any rate, had been his announced intention at his leave-taking with Ross. As to the details of the duet which had subsequently played itself under the roof of Number 76 Sefton Road, Ross, of course, could say nothing.

With Ross and his two companions everything had gone well at the start – in the end very ill. They had hoped to land some-where close to the Dutch frontier just before darkness fell; in point of fact they had developed trouble beyond Ross's diagno-sis some seventy miles from the Dutch coast and had nose-dived into a ugly sea. Beyond cries heard vaguely, Ross knew nothing definite as to what had happened to Manifold and Heberts. He himself had gone under seven or eight times before he had got a grip on a portion of the fuselage. To this he had clung for two-and-a-half hours before the trawler had picked him up – quite unnecessarily, in view of what happened to him a couple of months later in Parton Hill Prison.

The unfortunate Prescott had been an instance of Dr. Dorch's weakness for petty profit. Having somehow learned of the existence of the very obscure Johnson & Co., it had occurred to him that, with capital behind it, a business of that sort could be made to pay. He had opened negotiations with Prescott, the result of which had been that the latter had become manager instead of principal, at a salary with commission on profits. In a very few months Dorch had discovered that his manager had already contrived to defraud him of something close on two hundred pounds. He had not dismissed him, however, or prosecuted; he had always preferred subordinates who were securely under his thumb. In return for this grace, Prescott had revealed to his employer the possibilities of that sideline which, in a small way, had brought him in a considerable revenue over and above that derived from his registered business. The sideline had been an attraction just after Dorch's crooked heart, and had been the principal inducement to clemency in the matter of his manager's defalcations. Compared with his activities as a fence in New York and Chicago – or even in London – the profits of this kind to be derived from a provincial city like Westmouth were, Ross stated, contemptible. But Dorch had taken as much interest in Prescott's petty plunder as in the plotting of the schemes by which the Hartmann forgeries scooped in three quarters of a million of dollars. Just as, although an expert judge of pictures, he found as powerful a thrill in stealing valueless illustrations from other people's valueless books which happened to come by accident within reach of his fingers, as in negotiating for a client the purchase of a genuine Corot – a painter for whose work he had a passionate admiration.

Woodbine's find had been a somewhat elaborate version of the badge once worn by all good and true Q.E.D. gangsters. Ross and Peterson had been aware that Dorch carried this souvenir about with him as a mascot. But it had never occurred to them, until Lord had exhibited the badge to their surprised eyes, that this could have fallen from one of his pockets while he had been hoisted to the top of the ventilator tower and had been the object which Miss Higgins had seen Woodbine pick up. The immediately invented story Peterson produced for Lord's edification at all events did credit to his presence of mind.

Whoever the elderly man with the umbrella and the knocking knees had been who had met Gore in College Road on the night of his misadventure – Ross knew nothing of him, nor was he ever traced. He had been the merest accident, not any part of

Ross & Co.'s plan to subject the Colonel to the obliteration process. Certainly he had not been Prescott... whose suicide, it seemed, had been due to the realisation that, at the end, his long and avid pursuit of pounds, shillings and pence was to terminate in gaol. Inspector Lord was a little disappointed about this. The disappointment, however, was but the most microscopic of flies in the rich and glowing amber of his superiors' commendation. He is to go to the Yard very shortly, and a-honeymooning still more shortly.

But he admits that in one or two small points the Colonel gave him some little assistance.

Chapter Twenty-Two

ON CHRISTMAS EVE MORNING Colonel Gore breakfasted in bed and Simon Wyckham, in honour of the event, breakfasted with him. Simon Wyckham, who occupied what the breakfast tray left over of the counterpane, was highly diverted by his godfather's face, which had pieces of sticking-plaster all over it, two black lumps instead of eyes, several other lumps of assorted colours in unusual places, and looked a funnier face than it had ever made itself before. But Uncle Wyck, it seemed, was shy about it. He had taken great pains not to let the maid who had brought breakfast see as much of it as she had desired to.

And so, when the door opened a little again, and a voice inquired: "May I come in?" he said, "Well... er..."

The voice smiled audibly.

"Oh, very, well, you vain creature. It's about Duggie. Your man has called to take him away."

"Good," said the Colonel.

"But I don't know that I want him to go... now."

"Why not?"

"Because I've got too fond of him."

"Well – but," objected the Colonel, "I understood that was the reason why he was to go."

"I know," admitted the voice. It grew impatient. "Oh, I can't argue through a door. Anyhow, he's not going."

"But what will Duggie do for Christmas, Mums?" objected Simon Wyckham. "Gran hates dogs. We can't take him up to Wotton with us, can we?"

"We're not going up to Wotton, dear," said the voice. "We're spending Christmas here."

There was silence in the bedroom while light feet descended the stairs. When they could no longer be heard, Simon Wyckham and his godfather looked at one another silently and long. Silently they arose and descended together to the carpet. Silently they joined hands. Silently they danced a war dance.

THE END

Death on May Morning
Max Dalman

The Hymn Tune Mystery
George A. Birmingham

The Middle of Things
JS Fletcher

The Essex Murders
Vernon Loder

The Boat Race Murder
R. E. Swartwout

Who Killed Alfred Snowe?
J. S. Fletcher

Q.E.D.
by Lynn Brock

There's Death in the Churchyard
by William Gore

Murder of the Ninth Baronet
by J.S. Fletcher

Dead Man Manor
by Valentine Williams

The Man in the Dark
by John Ferguson

The Dressing Room Murder
by J.S. Fletcher

*Glory Adair and the
Twenty-First Burr*
by Victor Lauriston

The Tunnel Mystery
by J.C. Lenehan

Murder on the Marsh
by John Ferguson

The Fatal Five Minutes
R.A.J. Walling

*The Crime
of a Christmas Toy*
Henry Herman

Death of an Editor
Vernon Loder